ACKNOWLEDGMENTS

A world of thanks to my editor, Leah Hulten-schmidt, who helped make this book so much better; my agent, Holly Root, for her belief and excitement. Thanks also to my extended family at Romance Unleashed (www.romanceunleashed.com), especially Lori Devoti and Eve Silver, to Wendy Evans who braved the dark side of the online world, and to Andrea Snider, Laurel Jue, Laurie De Salvo and Lona Gordon for their honesty and encouragement.

And always, to Ron, Thomas, Michael and John—my real-life happily ever after.

CHAPTER ONE

Redemption, Texas
Summer 1881

I want *him*." Lucy pointed her long slender finger at the quiet man near the back of the restaurant, the tall one with the dark eyes and the wavy hair that begged to be touched.

Oh yes, he'd do quite nicely.

"I . . . Wha—?" The fat lady in charge of the auction whirled around. "Who . . . ? Where did you come from?"

"Lucy Firr," Lucy answered without taking her eyes off her man. "And I'll take *him*."

Necks stretched and craned as twenty or more men twisted in their seats to get a look at the man she wanted; the man with the long, unwavering stare; the man she'd chosen to be her savior—or her accomplice, depending on how you chose to look at it.

He didn't move a muscle, didn't nod in agreement or even acknowledge he was the topic of conversation. He just stared back at her with those too-dark-to-read eyes.

The fat lady sputtered, gaped, then stammered, "Y-you mean Mr. Caine?"

Lucy smiled and nodded toward the back of the room again. That was exactly who she meant.

Jedidiah Caine.

"Yes, him," she repeated.

Why did the fat lady keep staring that way—as if Lucy had suddenly sprouted horns?

Had she sprouted horns?

With calmness she didn't feel, Lucy fingered her hair back from her face, carefully probing for any unusual bumps.

Nothing.

Finally, the woman turned and stretched on tiptoe to see over the crowd, then teetered back on her heels. She fidgeted with her high lace collar, tucked the coin box tightly beneath her elbow and turned her wary gray eyes on Lucy.

The other women up for bid at the wife auction sought out Lucy's man, too, then bowed their heads in a circle as furious whispers buzzed among them. Each woman wore her hair pulled back in a tight knot or braid at the back of her head, with not a single bow or earbob in sight.

Lucy shuddered. How could any self-respecting woman, mortal or not, allow such dresses—if that's what you could call those horrid garments—to touch their skin? To make matters worse, each dress was exactly the same as the others, plain cotton frocks buttoned neck to waist, with plain straight skirts.

No imagination whatsoever.

These poor women didn't have a prayer. Then again, neither did Lucy, but that was an entirely different story.

She smoothed the deep green silk of her skirt and tossed her long, glossy black hair over her shoulders. The small restaurant-turned-auction-house was near to bursting with the crowd of men, but there were only four women on the auction block. Five if Lucy included herself, which she didn't. She was not up for auction. She was here for one man—and one man only: The man who stood between her and the baby she needed.

Mr. Jedidiah Caine wanted her. He *needed* someone else, but he *wanted* her. There was no doubt what was going on inside that gorgeous head of his; inner turmoil stewed beneath his frown and clouded his already dark eyes. He was going to be difficult, no question, but she'd overpower him soon enough. If she didn't, she would have to stand before her father empty-handed, and she could not let that happen. Again. The consequences would be far too severe this time.

Whether Jed Caine knew it or not, he was going to help Lucy avoid eternal damnation. He'd be sacrificing his own soul, but he didn't need to know that. Not yet, anyway.

The heavy stench of the unbathed crowd, mixed with cheap cigars and manure-covered boots, fogged the air. Yet even with the space of the room separating them, Lucy knew her man wouldn't stink. There was something about him, something about the way he stood there, so quiet, so sure of himself.

Lucy bit back her laughter. His lust would be easy enough to work with on its own, but he was obviously a proud man, too. This was going to be easier than she'd hoped. Was it possible her father had finally underestimated her abilities?

Grumblings between the men started low, then grew louder. Coffee cups rattled on the tables, and a few men motioned toward the door, but not a single person left.

Lust seeped from them like blood from gaping wounds. It was in the way they ogled her, the way they curled their lips and nodded toward her as they muttered among themselves.

But *his* want burned hotter than the rest. It smoldered in those dark eyes, in the firm set of his jaw and in his deepening frown. Oh, he wanted her all right, but he certainly wasn't going to admit it. And he certainly wasn't happy about it.

"Yes," Lucy purred. "He'll do just fine."

The woman in charge cleared her throat and adjusted her wire-framed glasses. "I'm sorry, Miss Firr, but that's not how the wife auction works." She indicated the room full of men, each one raking Lucy with shameless, lust-filled gazes. "The gentlemen decide which woman is suitable and then the bidding starts. Highest bidder wins." Her thin lips curled into a nervous smile. "The women don't get to choose."

Lucy seared the fat lady with a glare but refrained from commenting on the woman's easy use of the word "gentlemen."

"What if I don't want the man who buys me?" Lucy wrinkled her nose as the man closest to her spat a wad of tobacco juice toward a nearby bucket and missed. It splatted against the plank floor and spread out in a tiny, dark puddle where many others had obviously landed before it.

Again, the fat lady smiled in that nervous way as she took a step closer. A sour waft of body odor hit Lucy's nose as the woman stopped in front of her. "It doesn't matter what *you* want."

An odd aura surrounded the woman. Lucy was unable to define it, but whatever it was, it troubled the woman's soul something awful.

Lucy shook it off and focused her attention back on the group at hand. She was surrounded by souls in various stages of decay, yet the only one that mattered was *his*.

His clean, honorable, yet proud soul. She would use that honor and pride to get him. If she worked it right, he wouldn't even know what she'd done until it was too late. By the time he realized what had happened, she'd have secured his soul and his sister-in-law Maggie's as well. Individually, neither meant anything to Lucy, but together, they stood as protectors over the one soul she desperately needed—that of Maggie's baby. The second it was born, Lucy would claim its soul and secure her freedom.

The baby was key to everything. Without its soul, nothing else mattered.

Lucy held her gaze on her man, but spoke to the fat lady. "I will choose who I leave with, and the money he pays, instead of going to me, will go directly to . . ." She hesitated a second, knowing she had to choose her words carefully. After all, guilt was a great motivator with these God-fearing, conscience-bearing humans. "The school."

Another murmur rose, this time accompanied by a few more tobacco spits from several of the men and more whispering by the women. The fat lady's eyes bulged with excitement.

"New books," she breathed. "Oh my!"

"Furthermore," Lucy continued. "I'll only have *him*." She pointed at her man again. "If he doesn't want me, I'll simply be on my way."

Again, every head swiveled in his direction, waiting. Lucy waited, too. If she walked out of this auction now, she'd forfeit her only chance of succeeding, her only chance of retrieving the one soul she most desperately needed.

"This is highly irregular," the woman muttered, but she, too, stood waiting for the man to speak.

Every passing second deepened Lucy's doubts and deepened her man's frown.

An icy chill shot through her. Her man needed a woman, but surely he couldn't want one of these others instead of her.

That was ridiculous. They were as homely as hedgehogs

and there must have been month-old corpses that smelled better.

Lucy gave herself a hard mental shake and refocused on Mr. Jedidiah Caine. She knew two things about this man and two things only.

The first was that if it hadn't been for his brother's "disappearance," Jed wouldn't even be at the auction, bidding on a wife he didn't want. And the second was that he'd never let his own desires get in the way of what his family needed.

"Mr. Caine?" the woman finally said, her voice wavering. "Will you have Miss Firr as your wife?"

Amid heated murmurs and pointing fingers, he finally stepped through the crowd, weaving his way toward the front of the room. His gaze never left Lucy's, even as he bobbed a quick nod at the fat lady.

A hush fell over the room as everyone strained to hear.

Mr. Caine spoke quietly, his voice deep and sure. "You're a beautiful woman, Miss Firr. But you already know that, don't you?"

Lucy smiled. Of course she knew it—temptation would be one of her strongest weapons.

Strangely, he didn't smile back. His dark eyes never wavered from hers as he spoke. "Given the number of honest men here today, I appreciate your interest in me."

Yes! This was going to be easier than—

"And though it pains me to say it," he continued, "I've no need for a beautiful woman. I'm not even looking for a wife."

Shocked silence hung in the air. He must be toying with her. Every man wanted a beautiful woman—the proof sat all around them. What made Jed Caine think he was any different?

Humiliation wasn't new to Lucy, but she'd never gotten

used to it—and when it came from the likes of a mere mortal . . .

She swallowed her anger and forced a seductive smile.

"You have no need of a wife, you say." She coyly tipped her head a little to the right. "Yet here you are at a wife auction."

Her facial muscles pinched against the smile, but she held it in place as Mr. Caine explained what she already knew.

"I need to hire a woman to help my brother's wife. I need someone who's not afraid to get dirty, who'll work hard and who doesn't mind living without frills." Color crept up his neck and over his face. His lips curled upward in an awkward, uncomfortable smile. "If you don't mind my saying so, Miss Firr, you sure don't look the type to collect chips for the fire."

Snorts and chuckles filled the room, followed by giggles and twitters from the other women. Lucy silenced their taunts with a blistering glare. These people had no idea who they were dealing with; she was here to win, and whether he liked it or not, Jed Caine was going to help her do just that.

"Why is it then, Mr. Caine, that you are here and not your brother? She's *his* wife after all."

A painful hush fell over the room. Mr. Caine swallowed, his Adam's apple bobbing slowly with the movement, and his eyes darkened to near pitch.

"My brother . . . Sam . . . is missing, and until he returns, Maggie and I need a little help." His jaw clenched, as though waiting for someone to voice what the entire room was thinking: that Sam Caine was dead, and he'd probably killed himself to get away from his crazy wife.

With practiced ease, Lucy slinked closer until they stood toe-to-toe. Broad across the shoulder, he stood like a rock wall, his sleeves rolled to the elbows and his faded blue shirt tucked neatly into the waistband of his wool pants.

Yes, Jedidiah Caine was a man to behold—tall, but not towering. Lucy had only to tip her head slightly to look into his eyes. There was a warm, musky scent about him. He was what humans referred to as a "good man." A good man meant a good soul, a trusting soul, a weak soul.

Perfect.

"I can be ugly if you want me to."

He quirked his left eyebrow. "I doubt that."

She opened her eyes wide and blinked up at him with all the false innocence she could muster.

"The work is hard."

"I like things hard." She murmured as she toyed with the button nearest his navel.

"And dirty."

"The dirtier the better." She waggled her brow, and slipped her tongue out to moisten her lips.

Tiny crinkles formed at the corners of his eyes, but he didn't laugh. Instead, he cast a telling glance down the length of her skirt.

"And living without any frilly dresses?"

Lucy waved her hand down her skirt. "Do you see any frills?"

The fat lady cleared her throat again. Tension built throughout the room, but Mr. Caine remained perfectly calm, apparently unmoved by any of Lucy's actions or words.

"Move it along, Caine," someone called as grumbling began to roll around the room.

"Can you cook?" Mr. Caine ignored the other man and eyed Lucy suspiciously.

"Yes," she lied. The rest of the crowd, especially the

women, seemed disinclined to believe her, given the way they rolled their eyes and snorted, but Mr. Caine did neither.

"And you can keep the house?"

"Of course." Another lie.

One of the men near the back stood up. "Caine already said he don't want her, so let's give the rest of us a chance."

An odd look flashed across Jed's face, then disappeared. He hesitated a moment, and licked his lips.

"What about children?" he asked.

Lucy trailed her fingers up to the next button. "I believe that's what the dirty work will produce."

One of the women sucked in a shocked breath, and several of the other men grumbled louder, but neither Lucy nor her man spared them a glance.

He still didn't look convinced. "You're awfully skinny; you don't look strong enough for the work."

Lucy leaned closer and trailed her finger in a long, slow path down his cheek, laughing softly when his jaw twitched beneath her touch.

"I've got all the strength you'll ever need, Mr. Caine."

More gasps and groans filled the room.

"Miss Firr, please!" The woman in charge fanned herself with her hand.

A tiny smile tugged at his mouth. He was enjoying this as much as she was, yet there was still something wrenching him away, something he was bound to by honor: caring for his brother's wife.

"As tempting as that sounds"—Mr. Caine wrapped his fingers around her wrist and tugged her hand away from his face—"and as tempting as *you* are, Miss Firr, I doubt very much you'd last a week."

"Move on!" the man in the back yelled. "We ain't got all day."

"M-Mr. Caine," the fat lady stammered, "I need a decision."

After a moment's hesitation, with the internal battle playing out in his eyes, he sighed in resignation.

"I'm sorry, Miss Blake," he said to the fat lady, his smile gone. "As much as I'd like to agree to this, Miss Firr isn't the type of woman I'm looking for."

Desperation flooded Lucy's veins. He was a stubborn one, this human. Well, so was she. If only she could think of something else to tempt him with.

"B-but," Miss Blake stammered. "If you don't want her . . . what about the school?"

Mr. Caine tipped a short nod at Lucy and headed back to his place at the far end of the room as the other men all started calling out at once.

"I'll take her!"

"I like 'em skinny."

"Ten dollars!"

Miss Blake turned desperate eyes on Lucy, who shrugged nonchalantly, smiled and made like she was going to leave, all the while fighting the fear and anguish that had begun to overpower her. She had about five seconds to figure something out, something that would save her from her father's wrath and the desolate eternity that beckoned.

She hadn't taken two complete steps when Miss Blake started offering her own services.

"If it turns out she can't cook, I'll teach her myself." The woman sounded almost as desperate as Lucy felt. The school must really need those books.

Judging by the excited nods and murmurs going on around them, it was safe to assume the woman could cook. And from the size of her, she must cook well. Lucy cocked a taunting brow at her man's back and waited.

He continued to make his way to the back.

"And I'll help her with the cleaning and the wash."
Miss Blake's voice went higher with each word.

He stopped, but took his time turning around.

A loud whisper carried across the room. "Maybe Caine
should marry you instead."

Chuckles and snorts followed, but Mr. Caine held
Lucy's gaze, his lips pressed together as though fighting
back what he wanted to say.

"Mr. Caine, please." Miss Blake mopped her brow with
a lace handkerchief. "You need a woman to make you a
home, to give you a family, and to help you make something of all that land you bought."

He didn't look the slightest bit swayed.

"And think of the children." She lifted her chin and
pinned him with what must have been a well-practiced
frown. "One day your brother's child will attend that
school—do you not think it's your responsibility to help
ensure him the best education possible?"

Lucy felt the uncertainty ebb over Miss Blake's soul
first, then Mr. Caine's. He seemed to falter for a moment,
but remained rooted to where he stood. His mouth tightened into a thin line, his dark eyes staring straight back
at Lucy.

Guilt—it worked amazing feats in humans. Lucy was
certain that if the fat lady—Miss Blake—could produce
one of these bookless, unschooled children, the man would
no doubt hand over his last penny.

But Lucy had to give her man credit—he continued to
resist. Sure, he was tempted, but he held strong. If he
didn't want Lucy, he might end up taking home one of
these other women.

That would never do. Still, she held her tongue. Watching the guilt crash and ebb over his expression was almost
worth the anxiety of the wait.

"Mr. Caine," Miss Blake went on, "if nothing else, think about Maggie."

Every muscle in Mr. Caine's face and neck tightened.

"It's not good for her to be out there all alone in her condition. Obviously, if you could care for her yourself, you wouldn't be here."

When he didn't answer, Miss Blake cleared her throat and continued. "She needs a woman with her, someone to tend her needs, someone who understands." She adjusted her glasses and cleared her throat quietly. "And though it's not a nice thing to say, most of these other women . . ." she indicated the four behind her, "would not willingly want to take on a responsibility like that with someone in Maggie's . . . condition."

Mr. Caine's gaze flicked from Miss Blake to Lucy, then to the other four women who all suddenly found great fascination with the toes of their boots.

He mumbled something under his breath and pushed through to the front of the room.

"Have you ever done a day's work in your life?" he asked, taking Lucy's hands in his and turning her palms up.

"Yes," she answered with a definitive nod. Stoking fires and chiseling brimstone counted as work, even in a human world.

His brow furrowed slightly as he ran his thumb over her calloused and scarred fingers.

Lucy tried to tug her hands away, but he held them a moment longer, his gaze locked on hers. What did that look mean? And why did a tremble creep up her spine?

"There's plenty of other men here, Miss Firr." He spoke quietly, causing the others to shift and strain to hear. "Why are you set on me?"

Lucy lifted her chin and leaned close enough to whisper. "Because you have a good soul. I can see it." She hesitated a moment, then added, "And because you're the only one *not* set on me."

An odd look came over him, a small spark glinting in the depths of his dark eyes.

"Okay." He released her, then held up a hand to quell the burst of complaints. "So long as you understand it's going to be hard work, and you'll have to do your share."

"M-Miss Firr?" The fat lady stuttered. "Are you in agreement?"

"Of course—whatever Mr. Caine wants."

"Once the money's paid," Miss Blake hurried to say, "there's no refund."

Caine nodded in silent agreement.

"And," she went on, "annulments are not—"

"There'll be no need for an annulment," he interrupted with a hard glare.

Another loud groan sounded through the room, but before anyone could complain too loudly or, God forbid, change their mind, Miss Blake and Jed bartered an amount. Miss Blake had them both sign the slip, then ushered them through the crowd toward the door.

"Reverend Conroy is waiting at the church." She hurried them out of the restaurant. "Just give him this slip and the school's portion of the money. Good luck to you both."

She made to shut the door behind them, but peered through the last remaining crack for a long moment.

"Mr. Caine," she said quietly. "I meant what I said. I'll help in any way I can."

Lucy waited until the door was closed before speaking. There was something about the fat lady that Lucy didn't trust. Granted, she didn't trust anyone, but this woman was particularly odd.

"Do we have to be married in the church?" Lucy shivered, panic clenching at her throat.

Mr. Caine held out his arm for her to take, but she didn't move. She couldn't go inside a church. God would strike her down before her foot crossed the threshold, and any preacher worth his salt would know what she was the instant he saw her. If that happened, this whole plan would be finished before it began.

"Change your mind already?" He chuckled, setting his hat over his dark hair and tipping her a raised brow.

"No," she answered, her mind racing. "I'm not a particularly religious person is all." That was putting it mildly. "Couldn't we go see the judge instead and have him pass the money on to the school?"

Mr. Caine shrugged. "Makes no difference to me as long as it's done quickly and we can get back. Day's a-wastin'."

She released a breath and took the arm he offered. Warmth radiated from his skin, a welcome relief to Lucy as she shivered again. "Does it ever get warm?"

His laughter startled her. "It's the middle of July, Miss Firr." He waved towards the sun, directly overhead. "It doesn't get any hotter than Texas in July." He turned to look at her while they walked. "Where are you from, anyway?"

"Somewhere warmer than here," she answered with a smile.

He led her across the main street of town, steering her around potholes and horse droppings.

"What brings you to a town like Redemption?" he asked.

A lie jumped to her tongue, but Lucy bit it back. It would be much more interesting to see him figure it out bit by bit, even though his mind would refuse to believe any of it.

"I came here to save myself from a life of misery." She lifted her silk skirts higher than necessary to avoid another pile of dung. "I want to live what you'd call a normal life."

"And you didn't have a normal life where you lived before?"

"Normal for there, yes," she answered.

They passed by the bank and then the feed store, where two men standing outside leered openly at her. A pointed look from Mr. Caine had them scurrying inside, safe from the trouble his glare promised.

"What was so bad about where you lived?" he asked as though nothing had happened.

Lucy bit back a laugh, then watched his face as she answered. "It was Hell."

To her surprise, he didn't flinch at her language. Instead he chuckled softly. "I know what you mean. I used to think this was hell, too."

"Oh no," she muttered. "This isn't even close."

He led her inside the law office where, within minutes, the old whiskey-smelling judge made it official.

She was now Mrs. Jedidiah Caine. Granted, it wouldn't last long, but she'd never been a wife before.

This ought to be interesting.

CHAPTER TWO

*W*hat the hell had he just done?

Jed fought the panic creeping through his veins. He'd spent two long days thinking the whole thing through so carefully. He'd made detailed mental lists of what he needed—and didn't need—in a wife and how much he could afford to bid at the auction.

And then he'd spent the next two days talking himself out of that plan and trying to come up with a way to simply hire a woman to help out for a while.

Despite all his forethought, he'd just paid two and a half dollars more than he'd originally planned and given his name to a woman who was the exact opposite of anyone he'd ever considered wife-like.

Sure, she was a looker with all that long, black, glossy hair and those bright green eyes. But the fancy dress she wore, with its low-cut bodice and cinched waist, was about as impractical as could be, and as for those satin slippers on her feet . . .

This was a disaster waiting to happen. Even the way she spoke was wrong; gentlewomen didn't dare *think* the suggestive things that came out of Lucy's mouth. God knew Maggie never uttered words like that! And if Lucy spoke so freely about these things, how much of that came from actual experience?

Yup, Jed had definitely lost his mind when he'd agreed to marry Lucy. But his word was his vow, so now he'd have to find a way to make it work.

Several more dollars later, he'd outfitted her with two simple day dresses, a pair of sturdy boots, a cotton bonnet she refused to touch, and a pair of work gloves.

The dresses were designed for work, not looks, made with plain stitched cotton and not so much as a breath of lace. The black leather boots would no doubt hurt something awful until she broke them in, and the bonnet was, without question, unsightly, but it would keep the sun off her head, and that was more important than anything else.

She'd turned up her nose at all of it and flatly refused to so much as try the gloves on.

Jed rubbed the back of his neck and sighed. It had been the condition of Lucy's hands that pushed him into this marriage. She might look all silky and fancy, but those hands told a different story, one she hadn't wanted him— or anyone else—to know about.

"Just so you know," Lucy said with a sniff. "There's a considerable difference between dresses with no frills and ones that are down-right ugly."

"They're not ugly; they're sensible." Jed sighed as he collected the package and led her away from the mercantile toward his waiting wagon. "And besides, I think we both know you couldn't be ugly if you tried."

That seemed to appease her long enough for Jed to double check the rest of the supplies roped down in the back of the wagon, and then help his new wife up onto the blanket-covered seat. She pulled a second blanket from behind the bench and wrapped it around her shoulders, sending a waft of her unusual, exotic scent to tickle Jed's nose.

"When we get home, you'd best wash off your perfume," he sighed, swallowing back his regret. "It'll attract mosquitoes."

She laughed lightly. "I'm not wearing perfume. Besides, mosquitoes don't like me—I have bad blood."

The horses whinnied and tossed their heads nervously. What was that all about? Jed took a second to scratch their noses, which seemed to calm them a little.

He climbed up beside Lucy, released the brake, and clicked the horses forward. Why was she moving closer to him? There was plenty of room on her side of the bench.

"It's a bit of a ride." He cleared his throat to try to ease the tight knot that threatened to block his words and his breathing. "You should put that bonnet on."

Lucy slid closer until their legs pressed against each other through layers of silk and wool. "I told you, I'm not wearing that revolting thing—especially not through the middle of town where someone might see me."

"The heat'll make you sick," he said. "You need to cover your head."

"This isn't heat," she answered airily. "And I don't get sick, so you can stop fretting."

Jed's patience began to fray. "If I say the sky is blue, I'd wager you'd say it was yellow."

Lucy snuggled under the blanket a bit more, without the slightest disturbance crossing her expression. "What are you talking about?"

"You challenge every word I say!" he bellowed, then took a long, deep breath. "There are jobs that need to be done, Lucy, and it'll be your job to do them. They won't be fun, and they won't be easy, but you'll have to do them anyway."

Her only response was a shrug and a smile.

"You *will* wear that bonnet, and you *will* wear the dresses because that . . . thing . . . you're wearing now will only get ruined. And if you get sick from the heat, you can't work."

"I won't get sick."

"You don't know that!" He was yelling again.

"Yes," she answered plainly. "I do know that."

Jed needed to calm down. This was no way to start a marriage—and he sure as hell couldn't let Maggie see him so upset.

"You know that for certain?" he asked, forcing his voice to a normal level.

"Of course."

"Here's what I know for certain." He tightened his grip on the reins. "I just paid a helluva lot of money for a wife I didn't want because the school and my family needed me to. And for whatever reason, you were set on leaving that auction with me."

Lucy's smile lit up her entire face. "Yes," she agreed. "You were the one I wanted."

"Well, you got me," he grunted. "This is me, and this is going to be your life from now on. When we get home, you'll put on one of them other dresses, you'll tie that stupid bonnet over your head and you'll get to work."

"But—"

"No. No buts." He shook his head, but kept his eyes looking straight ahead. "You wanted me, and you got me. I warned you back there it would be a lot of work, and I'm not going to waste time arguing with you over everything I say."

He dared a quick glance toward her, just in time to see fire flash in the depths of her green eyes. A heartbeat later, it was gone, replaced with a smile she must have pulled out of nowhere.

"Whatever you say, husband." She pushed her hand out from the folds of the blanket and settled it on his thigh.

Jed tensed, but didn't say anything. Sweet Jesus, where did this woman come from? She couldn't have been from Texas, because Texas ladies were . . . well . . . well-behaved. Granted, it had been a while since he'd been with a woman, but he sure didn't remember any of them being so free with their hands.

'Course, Lucy wasn't even a little bit like any of those women; that was mighty clear and he'd only just met her, but at least he'd made his point. She knew what was expected now and, God willing, there'd be no more arguments over it.

Her slender fingers inched up a little more, then more yet, and tightened in a gentle squeeze.

Whoa! Blood ripped through Jed's system like a hurricane, and God help him it was going to be a helluva storm if he didn't put a stop to it right quick.

"Lucy," he struggled to say, lifting her hand from his leg and setting it in her own lap. "There's some things we need to get straight, and I think we'd best do it now before we get home."

"If you say so." Her eyes sparkled beneath dark lashes. "But remember, husband, I already agreed to do everything you want."

Despite his rant a moment ago, Jed wasn't near stupid enough to believe one word of that. He cleared his throat roughly and nodded. He shoulda never gone to that blasted auction.

"First things first, then." He reined in the horses, set

the brake and turned to face his new wife. "This is my side of the bench and that"—he pointed to the far side—"is yours. I need you to sit over there."

Confusion dimmed her eyes for a brief moment. "Why?"

"Because." He hesitated. Honesty was the key to everything, though she obviously didn't feel the same way. Regardless, he'd best start off on the right foot—set the example, no matter how uncomfortable it was to admit. "You're too distracting when you sit this close."

Lucy's face lit up. "Distracting? Oooh, I like that." She resettled herself a little ways down the bench, not completely on the other side, but far enough away that they no longer touched.

And more importantly, both of her hands stayed tucked beneath her blanket.

"Thank you." Jed set the wagon in motion again, and took two long, deep breaths before continuing. "There's some things you need to know before we get home."

"Such as?" She didn't look the least bit interested, but instead seemed more fascinated by a stand of mesquite bushes along the side of the road. It couldn't be good if his new wife was more interested in a prickly, hard-to-kill weed than in what he had to say.

Not good at all.

"Well," he stammered. "To start with, there's Maggie."

"Your sister-in-law."

He nodded. "She's a little frail right now, worse since Sam disappeared. She gets weepy and sometimes says things she doesn't mean."

No response. Was Lucy even listening?

"You need to be patient with her. She refuses to believe Sam is dead—"

"And you believe he is."

"I don't believe my brother would leave his wife in her condition unless he was dead." His voice uttered the words even as a tiny part of his heart pinched against them. He wanted to hope, as Maggie did, that Sam would come back to them, but he couldn't afford to hope anymore.

He had a pregnant sister-in-law and a spread to take care of.

"Maggie needs to rest," he said. "She's already lost two babies, and if she loses this one . . ." He didn't finish.

"What about you, husband?" Lucy tipped her head to the side and studied him until he squirmed. "What should I know about you?"

"Only that I'm a practical man. I don't have time for frippery and nonsense, and once we get home, neither will you."

"And by frippery, you mean . . ."

"I mean spending time worrying about how you look or what you're wearing." He took a slow breath. "There's only two things you need worry about."

"And those would be?"

"Tending to Maggie and getting the chores done."

"You're not one of the things I need to be worrying about, husband?"

Jed shook his head and shifted his position on the bench. "We're not in love, Lucy, and we don't need to be. All we need to do is build respect between us."

"Not love?" Surprise filled her voice.

"Love might become part of it," he nodded. "But two people can have a good marriage without any of that nonsense some girls look for."

She seemed to ponder that for a moment, a deep frown puckering her brow. "Are you telling me you don't think you'll ever love me?"

One of the horses snorted and tossed its mane as if it were laughing at him.

Deep breath. "If it happens, it happens, but it's not something I'd expect."

"That's not very romantic, husband."

"If you're looking for romance, you've chosen the wrong man."

Damn that no-refund rule.

Lucy continued to study the side of his face for a long moment. "You honestly don't believe we were destined to be together? That somehow, through the turning of time, we were meant to be, that we're . . . what is that silly expression . . . *soul mates*?"

Jed rolled his eyes heavenward. "I believe in reality, Lucy. And the reality of our marriage is that I needed help, you were being auctioned off, and I bought you. Period. Wasn't destiny, wasn't fate, and it sure as hell doesn't mean we're soul mates." He cast a quick glance her way, cursing himself for his acid tone. "I could just as easily be taking home one of them other girls."

She didn't seem the least bit affected by his words, and though he wished it didn't, it unsettled him.

After a few more deep breaths, he continued. "Maybe, in time, we might come to feel . . . some sort of . . . affection . . . for each other, but we need to get to know each other first. For the first while, we'll be too busy to even think about any of that anyway."

She raised her brow and smiled saucily.

"What about lust, husband? Is that part of a good marriage?"

Jed choked on his next breath. "I . . . uh . . ."

"What?" Lucy's laughter was low and throaty. "Do you think lust is something only a man feels?"

He fought to swallow. "I . . . uh . . ."

"It's not." She moved closer, sliding her hand across his thigh again. "Most women are told it's shameful to feel such things, so they don't speak of it." Her hand slid higher, her voice softer. "But we feel it, husband, just as much as you."

Jed ground his teeth together and pushed her hand away. One more touch from her and he'd surely explode.

"Stay. Over. *There.*"

He wished he could stand up and adjust his trousers, but that'd only give her more to smile about. "This is exactly what I'm talking about."

"Lust?"

"No, not lust." He shook his head. "Well, yes, but no."

"You're not making sense, husband."

Jed glared her way, then exhaled slowly. "If you'd just stay over there—and not touch me—I'll try to explain."

The scorching sun seared through his clothes and hat, making it near impossible to draw a clear breath.

"As I was saying," he sighed, "a marriage is better built on reality and respect than silly notions and romance."

She just shrugged.

"As for lust"—He tightened his hold on the reins until the leather pinched his skin white—"it's an important part, too, but that's not what I want."

A look of horror gripped Lucy's features. "You don't want to . . . ?" She gasped loudly. "Or do you mean you *can't* . . . ?"

"No!" He bit back a curse. "I mean, yes, of course I want to. And of course I can!"

"Thank goodness." Her saucy smile returned. "You had me worried there for a minute."

Every breath was a chore, every word a lesson in patience. "I just mean that in order for our marriage to be strong, we need to have something more than *that* between us."

Lucy yawned.

Yawned!

"Once we know each other better," he continued, "and have a good amount of respect for one another, then we can . . . well . . . I mean . . ." Heat raced up his neck and ears.

"Get lusty?"

Jed couldn't help but laugh. "Yes, Lucy. Then we can get lusty."

God help him, what had he married? A practical man would turn the buggy around and dump her back in Miss Blake's lap, refund or not. What had happened to that practical man? Somewhere between walking into the restaurant and touching Lucy's calloused hands, he'd disappeared, replaced by this stuttering fool who couldn't seem to put two words together without tripping over his tongue.

Lucy chewed her bottom lip for a moment, her brow furrowed slightly. "So you're saying you don't want to bed me?"

Jed gulped back a breath. Women didn't—or shouldn't—speak of these things so openly. "That's not what I said."

"Yes it is."

"No," he corrected. "I never said I didn't want to . . . bed . . . you." *Breathe*. "I said we need to develop trust and respect between us before we . . ."

"Get lusty and impassioned," she finished for him, a not-so-innocent smile tugging her lips upward.

Jed swiped his arm across his brow. If Lucy was trying to drive him mad, she was doing a damn fine job.

"Right," he finally muttered, then forced his breathing back to normal. "So we're agreed then."

They rode in silence for a long while, Jed trying his damnedest to control his thoughts and breathing, while Lucy seemed to be pondering the whole idea amid her confusion.

"What about kissing?" she blurted, her eyes wide with hope. "That's fairly harmless, isn't it?"

Jed groaned. Somehow, he doubted anything about Lucy would be harmless. With any other woman, kissing could undoubtedly be completely safe, but with her? Sweet Jesus, she'd likely devour him whole.

"How 'bout we just take it slow and see what happens?" He cast her a quick glance, just in time to see her frown.

"Don't you *want* to kiss me?" she asked.

"Lucy—"

Too late. She was already sliding closer again, pressing her body against his arm as her whisper breathed against his ear. "I've been wanting to kiss you, husband, since the moment I saw you at the back of that smelly old room."

"I—"

Swallow. Breathe.

She ran her finger around the edge of his ear, then down his jaw.

"Why don't we stop under that big tree there." She pointed toward a towering pecan tree about a hundred feet off the road.

Its huge branches cast the only significant shade for miles around; it'd be cool and comfortable, the perfect place to . . .

"No." He shook away from her touch and released the reins long enough to point her back to her side of the bench. Hadn't she heard a word of what he'd just spent so many tortured breaths explaining to her?

"You don't want to kiss me?" Lucy pouted. "Then why did you pick me?"

With a long sigh, he searched for the words to make her understand.

"It's not that I don't want to," he said finally. "I'm sure every man in town wants to."

That seemed to make her feel a little better. Her pout disappeared, and the frown began to fade.

"You're a very strange man, Jedidiah Caine." Lucy shook her head slowly. "Very strange indeed."

She was right. He was a little strange, especially compared to most of the men in town.

"Well," Lucy said, "even practical men want to bed a woman once in a while."

Jed sighed. He'd be willing to bet any one of the others would have taken a room at the hotel and made Lucy their wife ten minutes after marrying her. But Jed wanted more, more than just a woman in his bed, more than just a wife who did his every bidding.

Three years ago, he thought he'd found that wife. She was everything he needed: capable and caring, without any of the usual female sensitivities or need for undying love getting in the way. It was a sensible pairing, and he had been confident that the respect they felt for each other made up for any romance that was lacking.

But then he'd gone and introduced her to his brother. After that, he could only stand back and watch as the two of them fell head-over-heels in love.

He knew that kind of love didn't happen to everyone, and since he'd just up and married a woman who was his complete opposite, it sure as hell wasn't likely to happen to him. But he didn't need love to make his marriage work. All he needed was a basic mutual respect between him and Lucy.

Given that her main concern seemed to be nothing more than pretty dresses and sex, it would no doubt prove more of a challenge than he'd expected, but somehow—someway—he'd make it work.

God help him.

CHAPTER THREE

Is this it?" Lucy stared down from the wagon seat in dismay. Surely to Satan, there was more to Jed Caine's spread than a tiny barn and a slapped-together shanty. Somewhere beyond the sparse patches of grass and acres of dirt there had to be something more.

"Yup, this is it."

A tiny corner of Jed's soul flickered to darkness, then fought back to the light. To him, as a human, it would only seem like a moment's disappointment, but Lucy knew better. Too many disappointments darkened a mortal's soul until it was charred beyond recovery. A heartbeat later, a look of determination settled over him with such intensity, it rattled her nerves for a moment.

"It might not look like much yet," he said, "but it will. Just needs a little work."

"A *little*?" She let him lift her from the wagon and then followed him toward the small shanty. How did anyone live like this—and why would they want to?

"How long have you lived here?" she asked.

Jed shrugged. "Going on six or eight months I guess."

"And what—exactly—have you been doing out here all

that time?" He obviously hadn't spent the time working on the house.

"Settling in, stringing the fence . . ." he trailed off.

"The fence?" She wanted to scream, but bit it back. "You didn't think a proper house might be the better place to start?"

His lip curled in a small grin. "You're the one who told me you had all the strength I needed, so I saved the big work for you."

He was certainly handsome when he grinned like that, a delicious mixture of boyish charm and male determination.

"But—"

"No buts." He took her by the hand and led her into the middle of the yard, then turned in a slow circle, his arms spread wide. "It's going to be the best piece of land God ever set on the earth."

"But—"

"We'll build a house, a new barn," he paused, then added, "we can raise a family here."

She clamped her mouth shut, grinding her teeth together. Hell would freeze solid twice before she'd agree to bring a child into this world. She was here for herself and no one else, not for this new husband and certainly not to have a child.

She was here to claim three souls: Jed's, Maggie's and the baby's when it was born. The baby was the most important; the other two simply stood in the way.

Maggie should be easy enough to sway, given her fragile state of mind. But she had a feeling Jed was going to prove a bit more difficult.

Once she'd completed her mission, she could hand their souls over to Satan and be free to do as she wished.

And what she wished was for someone else to take her place in the bowels of Hell.

Jed interrupted her musings by waving his finger in front of her and pointing to the strings of barbed wire snaking off in the distance.

"I had to finish the fence first so we could start building a herd."

"A herd of what?" The stench of horse dung assaulted her senses, making her eyes water and her throat tighten against a gag.

"Cattle."

"Cows stink," Lucy groaned. "And they're stupid."

Jed shot her a wink and grinned. "True, but they're also money in the bank."

"But—"

"No buts."

As he took her hand and headed back toward the wagon, Lucy's next complaint fogged out of her mind. His hands were distractingly warm. And strong.

"Why don't you take this." He pulled the parcel of new clothes from the wagon and handed it to her. "You can get changed into one of them other dresses, and then we can get started."

He set about releasing the horses, speaking softly to each animal as he unbuckled the straps, taking a moment to scratch behind their ears and across their noses.

"Maggie might be sleeping," he warned. "So be quiet when you go in."

The mention of Maggie redirected Lucy's thoughts. She shouldn't focus on the horrid land and piles of dung surrounding her, but rather on what she could do to hurry things along. Maggie was the first step.

With a small flounce, Lucy took her package into the house and stood staring through the gloom.

A tiny window faced north toward the makeshift barn and main pasture, but whatever light it might have let in was shadowed by a narrow overhang from the roof. She lit the lamp, turned it as bright as she could, then took a good look around the cramped space that was now her home.

The one-room shack did nothing to boost her spirits. A small square table sat under the window, with two oddly crooked chairs tucked beneath it. Long narrow shelves hung on both the far wall and the one between the door and the table, each filled with cans of beans, bags of rice, and various other household items.

Three hooks in the near corner held changes of clothes: a pair of faded denim pants, a blue button-down shirt, a tattered pair of long gray underthings and two plain dresses.

The other corner of the pathetically small room was completely taken up by a narrow, lumpy bag of straw with a green blanket tossed over it.

The lump shifted and moaned.

"Jedidiah?" The voice coming from the bed was frail and feeble.

"No," Lucy said. "I'm Lucy, Jedidiah's wife."

"His what?" Maggie scrambled from the bed, then stumbled back into the wall, her nightgown tangled around her legs. Stringy blonde hair fell around her shoulders in a matted mess, and her skin was so pale, she almost appeared transparent.

"His wife," Lucy repeated as she stepped forward.

"Don't touch me." Maggie recoiled. She narrowed her eyes and squinted back at Lucy. "Who are you?"

"I told you, I'm Lucy."

"Where did you come from?" Distrust oozed from Maggie's every pore.

"You don't want to know," Lucy laughed.

"Why are you here?" Maggie hadn't moved from the wall.

"To look after you."

There seemed to be a barrier of some kind around Maggie's soul, one that made it impossible to read, but Lucy could still see the woman was obviously mad.

"Who sent you?" Maggie's voice grew tighter. Lucy was certain the other woman would have crawled through the wall if it meant she could get away from Lucy.

"Nobody sent me, Maggie. I'm here to help you."

Where was the stove? And the floor! Not a single plank of wood to step on, nothing but more dirt. How could anyone be expected to keep that clean?

Obviously, by marrying Jed Caine, Lucy had done nothing more than trade one form of Hell for another.

At least the other Hell was warm.

"I don't need your help."

"Really?" Lucy shrugged indifferently. "That's not what I hear."

Maggie turned a little more into the room. "What did you hear?"

With a heavy sigh, Lucy stopped and turned to face her. "Your husband ran off because he couldn't stand being married to a madwoman. The whole town is afraid your baby will be born mad, too, and I was the only one Jed could convince to come out here and help you." She paused, then waggled her brow. "Cost him plenty, too."

"How much?"

Lucy fought the snort. "Practically sold his soul to the devil."

Maggie gasped, her eyes round as dish plates, her

hands splayed protectively across her enormous belly. "Get out!"

"I can't do that, Maggie." Lucy planted her hands on her hips and shrugged. "Jed paid good money for me, and I have a job to do."

"Jedidiah will make you go if I tell him to."

"No, he won't."

"Yes, he will," Maggie screeched as she ran past Lucy and out the door. "Just you watch, devil woman!"

Shock stopped Lucy from chasing her outside. Surely Maggie couldn't know . . .

No. That was ridiculous.

Lucy didn't have time to worry about it anyway. She had a plan and she needed to make it work. Unfortunately, things weren't quite going the way she'd figured. The dress she'd so carefully selected now lay in a heap on the bed, and in its place, she put on the plainest, most boring cotton sack of a blue dress she'd ever seen. Its high collar nearly choked her, and the long sleeves hugged the length of her arms down to where they buttoned tightly at the wrists.

Even in Hell, she had better clothes.

Outside, Maggie's screechy voice continued to plead with Jed to send Lucy away. Though she couldn't make out Jed's end of the conversation, it obviously wasn't what Maggie wanted to hear.

Lucy searched the shelves until she found a knife sharp enough to serve her purpose. She slipped out of the dress and in seconds, left the itchy collar and half of each sleeve in a pile at her feet. Without the benefit of a looking glass, she'd have to hope for the best, but to help matters along, she yanked the top three buttons off, leaving it open to the V between her breasts, and fluffed her hair around her shoulders.

"There," she muttered. "Now we'll see how strong you really are, Jedidiah."

Lack of sleeves would only chill her more, but that was a small price to pay if it helped her plan further along.

With the dress remnants collected, she took one last disheartened look around the room, extinguished the lamp and stepped out into the late afternoon sunshine.

"See?" Maggie cried. "Just look at her!"

"What the . . . ?" Jed's gaze swept the length of Lucy, his mouth hanging open, his hat pushed back on his head.

Lucy resisted the urge to laugh. Men—show them a little skin and they all turned into drooling fools.

"Where's the stove?" she asked, pretending not to notice his reaction. But for added fun, she lifted her skirt high enough to scratch a nonexistent itch just above her knee.

Maggie cowered behind Jed, her loud whisper carrying across the yard. "She wants to cook me."

Jed stuttered for a moment, but recovered with remarkable speed. "Nobody's going to cook you, Maggie."

"You brought her here to cook me." Maggie's pale blue eyes widened as a fresh wave of fear crashed over her. "You got rid of Sam and now you want to get rid of me."

"I didn't do anything to Sam," he said quietly. "And I'd never hurt you, Maggie." He wrapped his arm around her shoulders and started back toward the house. "Please go lie down. You need your rest."

"I've had my rest," Maggie snapped. "That devil woman's going to cut me open and steal my baby."

Lucy watched in silence as Jed struggled to get Maggie inside the shack again.

"You'll be fine," he soothed. "I promise not to let her touch anything sharp."

He closed the door, then leaned his forehead against it. A second later, a loud thud sounded from the inside.

Jed looked up at Lucy and smiled sadly. "She sometimes likes to keep the door barred."

Lucy could have pretended to care, but it hardly seemed worth the effort. Maggie would be easy enough to take; it was Jed she needed to focus on. If he thought for one second something was amiss, he'd no doubt bring everything to a halt, and Lucy didn't have time for that.

"The stove?" she asked again.

Jed pushed away from the door and pointed toward a large circle of rocks with a spit set above a pile of cold embers. "We cook over the fire."

"What fire?" She offered him a saucy little smile, and even added a head tilt for good measure.

The slow grin that spread across Jed's face left Lucy unsettled.

"The fire you're going to build once you get the chips collected," he answered.

Lucy gaped. "What? You don't really expect me—"

"'Course," he interupted. "Thought we covered that back at the auction." He moved around the corner of the house and returned a moment later with a small wooden pushcart.

"Here you go."

"But—"

"No buts, remember?" When she made no move to take the handles from him, he set it at her feet and walked away.

"Wait!" she called. "I can't pick up . . . *that*."

"'Course you can," he answered over his shoulder. "Go get the gloves we bought and just make sure the chips are good 'n dry before you touch them."

Bile swirled up Lucy's throat. He had to be joking. She was Lucille Firr—the Devil's daughter! She'd done a lot of humiliating things in her day, but picking up *animal chips* wasn't one of them. And regardless of what she might have said back at the auction, she had no intention of starting now.

She tugged her collar open a bit more, fluffed her hair and worked up her most seductive smile.

"But, Jed," she said softly, following him back toward the wagon, "it's such a smelly thing for a lady to do, and my gloves are in the house with Maggie."

"No chips, no fire." He didn't stop to look at her—and she was putting on a fine show with her hips swaying and her head tilted to the side a little. She even set her lips in what she'd been told was a beautiful little pout.

She stepped around the wagon and slid her hands up his back, loving the feel of hard muscles against her palms.

"I'd rather light *your* fire," she purred.

Jed's hands stilled atop a large bag of flour. For a second, she thought she'd won him over, but then—

"We already talked about that, Lucy," he said, his voice a little tighter than before.

"No," she murmured. "You talked." She moved around him, trailing her finger over his shoulder, then across his jaw. When his Adam's apple bobbed hard, she pushed his hat off and slid both hands through his hair. "Now it's my turn to talk."

"Lucy . . ." he stepped back, but she wasn't about to let him get away. The sooner she finished this, the sooner she'd be rid of this ugly dress and that pathetic shack.

"We're married, Jed," she whispered. "We're out here in the middle of nowhere, with no one to see what we're doing." She pressed herself against him. "I could do things to you that'd make your—"

"Stop it." Jed pulled her hands away and stepped back

again, holding her at a safe distance. "We had a deal, Lucy."

"What deal is that?" She tried to tug her hands free, but his grip tightened.

He paused only long enough to lick his lips. "I made it pretty clear you weren't the woman I needed out here. One of them other girls was more what I wanted."

Once again, Lucy wasn't what anyone wanted. Not the mother who'd abandoned her, certainly not her father, and now not even her husband wanted her.

"They were ugly." She pushed her lip out a bit further, but Jed didn't look the least bit swayed.

Damn it.

"They were sturdy," he corrected, "strong, able-bodied women who'd have gotten right to work when we arrived here. That's what you agreed to."

"Did I?" No, she wouldn't have agreed to such nonsense. But, thinking back, she'd been awfully distracted by her man's dark eyes and clean smell. And, of course, the knowledge that she needed him to fulfill her plan.

Maybe she *had* agreed to it.

Lucy shrugged. It was irrelevant what she may or may not have agreed to. She didn't have to actually do it. Not *her*.

"Yes, you did." Jed released her hands and nodded toward the cart behind her. "It's getting late and Maggie could use a hot meal, so I suggest you get to work."

"Why can't you cut down a tree?"

He sighed heavily. "Look around, Lucy. There's not exactly an abundance of trees, and the ones we have will be needed for the house and a proper barn. We can't waste them on a fire."

There wasn't exactly an abundance of *anything* on Jed's land. Far in the distance, there were trees—big ones, too—but he obviously wasn't to be convinced. Surely there was something else they could burn . . .

"What about those?" she asked, pointing to the scatterings of prickly pears and thatches of mesquite bushes whose blooms had all seen better days.

"We're going to need those for corrals and the like." He smiled at her, but it only grated against her nerves more. "The buffalo herds were kind enough to leave plenty of things to burn when they came through, and Sam and I piled it up where we were working, so all you need do is go collect it. If you walk the fence line, you're sure to find plenty of piles to choose from."

"But—" She curled her fingers into tight fists.

"No buts." He moved around her and set to work on shifting more of the supplies toward the back of the wagon. "I'll get the supplies stored, and you'd best set to work on that fire. There's matches in the house."

House. Lucy choked back a snort. That dingy little shack was most definitely *not* a house—certainly not one she wanted to be living in, especially with a lunatic like Maggie.

"No." She *was not* going to touch buffalo dung, even with gloves. She risked her entire plan by refusing, but she couldn't do it. *Wouldn't* do it.

"No?" Jed chuckled, but there was no humor in it. In fact, he almost sounded indifferent. How could that be? She'd been seductive, she'd been sweet, and when that didn't work, she was adamant. Men liked those traits in a woman. Didn't they?

"Fine with me," he said. "I'm used to cold beans."

"Good, because I won't do it, Jed." She folded her arms over her chest and lifted her chin in defiance. "So you can eat all the cold beans you like."

He shrugged, but didn't respond.

If he thought for one minute he could be more stubborn than she, he was in for a rude awakening. "You can't make me do it."

"You're right," he agreed, without looking at her. "I can't."

He hauled the huge bag of flour out of the wagon and threw it over his shoulder. "Maggie and her baby could do with a nice hot meal, but they've survived so far on cold beans and pork, so I'm sure they'll be fine."

Did he honestly think guilt would work on her? Stupid man.

When Lucy didn't respond or move, he simply pushed past her as if she wasn't there and headed toward the barn.

No one treated her that way—no one! He'd be good and sorry when he realized who she was. It would make the final moments of his life that much more enjoyable.

And they could go ahead and eat their stupid beans cold for all she cared. Maybe they'd choke on them.

So long as they didn't die before she claimed that baby's soul.

CHAPTER FOUR

Maggie's means of barring the door consisted of dropping the Bible on the floor in front of it. Lucy pushed it aside with the edge of the door and stepped inside.

Over in the corner, Maggie lay curled up on the mattress again, whimpering in her sleep. Being mad must take a lot out of a person.

"Just look at you."

Lucy started at the unexpected voice.

Deacon. She should have expected him, yet seeing him there sent tremors through her veins. Before he sensed her fear, she slammed a wall up between them—she couldn't let him see into her soul. He might be her brother, but he was very much their father's son.

"What do you want?" She relit the lamp, low this time, then slumped down on the least rickety chair.

"Just came to see how my favorite sister's doing with her new *husband*." Deacon set his black bowler hat on the small table, then wiped the seat of the other chair with one of his pristine white gloves before sitting. A narrow, twitching nose poked out from inside Deacon's coat pocket, then wiggled its entire body out onto his lap.

"Ugh—why do you still keep that thing?" Lucy wrinkled her nose at the white ferret as it sniffed the air.

Deacon smiled down at the little rodent and scratched it gently behind the ears.

"You can't stay here," Lucy said. "If Maggie wakes up, or Jed sees you, he'll—"

"He'll what? Force me into an ugly old rag like that?" Deacon shuddered.

Lucy suppressed a grin; her brother was nothing if not vain. He wore only the fanciest of silk suits, the most stylish hats, and his boots showed nary a scuff. So why he let a filthy little ferret crawl all over him was beyond her.

Maggie sobbed quietly and rolled into a tight ball, pulling the blanket tight under her chin.

"Interesting choice you've made this time, Lucille." Deacon's gaze fixed pointedly on her, looking through her, down into her soul. "Are you sure you're ready to risk your future on this? If you quit now, I'm sure Father would understand."

"It was hardly my choice," she answered, straightening her spine and lifting her chin. Their father would definitely not understand, and she was not about to quit. "What do you care, anyway?"

He lifted the ferret in one hand until they were nose to nose.

"Surely you know me better than that," he sneered. "When have I ever cared about you or anything you do?"

A short moment of silence—barely a heartbeat—brought the reality of her brother's visit crashing down around her.

"No." Dread filled Lucy's lungs until she could barely breathe.

He didn't speak, but his silence screamed the truth.

"Deacon—he promised he wouldn't interfere."

All the strength drained from her body; this couldn't be happening. She'd planned everything so carefully, so cautiously, but she'd never planned for this.

"Lucille—"

"No," she repeated, anger replacing the dread. "He promised!"

Deacon shook his head slowly. She hated him most when he looked at her in that patronizingly superior way of his.

"We're talking about Satan, Lucille. After all these years, do you really think you can trust anything he says?"

Of course she couldn't. She knew that. Everyone knew that.

Heat flamed her skin, and her heart pounded against her ribs. "I'm his daughter. Surely that means something to him." *How could she have been so stupid?*

"Of course it means something." Deacon chuckled, completely unsympathetic. "It means he takes a more personal interest in seeing you fail."

As he spoke, his pale blue eyes remained fixed and unblinking on his pet's face.

Lucy eyed her brother suspiciously for a long moment before asking the question she wasn't sure she wanted an answer to.

"How are you involved?" she asked, forcing calm into her voice.

"You know the answer to that." As he rose from his chair, he eased the ferret back into his pocket, then reached for his hat, swiping invisible lint from its brim. "I'm here to ensure he gets what he wants."

She reached to touch him, but then pulled back. "Please, Deacon, you can't."

He shrugged. "Of course I can. I've already begun."

"How—" She stopped short. It made sense now. "You have Maggie's husband."

Deacon's head tipped in the barest of nods. "Stupid man. He honestly believed that by making a deal with me, his child would be born healthy and they'd all live the rest of their miserable lives together as though everything was fine."

It all made sense now. Deacon and her father had set her up, had given her a tiny flicker of hope, all the while knowing it was futile.

She wouldn't let Deacon have the satisfaction of winning so easily. "Of course you neglected to mention that he'd never see his wife or child again."

"It wasn't mentioned, no." Deacon shrugged again. "Humans trust too easily."

"And the part about me coming to take their child's soul, regardless of what he did or didn't do—"

"If he knew that, would either one of us be sitting here now?"

Lucy ground her teeth together. Deacon already had Sam, so all he'd have to do was dangle that knowledge in front of Maggie, and she'd no doubt take whatever bargain Deacon offered her, even if it meant giving up her own soul and that of her baby.

Once again, Lucy would be left out, only this time, she'd pay the eternal price for it. "I don't suppose you'd be willing to give Sam to me?"

"Dear, simple, stupid Lucille." Deacon set his hat back on his head and pulled on each glove with slow precision. "Why would I give up anything I've rightfully taken? We're talking about Satan!"

She knew full well who they were talking about. But she hadn't planned on Deacon's interference. Her father had promised her a chance at freedom, and she'd been foolish enough to believe him.

Dear, simple, stupid Lucille.

Deacon adjusted his gloves, keeping his gaze everywhere except on her. "You'd do the same thing if you were me, and we both know it."

She opened her mouth to argue, then clamped it shut. He was right. She'd take him down in a heartbeat if Satan told her to. At least Deacon had the decency to admit it.

"Maggie knows about us, doesn't she?"

"Of course. She's very perceptive, that one." Deacon smirked. "It's unfortunate the rest of the world thinks she's mad."

"Does she know what you've done to Sam?"

"There's a part of her twisted mind that knows." Deacon's eyes flashed with silent mirth. "Being human, of course, she refuses to believe it."

"And you're using that to push her over the edge into insanity."

Deacon nuzzled his stupid ferret again. "Your being here is helping me in that regard."

"I won't let you do it." Lucy's voice was low, barely audible to her own ears, but he heard her.

Finally, his eyes met hers again. "You can't stop it, Lucille. I already have the husband and we both know that woman"—he tipped his head in Maggie's direction—"will do anything to try and get him back."

"But she can't get him back."

"True." Deacon's expression remained impassive. "Lucky for us, she doesn't know that."

"So why not take her now?"

He hesitated before answering. "You know why."

The baby. They both needed the child's soul, and the only way to get it was to wait for it to be born. Too bad for

Lucy that Deacon had an ace up his sleeve in the form of Maggie's husband.

Deacon straightened his suit jacket and tipped his hat to the left just a touch. "You can't win this, Lucille. It's simply a matter of whether you give up now or make me take you by force, as I will with the entire Caine family if necessary."

Without another word, Deacon was gone, leaving Lucy to her despair and worries while the cramped room closed in around her.

Deacon was a powerful adversary, no question, and he'd do everything he could to drag her back to Hell with him. He'd win, too. Satan always won, and if he sent Deacon to do his bidding, he fully expected Deacon to win, too.

What made her think she was smart enough—or strong enough—to stand against him and try to win her freedom? She'd seen others attempt the same thing, others who were stronger and much more capable. Yet not a single one had found success.

Why should she be any different?

Failing would mean spending the rest of eternity in Hell with no hope of ever getting out. Not ever. She would never have the chance to live freely, doing as she pleased. Instead, she would be forced into the deepest part of Hell—a part no human could imagine—where the darkness weighed on a soul until it suffocated a million times over.

Lucy couldn't let that happen. Granted, as Satan's child, she would never feel emotions as humans felt them; she'd never experience peace or joy or love, but at least she would be free of the anguish and desperation she'd been threatened with her whole life.

Lucy's mind raced against a mixture of panic and determination.

With Deacon working against her, she'd have to double her efforts. She couldn't let Deacon or their father feel her doubts, not for a single second. If they so much as suspected her fear, it would be her downfall.

She needed Jed. She'd never needed anything or anyone before in her life, but she needed him now. She needed him to love her, even if for just a moment. A moment would be all she needed to win his soul. Once she had Jed's soul, Maggie would fall with little effort, and then Lucy could take the child.

The problem was that no one could love the real her. But maybe—just maybe—she could become someone else until she was free, someone Jed could respect. Someone he could love.

His love was the key to her freedom, plain and simple.

The thought of going back to Hell for an eternity with nothing but desolation—no, she couldn't do it.

She *wouldn't* do it.

Lucy inhaled a long, slow breath and tried to clear her mind.

It couldn't be that hard to win Jed over. If he wouldn't simply give in to his lust, as most men would have by now, she'd have to do things his way. If he wanted her to respect him, then that's what she'd do. She'd respect him if it killed her.

She'd make him believe anything he liked if it meant her freedom.

First things first, she needed to get outside and start collecting buffalo chips.

Damn it.

CHAPTER FIVE

Jed tossed another pile of oats into the feed bin and sighed. Damn, but he was hungry. He'd hoped to avoid cold beans for supper, but if Lucy wasn't going to do her part, then there was nothing he could do about it.

With the long days of tending Maggie and trying to keep up with the chores, he was too tired at night to be bothered with a fire. Maggie ate little but bread and cheese, so there was seldom a need to cook for her.

Sooner or later, Lucy would see her way clear, and then he'd eat to his heart's content. Until then, he could live on cold beans and dried pork a while longer.

But if her anger was any indication, it'd be a while before she saw clear to anything. He'd never seen eyes flash fire like that. It went beyond her tantrum, beyond him denying her advances again, and far beyond any normal woman's frustrations.

For a moment there, he'd almost thought she'd lit his back on fire with rage from that glare.

It'd be easy enough to let her have her way. And sure as hell it would ease her anger enough to make their first night together a lot more enjoyable, but he had to hold firm. By giving in to her now, he'd be letting her think she could do as she pleased whenever she pleased, and that was no way to win her respect. Worse, she'd never earn his.

While the horses chewed noisily, Jed checked over the tack and stored it neatly away. Why couldn't he think of anything besides food? Maybe he'd have an extra serving of pork to make the beans more enjoyable.

What he wouldn't give for a cup of coffee . . . no, he couldn't. He'd had two cups this morning before heading into town. To make more would mean he'd have to build a fire, and that would defeat the purpose of having Lucy do it.

Stubborn, unbending, and too damn proud for his own good—that's what he was. It was those exact qualities that forced him to believe he could make something of what others saw as a hopeless piece of land.

And it was those exact qualities he appeared to share with his new wife. God help them both.

With a final glance around, Jed stepped out into the fading afternoon light and inhaled a long, steadying breath.

What the . . . ?

He froze in place, lifted his nose to the air, and strained to listen for the familiar crackling above a lone whippoorwill's cry. *It couldn't be, could it? It smelled like it, but . . .*

Cautiously, he stepped around the corner of the barn, half expecting it was nothing more than his mind playing tricks on him, that he'd only imagined both the smell and the sound.

They had fire.

Lucy stood next to the pit, small flames dancing skyward and a fair-sized pile of buffalo chips stacked nearby.

She hadn't seen him yet, so he kept to the shadows, watching—and choking back laughter. A rag covered Lucy's mouth and nose, tied at the back of her head. Her cheeks puffed out, straining against the cloth, as her face went from pink to scarlet.

With her gloved hands, she picked up two more chips, tossed them on the fire, then turned and ran, dropping to her knees about a hundred feet away, gasping for breath.

It wasn't until she stood and began to walk back that Jed realized the rag she'd covered her face with was actually the bottom of her skirt. It used to hang to the toes of her boots, but now only reached about halfway down her shins. If she hadn't looked so ridiculous, Jed would have been angry at how she'd ripped apart a perfectly good dress.

But all he could do was grin.

He stepped out of the shadows and moved toward her with slow, steady steps.

"Laugh once and you'll be eating these chips for supper." Lucy swiped her hair back from her face with her forearm, carefully avoiding any contact with the actual glove.

Jed choked back a chuckle and took another step toward her. "You'd probably do it, too."

"How are we supposed to eat anything that's been cooked over a smell like that?"

"Buffalo chips don't smell."

Lucy snorted. "This from the man who won't collect them himself."

He ignored the argument that crept to his tongue. He'd built his fair share of chip fires before she came along and despite what she said, buffalo chips didn't stink.

At least not as bad as cow pies.

Brushing the smelly thoughts from his mind, he slapped his hat against his thigh, sending clouds of dust around him and the fire.

"Where's Maggie?" he asked.

Lucy shot a sharp glare at the house. "She won't come out of the house."

"Why not?" Jed started toward the door, but Lucy's words stopped him in midstep.

"She has it in her head that I've come here to hurt her. And she won't eat because she believes I'm poisoning the food."

"What?" *Had Maggie truly lost her mind? What would possess her to say these things?*

Lucy shrugged almost indifferently. "That's what she said."

"That's craziness."

Another shrug. "I tried to reason with her, but she only got more upset, so I thought it best if I left her alone for now."

Jed was at the cabin door before Lucy finished speaking.

"Maggie!"

No response.

He rapped his fist against the door and called again. "Maggie, you have to eat."

"She's trying to poison me." Maggie's shrill voice reached Lucy at the fire. "Go away."

"Fine." Jed sighed. "I'll make you something myself."

"No. I won't eat anything she's been near."

He pressed his forehead against the door, his palms flattened on each side. "Please, Maggie."

"Go away, Jedidiah."

"You have to come out sooner or later."

"No, I don't." Her voice sounded more determined. "I'm quite happy in here."

"You'll have to . . ." he glanced around frantically ". . . use the outhouse or get water."

A pause. "I'm not coming out so you and your devil wife can kill me and take my baby." A sob. "I'd rather die."

And that was Jed's biggest fear. He could walk in, of course, but that would just make her panic more. And he couldn't force food down her throat.

"Just leave her for now," Lucy said quietly. "She'll come around."

He wanted to believe that, yet a gnawing doubt kept at him, twisting his stomach and making his head pound. With another sigh, he rubbed his hands over his face and turned back to Lucy.

"So what are we having for supper?" he asked, his mouth watering at the mere idea of food. "I could eat the north end of a south-bound skunk right about now."

Lucy sank back to the ground and sighed. "Don't rule that out," she mumbled, barely loud enough for him to hear over the crackling of the fire.

Jed groaned. *No no no*.

He should have listened to his head. He should have stuck to his plan and taken one of the other women at the auction—one who could actually cook and who wouldn't have caused such a fuss over starting a fire.

The fact that none of the other women would have even considered coming home with him was irrelevant.

"You can't cook." It wasn't a question, since they both knew the answer.

"No." With a slow tug, she pulled the rag from her face.

He kicked a chip with his boot as the hopes of warm biscuits and apple pie drifted away like a feather on a spring breeze. Far, far away.

"You lied to me."

"Yes." She didn't look the least bit remorseful, and he didn't expect her to.

"Can you cook anything?"

Lucy's mouth twisted for a moment before she shook her head. "Nothing."

"Not even biscuits?" He could hope.

She shook her head.

"Pie?" *Please say yes.*

Another shake of her head.

"But surely you can make coffee." Desperation tightened his voice.

"No."

Jed blew out a long loud breath. "Can you clean? Do the washing?"

Lucy yanked the gloves off, rubbed her hand over the back of her neck and offered him an innocent little smile.

"Well, I never have, but how hard can it be?"

"You've never washed clothes before? Never kept a house clean?" His blood simmered just below a boil.

"No."

Jed paced beside the fire, his teeth clenched, his belly inflamed and knotted—and growling loud enough to wake the dead. "Why?" He wanted to grab her and shake an answer out of her, but doubted her answer would be anything he wanted to hear. "And where they hell did you come from that you didn't learn to cook or clean?"

Her silence fueled his frustrations until he thought he'd scream—at himself, not her.

Jed cursed himself sideways. Lucy was the only woman who would have left that auction with him. He needed her even if she couldn't boil water.

At first glance, he'd wanted Lucy for the same reason every other man at the auction had wanted her: she was sexy as hell. But he could have resisted that. Good looks didn't last under the hardships of Texas ranching. He'd been pulled in by something so ridiculous, he still couldn't believe it.

It all came down to pride.

She had calluses on her hands, evidence of hardship and years of work. Those hands tipped it for him, despite what the rest of her appearance said. Anyone with hands like that knew hard work, and that was the kind of woman he wanted working with him.

And he'd enjoyed that she only wanted him and no other man. That alone should have been a warning.

Pride cometh before the fall, after all.

When he turned to face her, she didn't even have the courtesy to look contrite.

"What about children?" he finally asked. "Was that a lie, too?"

So help him, if she admitted to that lie as well, he'd load her into the wagon right this minute and haul her back to town so fast she'd be dizzy for a week.

No matter what Miss Blake said, annulments were easy enough to get these days—especially if it involved a woman who lied as Lucy did. He might not ever be able to hold his head up in town again, but that was just all the more reason to avoid town.

"No." She looked him square in the eye and smiled. "That wasn't a lie. If it's truly my lot in life to have children, I'll welcome them."

"*Your lot?*" The faint glimmer of hope he'd felt a second ago flickered out. "Do you mean to tell me you don't want children?"

"There was a time . . ." She shrugged slowly.

"But—"

She silenced him with a raised finger. "No buts, remember? I told you I'd do whatever you wanted, Jed, and if that includes children, then that's fine with me."

Despite his anger, despite her lies, she had the audacity to smile back at him.

"Of course," she added, "if you want children, you'll need to bed me first."

*   *   *

Lucy choked back her last mouthful of burnt beans, then downed it with another cup of water. Maybe Jed would see the light now and take over the cooking; surely he wouldn't let his darling sister-in-law starve to death.

He'd been awfully quiet since learning she'd deceived him, but he'd as much as licked his plate clean, so perhaps he wasn't as angry as she'd thought.

"Thank you." He set his plate on the blanket next to him. "That was a fine supper."

She fought the urge to snort. Instead, she set her plate on top of his and looked up at him with a wry smile.

"What?" he asked. A quick splash in the creek had rid his hands and face of the afternoon's dust and sweat, but not the frown etched across his brow.

"I never would've taken you for a liar."

A look of absolute umbrage froze his mouth in an *O*. "I don't lie."

"Oh really?" She rolled her eyes for effect. "'A fine supper'?"

Jed sputtered for a second. "But it *was* a fine supper."

"What we just ate, dear husband, was anything but fine." She lifted her chin a notch, then pushed up from the blanket. "You needn't waste time trying to appease me, Jed. I'm a horrible cook and we both know it."

She walked over to the side of the fire pit, where she'd left a pot of boiled water to cool, and set to washing the dishes.

"Lucy."

Hunched over the pot, she bit her lip to stop from

smiling. Miss Blake knew what she was doing with the whole guilt idea. Jed would no doubt give in and relieve her of all future cooking duties. Maybe the dish duty, too.

His huge fingers wrapped around her arm, gently pulling her to her feet.

When she was standing next to him, he released her. Lucy could only hope she looked as hurt as she was trying to be.

"Supper *was* fine," he said, then held up a hand when she opened her mouth to object. "I told you earlier, I've been eating nothing but cold beans and a little dried pork for weeks." He paused a second, then added with a drawn out sigh, "Long, tiresome weeks."

"And you want me to believe what I served you tonight was better than that?"

Color crept up Jed's neck as he chuckled softly. "Well, now, I never said it was *better*, did I?"

Lucy opened her mouth to argue, then snapped it shut.

"No," she admitted, looking down at his boots. "You never did."

He tipped her chin back up with the crook of his finger and smiled down at her. "I didn't say it was bad, either. It was fine."

"It was burnt."

"It was cooked, which is a darn sight better than what I've been living on lately."

"But—"

Jed pressed his finger against her lips. Her heart stuttered, her breath held, and for a long moment, they simply stood there, Jed seemingly mesmerized by the mating of his finger against her lips.

Lucy stood rooted to the spot, willing him to kiss her, to press his lips against hers and take everything he wanted.

His mouth opened and shut twice. Then he licked his lips and swallowed hard.

"No buts," he murmured before pulling his finger away and stuffing both hands deep in his pockets.

An odd feeling coursed through Lucy's body. Her lips tingled from his touch, and it took every ounce of strength she could muster—and then some—to not slide her tongue out to taste where he'd touched.

Startled, she shook herself hard. *What the—?*

Biting back a curse, she turned away from Jed and set back to work on the dishes. She needed to focus. With Deacon working against her and her husband worrying about a long and fruitful marriage, she definitely needed to rethink her plan.

Lucy had no intention of going back to Hell with Deacon, but she sure as Satan wasn't going to have a long and fruitful commitment to *any* man, least of all one who made her collect buffalo chips. Only a few hours into this marriage, and she'd already had enough of being told what to do and when to do it, especially by a mere mortal.

He'd be sorry.

They'd all be sorry.

CHAPTER SIX

Lust. That's all it was.

He'd been a long time without a woman, and Lucy was a hundred times more woman than he'd planned on bringing home.

Jed scooped the two large buckets from the ground and began the short walk down to the creek, leaving Lucy staring after him. With any luck, the distance would give him time to regain his senses.

He hadn't set out to touch her. Hadn't even meant to stand that close, yet before he knew it, he'd done both. Her lips were softer than any he'd ever felt, and if he hadn't regained his control when he did, sure as hell he'd have kissed her. But kissing her wouldn't be enough—he knew that, and apparently so did she.

He tried not to wonder how many other men had touched her lips, or worse . . .

Jed shook his head. It didn't matter. He needed to be patient, to create a bond with Lucy before they let themselves fall into bed—or onto the hard ground, as was more likely to be the case with her. How long could he resist her, though? Even when she wasn't intentionally trying to seduce him, she was far more than he was prepared to handle.

What he had was a wife who didn't think the same way he did. He had a wife who was only interested in the physical end of a marriage—and that was something no man could resist.

The other men at the auction would lynch him if they knew he hadn't taken her to bed the moment they'd arrived at the house—or sooner.

But he couldn't. Well, he *could*, but a marriage needed to be built on respect. It was a hard-learned lesson, but one he'd never forget. How many times had he seen the disgust in his mother's face when she looked at her husband? And how many times had his father taken up with a girl in town simply because she *didn't* look at him that way?

It was a life Jed wanted no part of. He'd always pictured himself married to a gentle woman, settled down on a big, beautiful ranch somewhere with a whole passel of kids.

Yet suddenly he was married to a woman he knew nothing about, living on a parched piece of land that showed little to no promise at this point. He might never have love in his marriage, but he damn well would be respected.

And if he had any hope of earning Lucy's respect, he needed to prove he was interested in more than just her body. But that body . . .

He followed the familiar path worn down by his many trips to the creek. Oddly shaped prickly pear cacti grew along the way, but his favorite was the one shaped like a hand. Its five elongated, flat pads seemed more like green fingers pointing toward the sky, and each tip—or fingernail—boasted a single yellow bloom, except for the fourth finger, which had yet to bloom at all.

When he reached the creek, Jed knelt and splashed his face with the cool clean water. This creek was one of the main reasons he'd bought the parcel in the first place. About eight feet across and four feet at its deepest, it ran diagonally across his property and, according to the previous owner, had never once run dry, nor had it ever overflowed its banks. That was good enough for Jed.

He filled the buckets, took a long steadying breath, and started back to the house and his new wife. The sun hung above the horizon, leaving the sky awash in winding ribbons of red and pink. Wouldn't be long 'til night set in—one more day Maggie had survived without Sam, one more day she'd carried that baby, one more day she teetered closer to the brink of madness.

Lucy sat on the blanket, facing the fire, seemingly lost in thought. The light from the flames danced across her face, casting odd shadows one second, then illuminating it the next. He'd give almost anything to know what she was thinking.

He set the buckets beside the fire, took another deep breath, and lowered himself to the blanket beside her, his legs stretched out in front.

"I made coffee," she said. "I think."

"You think?" His mouth had already begun to water at the mere mention of the word. Funny how he hadn't smelled it brewing, though. It was usually a scent he could pick up a mile out.

Lucy nodded toward the small pot of boiling water. "I've never made it before, so I just guessed."

Jed cringed. Coffee was like liquid gold to him. He cherished every cup, savored every drop. But he could tell from where he sat that what she'd made wasn't coffee. *The brew* was little more than dirty water—cooked in an open pot no less!

And why the hell were the beans floating in it?

He didn't want to taste it, and he sure as hell didn't want to down a whole mug. But Lucy had gone to the trouble of making it, so the least he could do was drink it, even if it killed him.

The first sip sat on his tongue a long time before he mustered the will to swallow.

Eyes wide, almost hopeful, she watched his throat until he'd swallowed completely. "How is it?"

God-awful.

"It's fine," he answered. He took another sip, then tried to spit the beans out as discreetly as he could.

"Fine." The word fell from Lucy's tongue like a rock. "Just like supper was fine."

He couldn't help laughing, seeing her sitting there in her ripped dress, her long silky hair hanging in tangles around her shoulders, and her boots covered in dust and buffalo dung.

She was a far cry from the woman he'd met earlier that day. Of course, if she'd had any idea what kind of life she was in for, Jed would've bet his entire spread she'd have high-tailed it outta that auction faster than he could spit.

"First thing tomorrow," he said. "I'll teach you how to make coffee. But for now, this is just fine."

"Fine," she repeated with a disheartened grunt. "I'm so sick of that word."

Jed stared into the fire a moment longer, choked back the rest of his coffee, then refilled his mug.

"You don't have to—" Lucy began.

"I want to." With a quick wink in her direction, he lay back on the blanket, hands cupped beneath his head, the mug set on the ground beside him. "Has Maggie come out yet?"

"No, but I saw her peeking out the window a few times."

Jed exhaled a long breath. What was he going to do with her?

"She'll be fine," Lucy said matter-of-factly. "I imagine it's difficult for her to have a strange woman show up unannounced."

She was probably right; all Maggie needed was a little time to get used to the idea of having Lucy around.

One thing at a time, that was all Jed could do. If he could get comfortable around Lucy, maybe Maggie would follow his lead. Maybe it would help her understand that they all wanted the best for her and the baby.

He leaned up on his elbow, took a long drink of the coffee swill, and watched Lucy's expression as the light from the flames licked and danced across her face.

"Tell me about yourself, Lucy." Even as he spoke the words, he wished he could take them back. Did he want to know about her past, the details behind the scars on her hands, or about any other men she may have sat under the stars with?

It took her a while to answer, almost as if she was trying to decide what she should say—or perhaps what she shouldn't. After a while, she turned to him and shrugged.

"What would you like to know?"

"Everything." He tried to smile, but it took too much energy. "If we're going to be husband and wife, we should probably get to know each other."

"Okay." She tipped her head a bit and looked down at him, her green eyes smoldering like fiery emeralds. "But we don't have to talk to get to know each other. We can learn all we need by just—"

Jed sat bolt upright. "No." He took a few deep breaths before looking at her.

A small pout pushed at her bottom lip. "You're so stubborn—"

"Me?" he choked. "You're the one . . . you . . . what are you . . . ?"

Lucy crept closer until she knelt directly in front of him. Jed tried to scramble back, but she pulled his hat off and tossed it aside, then slid her fingers through his hair, caressing his scalp and tickling the skin behind his ears.

A soft moan floated around them. *From him?*

"There," Lucy cooed. "Isn't this better?"

Why couldn't he swallow? Her fingers were like magic, making all coherent thought vanish.

"Lucy . . . I don't think . . ."

"Shh." Instead of silencing him with her finger, as he'd done to her earlier, she cupped his face in her hands and pulled him closer. *What the hell—?*

He swallowed hard, his throat as dry as the ground beneath him. Her face hovered closer, her calloused palms cool against his cheeks.

Sweet Jesus.

She was like velvet against his mouth, her lips soft, full, and open to him. She intoxicated him with her scent, her touch, her taste.

He should stop this. He should set her back and try once again to make her understand that they needed to be practical.

He sure as hell shouldn't be pulling her closer or moaning when her tongue met his. That wasn't practical at all. But hell if he could stop himself.

Cradling her in his arms, he lowered her to the blanket, then braced his elbows on either side of her, their bodies barely touching. He brushed his mouth over hers, just enough to tease, just long enough for her fingers to find his hair again. Then he took the kiss deeper, longer.

He teased her lips open with the tip of his tongue, then traced the edges of her teeth, pausing only when she whimpered beneath him.

Light from the fire flickered softly across her face, revealing eyes heavy with desire, and cheeks reddened from his stubbled beard.

He was lost. Somewhere in the ten minutes between that first cup of swill she called coffee and her fingers sliding through his hair, he'd dismissed his entire plan.

How could he refuse her now? She'd gone from a silk dress and fancy slippers to buffalo chips and dirt—all for him. And as much as he knew he should walk away from her, he also knew there wasn't a man alive who had that kind of strength.

Lifting her head off the blanket, he used his left hand as a pillow, then eased her back down. Her lips parted, inviting him to another taste. And like a man starved, he indulged. Then went back for more. Her long slender fingers slid over his shoulders, down his arms, then back to his hair, keeping him close, not giving him a chance to escape—as though he could.

Had he ever wanted another woman this much? Had he ever been so shameless in his need? No.

No.

Jed eased back just enough to look down at Lucy, her lips swollen from his kisses, her hair fanned out in a tousled mess.

Damn it.

Her brow furrowed, then eased, a look of disappointment falling across her beautiful, dirt-smudged face.

"Jed?" Her breathy voice, filled with confusion, whispered against his skin.

If he had any sense at all, he'd see her into the house for the night. Problem was, he couldn't bring himself to let her go yet. He rolled onto his back and pulled her up beside him, settling her head on his shoulder, while his other arm pillowed the back of his head.

"Maggie might see us."

A low sigh was her only response.

They stared up at the stars for a long time, Jed's heart thundering beneath her ear, his fingers drawn to her skin like bees to flowers. He traced the length of her arm with slow strokes, wondering how long he'd have to wait before he could trust himself to kiss her again.

The neglected fire simmered in the silence. Wouldn't be long before it went out completely, and with it, the last of their light. Then he'd have only the memory of her desire—and the heat of his own—to keep him warm.

"Maggie's not going to let me sleep in there," Lucy whispered into the night.

Maggie. Shame coursed through Jed like a flash flood. He should be thinking about Maggie, not his own urges.

"Of course she will." Easy to say, another thing entirely to believe. He eased Lucy away from him and stood, taking a moment to adjust his trousers before walking toward the house.

"Maggie." He rapped his knuckles on the door and waited. And waited.

From behind the door came the muted sounds of shuffling feet and whimpers.

"Maggie." He opened the door and stepped inside. His sister-in-law didn't look up as she paced the dirt floor in front of the bed. Only took her two or three steps before she had to turn and go the other way, and after watching her for about ten seconds, Jed was dizzy enough for the both of them.

He stepped close enough to touch her arm. "Maggie."

She started, jerked back, then looked up. "Jedidiah," she exclaimed. "How did you get in? I barred the door."

Jed cast a quick glance at the old Bible on the floor, then looked back at Maggie. When was he last time she'd washed her face or brushed her hair?

He took her hand and led her to the table, then waited until she was seated before he sat across from her.

"It's getting late," he said quietly.

"Yes." She nodded quickly, her gaze darting around the room, never settling on any one thing for more than a second.

"Lucy needs to get ready for bed."

"No." She smothered her belly with the length of her arms. "She's not coming in here."

"Maggie . . ."

"No!" Maggie pushed away from the table and began to pace again. "She's evil, Jedidiah. Evil."

"No, she's not. She's here to help."

Maggie shook her head with thunderous force. "No! You need to send her away before she makes you evil, too."

"I can't send her away, Maggie. She's my wife."

"She's evil." Her voice was little more than a harsh whisper. "If you let her in here, she'll take my baby."

"Maggie." Jed rose wearily and moved to take her hands, but she pulled away from him. "Nobody's going to take your baby."

She continued to pace, continued shaking her head. "Sam will come back. He'll make her go away."

It had been almost two weeks since Sam disappeared. The whole town believed him dead, everyone except Maggie. She clung to her husband's memory as though it was her last thread of sanity.

"You can't make Lucy sleep out in the barn."

"Yes, I can," Maggie hissed. "She's an animal."

"Maggie . . ." Jed couldn't say anything else. He'd never seen Maggie so upset, so crazed. Maybe Lucy would agree to the barn for one night. It'd probably mean he'd have to find a way to make it up to her, but at this point, what choice did he have?

"Fine," he sighed. "I'll set Lucy up in the barn tonight, but tomorrow she sleeps in here."

"No." Maggie didn't blink. "I won't ever let her in here. I'll keep the door barred."

When he opened his mouth to argue, she waggled her finger in his face. "I'll kill her before I let her hurt my baby."

She really was crazy. The realization settled over Jed like an unbearable weight. What was he going to do with her? No one in such a state would be capable of raising a child.

"I think we both need to get some rest," he finally sighed. "We'll talk some more tomorrow."

He gathered the items Lucy would need for the night and morning, then stepped out into the still night air, out to where Lucy sat waiting.

Before Maggie shut the door behind him, she laid her hand on his shoulder and smiled up at him with the same sweet and gentle smile that had first attracted him to her so many years earlier.

"Good night, Jed. Have a good sleep."

A second after the door closed, a soft thud signaled she'd barred the door. He didn't move for a long time, just stood staring toward the fire, caught between two completely different women, both of whom he'd made promises to.

It took him a while to gather his wits. His wife would not be happy about sleeping in the smelly, cold, barn, but—

Was she sleeping already? He strained to hear as he moved closer, quietly as possible. Sure enough, Lucy had curled up in the blanket, and lay snoring on the hard ground. There would be no argument about sleeping arrangements tonight.

Thank you, God.

He took the supplies into the barn and set them in a neat pile before returning to Lucy. With the blanket cocooned around her, head to toe, the only part not covered was her face, and still her lips had taken on a slight blue tinge. How could she possibly be so cold?

After a long moment of staring down at her, he lifted her into his arms, careful not to wake her. Better to ask forgiveness in the morning than permission in the middle of the night.

She'd be plenty mad when she realized where she'd slept, but he'd deal with that in the morning. Right now he was too damned tired to even think about it. All he wanted to do was get his wife into bed. Any bed.

Of course, he hadn't planned on sleeping in the same bed yet, but he couldn't very well leave her out there on the hard ground. Surely he could manage one night of lying beside her; after all, they'd both be dressed . . .

Dammit. Was he being punished for something? He didn't *want* to want his wife so soon. He needed to be stronger. He would *not* be the man his father was.

No matter how much effort it took, no matter how much Lucy fought him, and no matter how many dips in the creek he'd need to take, he would make this into a good marriage or die trying.

With that thought lingering in his brain, Jed carried Lucy through the darkness of the barn and settled her on top of the lumpy pile of straw he'd been using as a mattress.

What a contrast she was to Maggie; she so dark and headstrong, Maggie so fair and gentle. Like night and day.

He tucked a second gray wool blanket up under Lucy's chin and stood staring down at her for a few more minutes, his brain waging war against every other part of him. It'd be so easy to take her back in his arms and make them man and wife in the most basic way.

But life wasn't meant to be easy—and Lucy was living proof of that. With her lying next to him, he'd never get any sleep, especially with her kiss still fresh in his mind. And still fresh on his lips.

All these years he'd thought he wanted a woman like Maggie; one who wouldn't argue with him at every turn, and who would make life easy and trouble-free. Who'd have thought he'd find himself married to a woman so completely the opposite, or that his new wife would cause flickers of doubt to creep through him so soon?

Maybe a quiet, gentle woman wasn't what he wanted after all.

CHAPTER SEVEN

Lucy's first night as Mrs. Jedidiah Caine hadn't exactly fulfilled her expectations.

She should have woken up in her husband's arms, after having spent the night securing at least part of his soul as her own. But he'd simply tucked her in to the hell he called a bed and turned his back to her.

Waking up in the barn—the barn, for the love of Satan!—was not something she was terribly happy about, but at least Jed hadn't left her outside on the cold, hard ground.

Memories of the night before flashed in her mind, the way Jed had looked at her with such hunger and confusion. And the way he'd kissed her. Lucy lifted her finger to her lips. She'd never been kissed like that before. Gentle yet strong. Slow yet intense—very, very intense.

He could have taken her right there by the fire if he'd wanted to—and she was quite sure he'd wanted to. But instead, he'd stopped himself, and done the most confusing thing.

He'd lain on that horrible blanket and pulled her close to his side, making sure she was comfortable even though he wasn't.

What purpose could that have served? She'd been ready and willing to do his bidding, but he'd refused her.

Again.

She wanted to laugh at his determination, to mock the way he fought so hard in a battle he was destined to lose. But she couldn't. Jed Caine was turning out to be a complicated man whose single-minded resolve was infuriating.

But it couldn't be just the will of a mere human who caused this odd feeling in her stomach; a gnawing twist, making her doubt everything about herself.

No, it had to be Deacon. His presence always threw her into an upheaval and now was no different. In fact, it was worse. He not only had control of Sam, but he was using Maggie, too, wheedling his way into her mind.

And so far, an entire day into her plan, Deacon was winning.

Pushing it all aside, Lucy pulled her blanket around her shoulders and stepped out into the early morning air.

Jed stood next to the fire—one he'd built himself instead of forcing Lucy to do it. From the dark circles under his eyes and the frown on his lips, he must not have slept any better than she did.

He tipped his head in a short nod. "Ho͏͏ ͏ ͏u sleep?"

"Fine," she lied. Sleeping on that ͏ ͏ ͏ ͏ ͏ ͏ was about as comfortable as sleeping on ͏ ͏ ͏ ͏ ͏ ͏ ͏ ͏e wouldn't let him know that. He ͏ ͏ ͏ ͏ ͏ ͏ thing was wonderful. The soone͏ ͏ ͏ ͏ ͏ faster she'd win him over, and ͏ ͏ ͏

"Fine like supper was fine?͏ ͏ ͏ ͏ ͏ ͏ like . . . well . . . fine?" Dar͏ ͏ ͏ and chin, and his eyes ͏ ͏ ͏ never actually looked d͏ ͏ ͏

She couldn't bla͏ ͏

night being poked and jabbed by wayward pieces of straw, had been woken up five times by the horses snorting and carrying on. And then she hadn't had the necessary items to wash up with before stumbling out of the barn.

"I can sleep anywhere," she said with what she hoped was a smile and not a grimace.

"You proved that well enough last night." His soft chuckle floated through the surrounding quiet. When she frowned, he went on. "You fell asleep out here on the ground."

Lucy tightened the blanket around her arms, trying to ward off the cool morning air. Jed wore the same shirt as yesterday, untucked and hanging half-buttoned, his sleeves rolled to the elbow. He couldn't possibly be warm enough.

Moving closer, she nudged against him until he settled his left arm around her shoulders.

"This is where I wanted to fall asleep."

Jed stiffened slightly. "Right." His voice sounded rather strangled, but his arm tightened around her for a moment before he let it fall back to his side, leaving a cold, yawning space between them.

"So, are you ready to learn how to make coffee?" He stepped farther away and reached to toss a few more chips on the fire.

No. She was ready for a proper bed, a big feather one with a thick down quilt. Or better yet, a hot bath and a clean dress, preferably silk.

"Can I clean up first?"

" ʼ "

"ʼ gaped. "But look at me—I'm disgusting."
'n't look up at her, Jed's brow shot up as
ʼoss his bottom lip.

"I *have* looked at you," he muttered. "And you're even more beautiful this morning than you were last night."

An unfamiliar warmth trickled through Lucy's veins, but she ignored it. This was good, this was very good. Jed was already turning her way, and she hadn't done a thing.

"Well, now." She stepped next to him, folded her hand in his, and smiled up into his blushing face. "That's the best thing a girl can hear first thing in the morning, even if it is a lie."

His Adam's apple bobbed twice before he looked back at her. "I won't lie to you, Lucy. Ever."

Shocked into silence, she couldn't think of what to say. He couldn't possibly think she looked beautiful. Beneath this hideous blanket, her dress—still filthy from the previous day's work—was wrinkled and bunched in the most unappealing way possible. Her hair couldn't look any better and her mouth tasted worse than last night's supper, if that was at all possible.

Lucy forced herself back to reality. Jed might not lie, but she would if need be. Fortunately, at the moment, it wasn't necessary.

"Thank you, Jed." She pressed a soft kiss on his cheek.

Their eyes barely met before he looked away.

She slid up against him, belly to belly, and wrapped her blanket around both of them.

"Lucy . . ." Jed's voice was barely a whisper now. "We can't."

"Mmmm," she chuckled. "I think we can."

Strong fingers squeezed her upper arms for a heartbeat before pushing her back. "No."

Ugh—he couldn't be more infuriating. Last night he'd bent to his desires, though only for a moment. This morning, he was back to his old stubborn self, back to being a wall of "no's."

She needed to keep Jed moving in one direction, but obviously she was going to have to make that happen with several different angles.

"Fine," she pouted, taking a step back. "Then let's get started on that coffee lesson."

Jed's shoulders relaxed as he sighed. He held up a tubular-shaped pot with a spout and instructed, "Fill it with water, to just under the spout." He poured water from one of the buckets into the pot, tipping it slightly to show her where he'd filled to. "Then you set it over the fire to boil."

He hung the coffeepot from the spit over the fire, then sat Indian style on the ground and reached for the bag of beans.

"Shouldn't those go in the water?" So far it didn't seem like she'd been too wrong last night.

His mouth twitched, his eyes crinkled, but he didn't laugh—at least not out loud.

"We need to grind them first."

"Grind them? Really?" Her cheeks heated at the realization of her error, and at how he'd guzzled two cups of the bean-filled brew. "Oops."

Jed held up an odd-looking contraption and nodded briefly. "Coffee grinder."

The grinder was a small wooden box, with a drawer on the front and a black metal bowl on the top. Sticking out of the middle of the bowl was a long, thin handle with a knob on the end. As Lucy watched, Jed poured beans into the bowl, set it in his lap and began cranking the handle.

Lucy stepped closer and peered into the bowl. Sure enough—the beans were being ground down until they disappeared through a tiny hole in the bottom of the bowl. When the last bean's pieces slipped out of sight, Jed set the grinder next to him and slid out the drawer.

"Smell that," he said, lifting it toward her nose.

Lucy jumped back, twisting her head away from the odd stench. "Yuck."

"Best smell in the world," Jed chuckled. A flash of something—regret?—crossed his eyes as he stared at her.

"If you say so." Fighting against the need to shiver, she moved closer to the fire. If it meant she'd warm up, she might even consider drinking a cup of this revolting concoction herself. "Now what?"

"We wait for the water to boil."

"I hate waiting." Another oops—she hadn't meant to say that out loud.

Jed grinned up at her. "Patience is a virtue, Lucy."

"Yes," she agreed with a sigh. She'd been called a lot of things in her life, but virtuous was never one of them. "And you're probably wishing you'd taken one of those virtuous women from the auction yesterday instead of letting Miss Blake guilt you into buying me."

Jed rose to his feet slowly, his grin gone, his face stern and tight.

"Nobody forced me into anything." His jaw tightened, then eased just enough for him to add, "I chose you for my own reasons, not because of anything Miss Blake said."

"Then why?" She probably didn't want to know the answer, but since it obviously made him uncomfortable, she needed to hear him say it aloud. Pride be damned.

"Because," he licked his lips and watched her for a long moment before he continued, "you were trying too hard to be something you're not."

"What do you mean?"

Jed tugged the blanket out of Lucy's hands and let it

fall to the ground. Before she could grab for it, he had both her hands in his.

"This." He turned her hands over, palms up.

"What—" She tried to pull back, but he held her fast.

"These are not the hands of the spoiled princess you wanted me to think you were." His thumb brushed over the large callous beneath her index finger and then moved over the others. A long shiver worked up her spine, but it wasn't from the cold. In fact, this was the warmest she'd felt since leaving the auction yesterday.

Jed continued to smooth his thumbs over her palms, working slow circles across every inch.

"These are the hands of someone who's known hard work."

Lucy forced an indifferent snort.

Jed ignored her. "These are the hands of the woman I want working with me."

"But—"

"No buts." He curled her hand inside his own and smiled down at her, but it wasn't a happy smile. Worry and concern reflected through his dark eyes.

As Lucy released the breath she didn't realize she'd been holding, guilt gnawed at her. For all his honorable and righteous ways, Jedidiah Caine was impossible to dislike—and that wasn't making her job any easier.

She wouldn't fail. She wouldn't.

Blinking hard, she tossed her ratty hair over her shoulder and offered him what she hoped was a bright smile.

"So once the water boils . . ."

A small frown puckered Jed's forehead until he caught up with her change of subject.

"Right. The water." He released her hands and turned back to the fire. "Lift the pot off the fire, and add the grounds to the water."

"How much?" Her voice felt jittery, almost nervous. Why did she get so jumpy every time Jed touched her?

He glanced back at the full drawer of grounds and shrugged. "I've never measured," he admitted. "But you can never make it too strong for me, so that's not a worry."

Obviously he still hoped her cooking skills would get better.

Stupid man.

"Stir it up," he continued. "Then let it sit for a couple minutes."

"Okay," she nodded. "Is that it?"

"Not quite."

Lucy fought back a groan. The more instructions he gave her, the more likely she was to forget them. Still, he kept talking.

"Set it back over the fire and let it boil again. You might have to stir it some more to push the grounds down."

Boil it, stir it, she could do that.

"How long does it boil?"

"Couple minutes."

"Right. Then it's ready?"

"Not quite."

Lucy let out a loud sigh. "What now?"

He motioned toward the bucket of fresh water beside the fire. "Just before you serve it, pour a little bit of cold water in the pot and you're done."

She narrowed her eyes at him and fisted her free hand against her hip. "You're telling me I'm supposed to boil this . . . mud . . . twice, and then once it's good and hot, I'm supposed to dump cold water in it?"

He grinned. "Cold water helps the grounds settle."

He pushed to his feet and nodded toward the pot of water, which had yet to boil the first time. "Make sense?"

No.

"Of course." *What was she supposed to do once the water boiled?*

"Good. I'll start on the chores then." He headed toward the barn, then stopped and turned back, a mischievous grin on his face. "Suppose this means I shouldn't hope for eggs or biscuits for breakfast?"

"You can hope all you like."

* * *

With the animals tended, Jed spent a few minutes at the creek ridding himself of yesterday's dirt and sweat. And yes, trying to wash away some of the confusion clouding his brain.

Unlike Maggie, Lucy was difficult and trying, but she was also candid and direct; and despite everything, she had made an honest effort to help.

Maggie was usually mild-tempered and agreeable, Lucy was anything but. Both were beautiful women, but in vastly different ways. Maggie's was a gentle, womanly beauty, the kind that made a man want to protect her, shelter her. Lucy's had a strength behind it that demanded attention. She didn't need to be taken care of, and she had no need of a protector.

Even wrinkled and filthy, there was something about Lucy that drew Jed to her. He hadn't expected it, and though it was a good thing, it also scared him to death.

Strangest damned thing.

He was supposed to be focused on helping Maggie. Instead, he was thinking about his new wife and how much he'd like to . . .

Jed pushed his head under the water and held it there 'til his lungs threatened to pop.

There was no denying it. A day into their marriage, and

he already liked his wife. It was more than just a physical need—though that was strong enough on its own. He liked that she didn't need to be protected. He liked that she had opinions and she wasn't afraid to express them.

And he very much liked the idea that she wanted him as much as he wanted her.

If only she could learn to like him, too.

Jed walked back toward the house cleansed of dirt and grime, but still thick with need.

Long before he saw it, he smelled it. Strong coffee—*really* strong coffee—or some variation of it, anyway. He'd given her instruction, so how bad could it be? No matter—it would be hot and that was the main thing.

Lucy stepped out of the barn as he walked up. Her face had been scrubbed, her hair brushed back, and though she was wearing the other new day dress they'd bought, it seemed to have fallen under the same knife as the first one.

"I smell coffee," he said, grinning broadly. "My mouth's been watering the whole way back from the creek."

Lucy's eyes flew wide. Her mouth opened, then slammed shut as she hurried toward the fire.

A long groan worked its way up Jed's throat, but he choked it back. She'd added the grounds to the pot, then put it back on to boil and promptly forgotten about it. Brown water bubbled out the top of the pot and sizzled against the dancing flames.

Lucy's shoulders slumped. "I just went in to get cleaned up a little and . . ."

"That's okay," Jed struggled to get out. "I like it strong, remember? And it'll be good 'n hot, too."

Before he could stop her, Lucy lifted the pot from the fire, scooped a mug full of cold water from the bucket and dumped it inside the pot.

Least it *used* to be hot.

She retrieved the mug from beside the water bucket, filled it to the rim with what had started out as coffee, and held it toward him.

The first small sip sent his taste buds running for their lives.

"How is it?" she asked, her face full of nervous anticipation.

He took another sip in the hopes that the first had simply been off. Nope. The first sip had actually been better.

"It's, uh . . ." he hesitated long enough to take another sip. Not because he wanted to, but because his own words were kicking him in his conscience.

I won't lie to you, Lucy. Ever.

He nodded briefly before answering. "It's not the worst coffee I've ever tasted."

The smile that lit Lucy's face was enough to make him down two full cups of the cold, thin, murky substance.

CHAPTER EIGHT

Over the next several days, things didn't improve. Nothing Lucy cooked or boiled tasted as it should, and Maggie hadn't set foot outside the cabin, despite Jed's continued pleas.

"I'm going to town today," he said over Lucy's latest disaster of breakfast. "Maggie's agreed to let Miss Blake come and stay with her."

"Miss Blake? From the auction?" What was this odd fear that suddenly ripped through Lucy's veins? "Why her?"

"She promised she'd help if I needed it." Jed's frown deepened. "And God knows we need it."

"I think she meant she'd help with me."

"I know," he agreed quietly. "But she's our only hope. If she won't come, Maggie's going to starve herself and that baby."

He downed the rest of his coffee, set the mug by the water buckets, and offered Lucy a weary smile.

"I should be back by early afternoon."

Something in Lucy's heart twinged, but she dismissed it. This was her chance to prove her worth to him, to make him respect her, maybe even like her.

While he was in town, she'd work like a madwoman. If that didn't prove something to him, what would?

Half an hour later, he climbed up on the bench of the wagon and steered the horses toward town. The dust hadn't even begun to settle before Lucy set to work.

Dishes were scrubbed and stacked near the fire, since she couldn't put them away inside the cabin. The blanket, which now served as their outside table, was shaken out, repositioned, and secured with the largest rocks she could find. Then she set to work on the wash.

How could something so simple be so exhausting?

She plunged Jed's shirt back into the wash bucket, scrubbed it over the board again, leaving the top layer of her knuckles behind as she did.

This was almost as bad as . . . no, it wasn't. She pushed her hair back from her eyes and cursed the shirt, the board and the man who'd dirtied the clothes in the first place.

And even as she worked to clean this shirt, she'd no doubt have to wash his other one tomorrow. Lucy bent back over the wash tub, dunked the whole shirt into the water, lifted it out and did it all over again. Why wouldn't the soap come off?

With a long sigh, she wrung the shirt between her hands, shook it out, then hung it next to Jed's trousers and her other ugly dress.

Blood oozed from her scraped knuckles and her back ached from the constant bending, but she couldn't stop. She had to keep working; the more she accomplished in his absence, the happier he'd be.

Consequently, the happier she'd be.

After dumping the washtub out back, she set to work around the yard. By the time she stopped for a drink of water, she'd piled up enough chips to last them a week, and in the process had cleaned the yard of every last nasty bit of dung.

Next she set to work on the barn. If she was going to have to live out there for the next while, she'd damn well be comfortable. A quick search produced Jed's hammer and a handful of nails, which she pounded into the wall farthest from the stalls. Once the wash was dry, she'd hang the clean clothes inside, instead of leaving them folded in the dirt.

Next, she rearranged the straw they used for a mattress, added more, then covered it all with one of the blankets. It wouldn't be a huge improvement over sleeping on the straw itself, but it would be something.

When she'd satisfied herself with the new arrangements, she returned the hammer to its spot and retrieved the saw. Jed wanted to use the mesquite for a corral, so she'd help him out a little.

It only took three or four serious jabs of the thorns before Lucy finally gave up and put her gloves back on. Then she set to cutting down the nasty bushes with a vengeance. She didn't stop for her noon meal, nor did she pay Maggie a second's glance.

If the woman wanted to stay holed up in that disgusting little cabin, then so be it. Lucy would get to her eventually.

By the time the wagon creaked toward the house, Lucy was scratched, poked, filthy and almost warm. Almost.

Miss Blake sat on the bench next to Jed, her round body jostling against the seat with each dip and jerk the wagon made.

The woman's gaze darted to the house, the barn, Lucy's feet, then to Jed, but never once did she look Lucy in the eye.

"Mrs. Caine," she said quietly. "It's nice to see you again."

"Hello, Miss Blake," Lucy answered. "I'm sure Maggie will be happy to have you here."

"Please, call me Berta."

Lucy tried to smile, but failed. "I'm Lucy."

Jed helped the woman down from the bench, then pulled her small bag from the back of the wagon. He had yet to say anything, but his frown wasn't exactly encouraging. Now what had she done wrong?

He probably expected her to have more done, but what?

"How are you managing out here?" Berta still didn't look directly at her.

"Well . . ." Lucy laughed lightly. "It's certainly different." Her forced smile was a wasted effort as neither Berta nor Jed would look at her.

They stood in the yard for a moment, but no one said anything. Finally Berta cleared her throat.

"I best see to Maggie."

Jed nodded distractedly and led her toward the cabin.

"Maggie," he called through the door. "Miss Blake's here."

Lucy stayed where she was, watching, as Maggie cracked the door open just enough to see out, then wider to let the other woman inside. Berta's skirts had barely cleared the opening before Maggie slammed the door shut and Lucy heard the now familiar thud.

The Bible was in place.

With slow, measured steps, Jed made his way back to Lucy, but still he didn't say anything.

She'd ruined it. Her chance to prove something to Jed and she hadn't done it.

He rubbed his palm across his face and let out a long, low whistle.

"You've been busy."

A bubble of something—pride?—swelled inside Lucy. She half-nodded, half-shrugged as she followed his gaze around the yard.

"What d'you think?" she asked, fighting back the hope from her voice.

"I think I'm glad you're the one who wrestled those prickles and not me."

Jed's deep laughter filled her with an odd, unsettling feeling that almost had her laughing with him.

Almost.

He wrapped his arm around her shoulders and gave her a soft squeeze. "Suppose it's too much to hope you wore your bonnet while you were out here working so hard?"

Lucy grinned back at him and shrugged. "I told you before, husband, you can hope all you like."

The look in his eyes proved he did just that—hope. She snuggled against him, lacing her fingers through his as they dangled off her shoulder. It wasn't something she planned to do, but it felt natural.

How strange.

"Have you eaten?" she asked. "I could make—"

"I'm fine," he answered, a little too quickly. "Miss Blake brought some food for the ride back, so we ate in the wagon."

Though a tiny part of Lucy resented it, she couldn't help but breathe a sigh of relief.

"Back to work," she said, offering him a smile. "The boss doesn't put up with slackers, you know."

"Is that right?" Jed pulled her up tight and gazed down at her. She was filthy and wrinkled, but Lucy didn't care. She'd made Jed happy, and that was all that mattered. It put her one step closer to her goal.

"Yes," she sighed teasingly. "Work work work. That's all he thinks about."

A soft rumble began in Jed's throat as he leaned closer. "That's not *all* he cares about."

His kiss was soft and tender, his hands strong. She leaned into him, letting him lead her until the last of her strength drained away and she was left clinging to the front of his shirt.

He moaned softly. "This isn't helping me get the chores done."

"There's more to life than chores, dear husband."

Jed's laughter breathed through her hair. He kissed her neck, then the top of her head before releasing her.

"All right," she muttered. "We wouldn't want the boss finding us here doing nothing."

She waggled her brow at him, then headed back to the partially destroyed mesquite bush. She'd certainly rather be doing something else, but at least she had something to look forward to later.

*　*　*

Lucy lifted the coffeepot above her head, all set to hurl it into the fire, when Jed's voice stopped her.

"Please don't." His gaze flicked between her and the pot as though she were holding a priceless treasure.

"I hate this stupid thing."

Even though Jed drank it without question or comment, she knew the truth. Every pot was worse than the one before.

Of course, coffee was but one of her frustrations. Her husband had yet to do anything more than kiss her. Yes, his kisses were amazing, and yes, she welcomed each one. Worse, she found herself longing for the next.

But she needed more.

Too many times she found herself so caught up in his

kisses, she forgot why she was really there. She needed to remember the plan.

And if it meant she had to control her temper and learn patience, then that's what she was going to do, even though the temptation to stomp that coffeepot into the earth was more than any being should bear.

"What am I doing wrong?" she demanded. Still clutching the pot in her fist, she whipped it through the air, spilling thick brown sludge down her skirt and over the toes of her boots.

Great. More washing.

"Nothing." Jed stepped closer and reached for the pot, but she moved it out of his reach.

"Then why can't I do it?"

"You just need to have patience." He continued to flick his gaze between her and the annoying piece of tin he loved so much.

"Patience?" she cried, tightening her grip on the pot. She shoved it against Jed's chest and pierced him with an accusing glare. "I've been making pot after pot for over a week now, and it's still horrible. Are you sure you gave me all the directions?"

"Yes." He reached for the pot, but she yanked it away again.

"And I'm not forgetting any steps?"

"No."

She fought the urge to scream at him. How could he stand there so calmly when something as simple as making a pot of coffee was driving her completely mad?

"It's okay." Jed wrapped his arm around her shoulder and pulled her into a tight squeeze, but Lucy was no fool.

"Nice try, Jed, but you're not getting this stupid pot back."

He made a dive for it, but she jerked her arm back, out of his reach.

"Some people just don't have the knack for it."

A soft breeze whispered his scent under her nose. She inhaled deeply, momentarily lost in the warm, musky smell.

"But I'm doing it right!" Lucy pushed away from him and stamped her foot. "There's no reason for me to fail at something as simple as this."

He reached for her again, but she slapped his hand away. "Don't."

A look of shock flashed across Jed's face. She'd never refused his touch before. In fact, she'd always been the one asking for it.

"I'm sorry," she muttered. "But this is madness. It's just a stupid pot of coffee!"

"Ah." He nodded solemnly, but those dark eyes of his crinkled anyway. "I think we've just discovered the problem."

Why was he smiling? He better not be mocking her.

"It's not 'just' coffee, Lucy."

"Yes, Jed, it is." She tossed the pot beside the water bucket and let out a low growl.

He rescued his precious pot, rinsed the leftover sludge from inside it, then refilled it with clean water and set it over the flames.

"Making coffee," he explained, "making *good* coffee, is a talent. You either have it, develop it, or keep as far away from it as you can."

He couldn't be serious.

"It's coffee," she repeated. The urge to kick the grinder out of his hands was almost too much to bear. "If you follow the recipe, it should taste the same every time you make it."

Jed glanced up long enough to wink, then shrugged. "And yet we've proven that's not exactly true, haven't we?"

"That's ridiculous!" She took a breath, readying herself to continue the battle.

"Temper, temper, Lucille." Deacon's voice taunted from the darkened shadow beside the house. She should have expected him; she should have known he'd wait for her to lose focus for a moment, then slither in like the slimy snake he was.

Jed whirled around just as Deacon stepped into the light. The horses whinnied nervously and stomped inside the barn.

"What the . . . ?" Jed moved between Lucy and her brother. "Who the hell are you?"

A smirk twitched against Deacon's lips, but Lucy couldn't be sure if it was because of Jed's reference to Hell, or because he thought he could protect her from Deacon.

"Lucille—you haven't told him about me yet?" Her brother stepped closer, hat in hand, and offered a short bow.

Jed didn't flinch. "No, she hasn't."

Deacon smiled in his mocking way and shrugged. "That's odd, since she's told me quite a bit about you."

"Jed—" Lucy tried to step around him, but his arm shot out, blocking her way.

Deacon's eyes flamed for a second, then cooled. "I'm Lucille's brother, Deacon." He eyed Jed with icy disgust. "And you are Jedidiah Caine."

"We're not exactly close," Lucy hastened to explain as she stepped around Jed's arm.

The worst thing she could do would be to show Deacon fear; he'd devour them both as they stood there. She had to act as though his presence meant nothing to her, as though he dropped by every night for coffee.

Jed's entire body remained tense, his dark eyes scrutinizing every breath Deacon took.

"How'd you get here?" he asked. "Didn't hear a horse or wagon."

Deacon's gaze flicked to Lucy for a moment, then back to Jed. "I've never been particularly taken with beasts of burden."

"And as you can tell," Lucy said pointedly, gesturing toward the barn, "they're not particularly taken with you, either."

Deacon brushed unseen dirt from his spotless lapel, then frowned at the toe of his shoe, set deep in the middle of a crumbled buffalo chip.

"Sorry," Lucy smiled. "Must've missed one."

He raised his eyes slowly, the movement deliberate. With his right hand, he reached inside his coat pocket and pulled out his ferret, which he cradled like a baby as he stroked its neck.

Deacon meant to unnerve her and Jed, but Lucy would have no part of it. She'd barely moved a breath before Jed's hand closed around her arm and tugged her closer, his hard glare never leaving Deacon's face.

"You're saying you walked the ten miles from town?"

Deacon hesitated briefly, then shrugged. "Okay."

"That's an awful long walk." Jed didn't seem to pay any mind to the rodent sniffing its way around Deacon's neck.

Deacon shrugged again. "'Suppose."

"And yet your clothes look like they've just come back from Mrs. Lee's laundry."

Lucy released a soft chuckle. "Except his shoe, of course."

Deacon's expression didn't change, but the fire in his soul belched enough steam to reach Lucy's. Jed held

Deacon's gaze, not challenging him, but simply making it clear he would not be intimidated.

If she didn't need his trust and his soul, Lucy might have laughed at him. Jed seemed to think Deacon was no threat to any of them, a mistake he'd soon regret.

Jed relaxed, but barely. "Any family of Lucy's is welcome here, of course."

As Lucy fought back a groan, Deacon's face lit up.

"Excellent," he said, his gaze still fixed on Jed, almost testing him. "There's nothing more important than family, isn't that what they say?"

Lucy and Jed both snorted, then glanced at each other in surprise.

"Yeah," Jed agreed. "That's what they say."

The fire crackled gently behind them—the only sound for a few very long seconds.

"Where's our manners, Lucy?" Jed finally spoke. "I'll bring out the chairs and we can all sit down for a visit. It'll give me a chance to get to know your brother."

"Yes," Deacon sneered. "Wouldn't that be . . . nice?"

He eased the rodent from around his neck and set it back in his lap. It leapt to the ground and scurried off toward the barn, yet still Jed paid it no mind.

With a short nod at Deacon, Jed gave Lucy's hand a quick squeeze before heading to the house.

Lucy turned on her brother the second Jed disappeared behind the door. "What do you want, Deacon?"

Her brother's eyes were void of any emotion. "Just wanted to stop by for a little social time with my sister. Is that wrong?"

She cast a glance toward the house, then lowered her voice to a tight whisper. "Let's not waste each other's time."

"It's not me wasting time." He flicked an ash from his sleeve, and looked up at her with complete indifference. "You're the one who insisted Mr. Caine's pride would be his downfall. Either that or his lust. And yet here we are, a week later, and you've made little-to-no progress."

Before she could answer, Jed pushed open the door and carried the two chairs toward the fire.

"Have a seat," he said, offering Deacon the first one, and Lucy the other. "Miss Blake will be out in a minute."

Deacon wiped the chair with his gloves as he'd done before, then perched himself on the edge, his bowler hat balanced upside down on his lap. His ferret darted back across the yard, up Deacon's pant leg, and disappeared inside his bowler hat.

Deacon reached inside to touch his pet, then jerked his hand back, a single drop of blood falling from his fingertip. Instead of reacting violently, as Lucy expected, Deacon simply wiped the blood on his handkerchief and smiled down at the ferret.

Suppressing a shudder, Lucy took the other chair as Jed bent to the coffee.

"Do you live in town?" Jed asked, not looking up from his task.

"No." Deacon rolled his eyes, but only Lucy saw. "I don't really have a place to call home."

After a moment's hesitation, Jed's gaze swung uneasily from Deacon to Lucy, but even as she shook her head, the words fell from his lips.

"So will you be needing to stay here, then?"

The grin that split Deacon's face was enough to make Lucy want to hit him. Hard.

"Wouldn't think of it," he said.

"Of course not." It was Lucy's turn to grin. "Couldn't let those clothes get dirty, could we?"

She looked over at Jed just as he released a long breath. Damned manners of his could have gotten them into serious trouble.

He bent back over the coffeepot, and for a moment the only sound in the cool night air was him carefully tapping grounds into the rapidly boiling water. There was a certain rhythm to his movements, a gentle yet continuous motion that slipped the grounds into the water in an even pattern, not anything like the way Lucy dumped them all in at once.

Maybe that was her problem.

Her thoughts were interrupted by Deacon's forced cough.

"It's a lot of land you've got here, Jedidiah." His expression showed naught but indifference. "Lot of wide open, *empty* land."

Lucy's hard glare went ignored.

"It's a fair size." Jed straightened from the fire and looked around with that air of determination he always wore when talking about his land.

"Yes, but what will you do with so much emptiness?" Deacon wrinkled his nose, one brow arched in distaste.

This was a tactic Deacon used all the time, and in fact, one Lucy had used herself when she first arrived. With each small insult, a tiny bit of darkness pressed into Jed's soul. She needed to prevent Deacon from causing too many of them, or Jed would fall to her brother instead.

"Might seem empty now." Jed shrugged. "But not for long."

His face shone with resolve and pride, and for a moment, Lucy wanted to share those feelings with him, to be so sure of something—so sure of *anything*—that she could ignore the dissenters and make her plan work. Problem was, her dissenters wielded more power than she did.

"We're going to turn it into the best spread this county's ever seen, ain't that right, Lucy?"

She couldn't answer. Words formed, her mouth opened to say them, but the smile he shone her way burned each syllable to her tongue.

"Miss Blake." Jed stepped away from Lucy and toward the other woman as she closed the cabin door behind her.

"This is Lucy's brother, Deacon."

Berta's face froze against a smile that started but never finished.

"Deacon," Jed continued. "Miss Blake is here to help out with my—"

"Cooking," Lucy interrupted, then ignored Jed when he rose his brow in question. "She's here to teach me some new recipes."

Deacon made no move to rise, but instead bobbed his head in acknowledgment, then laughed coldly. "Jedidiah and Lucille were just starting to tell me about their plans for this . . . land."

Pale and skittish, Berta looked on the verge of collapse. Jed was so occupied with staring at Deacon, he didn't seem to notice. Lucy pushed off her chair and led the other woman to it. Berta sat down hard, then twisted away from Deacon's direct line of vision.

"Not feeling well?" Deacon asked with slight sneer.

"She's fine," Lucy answered, putting herself between them. "Just tired."

This was Lucy's job, not Deacon's. These were her souls to take, not his.

"Yes," he said dryly. "I imagine it must be exhausting to work a place like this."

"It's nothing Lucy and I can't manage." Jed's voice was far from friendly.

"Lucille works?" Deacon snorted. "Doing what?"

Shame rose within her like a massive tidal wave. It was no secret she hated any kind of work, but the last week of helping Jed had done something to her.

She still didn't want to do chores. She'd much rather have someone else do them, but once they were done, she felt . . . well, she wasn't quite sure what to call it, but it made her want to hold her head up higher.

Strange.

"She cooks, tends the wash, and keeps the place tidy."

Deacon didn't look the least bit convinced. "*This* Lucille?" He waved his gloves in her direction. "I don't think I'd risk eating anything out of her kitchen. You've never been much good at that sort of thing, have you, sister?"

She started to fire an answer back, but Jed stopped her. The fury in his voice was nothing compared to that in his eyes.

"You'll mind what you say in front of my wife."

Lucy's shock was matched only by Deacon's.

"Lucille doesn't mind." Deacon snorted, straightening in his seat. "She knows she has no talent—"

"That's enough." Jed's tone left little room for interpretation.

"It's okay, Jed." Lucy slipped her hand under his elbow, trying to tug him back a little, but Jed was immovable. In fact, his entire body seemed to harden before her eyes.

The air between the men crackled with anger and something else only men could project. Jed stood rod straight beside Lucy, but Deacon remained in his chair, his ugly sneer fueling the tension.

"I'm sure Lucille appreciates your protection, Jedidiah," he said. "But I don't think chivalry is what she needs."

"No?" Jed crossed his arms over his chest. "Well that's funny, because I don't think she needed to be left at an auction. I might not have much to offer her right now, but at least I care for her."

He cared for her. Lucy fought to swallow. He cared for her. That was good.

No, it wasn't. It'd mean . . .

Yes, it was!

It was what she needed. It was a starting point.

Flames danced in Deacon's eyes—a sight Jed no doubt believed to be a reflection of the fire crackling nearby, but Lucy knew better.

The ferret poked its nose out of the hat, but Deacon's gentle touch settled it back down.

"It was her choice to be there," he said.

"Doesn't make it right that you let her."

Deacon rolled his eyes and gave a very ungentlemanly snort. "Regardless, Jedidiah, surely you don't think *this* is the kind of life Lucille is used to."

The vein in Jed's temple began to throb. His jaw muscle clenched, then released. Then clenched again.

"If you had taken proper care of her," Jed's voice was steely cold, "she wouldn't have felt the need to sell herself off in a wife auction. And then maybe she could still be walking around in her fancy silk dress instead of working her hide off out here with me."

Deacon tipped his head slightly, his eyes glowing with anger. As only Deacon could, he shut down his fury and shifted his attack.

"You misunderstand me, Jedidiah." Deacon's grin was anything but friendly. "I believe Lucille is finally living the kind of life she deserves."

"Mind your tongue." Jed's arms dropped to his sides, his hands fisted against his thighs, his voice a low growl. "You'll show Lucy the respect she deserves, especially when you come—uninvited—to our home."

Berta inhaled sharply, but Deacon eyed Jed's fists and simply smirked.

"If you mean to strike me, Jedidiah," he said quietly, "I would advise against it."

"Of course not," Lucy interceded, then turned to Jed. "Deacon's right."

"No, he's not." Jed wrapped his arm around her shoulders and pulled her close.

A tiny shot of warmth burst inside Lucy's heart—is that what pride felt like? Surely not. Pride was for humans who didn't know better. She'd learned long ago that she had nothing to be proud of, and it was a lesson Deacon reminded her of every chance he got.

Deacon studied Jed for a long moment before he eased back. "My apologies," he lied. "I meant no disrespect."

Jed nodded slightly, but held his stance. "So long as we understand each other."

"Perfectly." He turned to Lucy, the flames still licking the depth of his eyes. "It would seem your husband has a soft spot in his heart for you already, dear sister."

Lucy blinked.

"And I'd wager you have the same soft spot for him." His icy grin forced a sharp shiver through Lucy. She couldn't prevent him from reading Jed's soul, or any other human's, but she had to make damn good and sure he couldn't read hers.

A second is all it would take for him to get in.

Silence fell over them, Jed and Deacon staring each other down until Deacon finally blinked and moved his glare back to Lucy.

"How about that coffee?" he asked over a forced chuckle.

Jed squeezed Lucy's shoulder barely enough for her to

notice, but it was enough to leave her feeling stronger and yet more vulnerable at the same time.

It was one thing for Jed to have a soft spot for her, but it was another thing entirely for her to feel the same.

She forced herself to hold her tongue when Jed moved toward his precious coffee. More than anything, she wanted to call him back, to have him pour more of his strength into her and help her through the rest of Deacon's visit.

Instead, she lowered herself to the ground near Berta's feet, forced her spine straight and her glare to harden on Deacon.

"It's sure been hot lately." Jed filled the coffee mugs and handed one to Deacon.

"I suppose." Deacon didn't bother to thank Jed, nor did he raise the mug to his mouth for a sip.

"Seems your sister doesn't agree." He sat down beside Lucy and offered her a small smile. "Always cold, aren't you, Lucy?"

She smiled back and nodded, ignoring the twisted smile on her brother's face.

When Deacon made no attempt to continue the conversation, Jed changed topics.

"Pretty soon we'll have a good sized herd," he said, then swallowed a large gulp of coffee. "Army's looking for good-quality beef to feed the Indians they've pent up, so we'll work out a deal with them that'll keep us busy for years to come."

Deacon snorted. "Seems a waste of perfectly good beef if you ask me."

Every muscle in Jed's face tightened. His knuckles whitened around his mug, and it was a long moment before he spoke. Lucy held her breath. Berta remained ashen and silent.

"Would you feel the same if it was your family the government had rounded up like a bunch of wild animals?"

"But that's all they are anyway," Deacon scoffed.

Lucy lay her hand on Jed's knee, then shook her head slightly. His lips tightened into a thin line, and his eyes hardened, but he held his tongue.

"Does your plan for the land include a decent house?" Deacon tipped his head in the direction of the shanty, but kept his eyes focused on Jed and Lucy.

"We have a decent house," Lucy quipped.

Jed's expression was hard to read. For a moment she thought he was appreciative of her answer, but a heartbeat later, he looked different, regretful.

"We're only going to start the house when we've saved enough to do it right," he finally said.

"Oh really?" Deacon's tone left little doubt as to how much he believed that.

"Yes, really," Jed ground out. When he looked back at Lucy, his features softened. "I'm going to build Lucy a big house with everything she could ever want."

Her pulse sped up; her stomach tingled.

"We're going to have wood floors, lots of glass windows, curtains, sturdy furniture—" He paused, then added, "And one of them fancy bathtubs inside."

Lucy fought the light growing in her soul. She sat stock-still, returning Deacon's cold stare with one of her own. She could be indifferent. She'd had a lot of practice, and she'd need every ounce of her skill to pull this off.

If Jed noticed that he was the only one talking, or that Deacon didn't even lift his mug to his lips, he didn't let on. He simply kept talking as though his argument with Deacon had never happened. But every time his head was turned, Deacon made faces or rolled his eyes.

She had to get rid of her brother. The longer he was

here, the more questions Jed would have about him—questions she had no good answers for.

"How long are you planning to stay?" she asked, hoping Deacon caught her underlying tone.

"I'm not sure yet," he said. "Depends on what happens."

Jed frowned. "How do you mean?"

"Well, Jedidiah," he said simply. "I hear there's been some excitement in town lately what with that poor man disappearing recently." He paused for effect, then widened his eyes in false shock. "Wait—his name was Caine, too. Brother perhaps?"

Jed nodded slightly.

"Then that would mean the crazy woman they speak of in town . . . she's your family, too."

No one answered, but Jed's jaw clenched tighter.

"Very sad," Deacon went on, pointedly looking at Lucy. "I think I'll stay a while, just until the truth is revealed."

Jed frowned, but he held his tongue. It was all the opportunity Lucy needed to end things before the two men started in on each other again.

"It's getting late." She rose from her chair and relieved her brother of his still full mug. "You best be heading back before it gets too dark."

The sun hovered above the horizon, but they both knew it didn't make a stitch of difference how many more minutes—or hours—of daylight they had left. Deacon didn't walk anywhere. He just appeared. Or disappeared.

"You're right." He pushed to his feet and eased his ferret back into his pocket before setting his hat at a slight angle on his head. With a short bow in Jed's direction, he sneered again. "Thank you for your hospitality."

The sounds of the horses moving restlessly in the barn filtered around them.

"You're welcome." Jed's jaw twitched slightly before he

asked, "Want a ride back to town? We can hitch up the wagon if you like."

Lucy caught her jaw before it fell open, but Deacon's brow shot upward in surprise.

"No. Beasts of burden and all."

Relief washed over Jed's face. "Right. Well, it was good to meet you."

Why was he being so kind to the same man he'd seemed ready to rip apart just an hour earlier?

Jed held out his hand, but it was a long, strained minute before Deacon gave it a quick shake.

"Yes," Deacon said, his tone in complete disagreement with his words. "It's been *interesting*. Good night to you, Lucille. Miss Blake."

Lucy tried to cover Berta's whimper with a cough, but there was no fooling the likes of Deacon. With another short bow, he walked into the shadows of the house and out of sight.

Jed blew a long, low breath and scratched his head.

"Think I know why you didn't tell me about him sooner."

"Deacon's, um . . ." Lucy's heart hammered against her ribs, "different."

"That's one word for it."

She studied his profile, watching him stare into the darkness that a moment before had been Deacon.

"Berta?" She turned to the woman, who remained on her chair, frozen in place. "Are you ill?"

Berta shook her head slowly, her eyes never blinking away from the darkness that Deacon disappeared into.

"I need to see to Maggie." With that, Berta lifted her chair and the one Deacon had used and carried them back to the house. A second after the door closed, the Bible thudded against the ground.

Was Berta going mad, too?

Lucy sighed. She didn't trust Berta any more than she trusted any human, and having her here meant one more person she'd need to get through to get to Maggie.

Sitting on the large boulder near the fire, Jed held his arms out and eased her onto his lap.

"When did you speak to him?" Jed asked.

"Hmm?"

He nodded toward the darkness. "He said you'd told him all about me."

"Oh, that." Lucy forced a laugh, shaky though it was. "He stopped by a few days ago."

"He what?" Jed roared. "How did he know you were here? Where was I? And why didn't you tell me?"

"Hush or you'll frighten Maggie and Berta."

Think.

Jed would not be put off. "Why didn't you tell me?"

"In case you didn't notice," she said softly, "Deacon isn't someone I'm terribly fond of—even if he is my brother. And I was hoping you wouldn't have to ever meet him."

Jed half-nodded, half-shrugged. "You should have told me."

"You're right." She moved closer and rested her hand on his arm. "You surprised me when you offered him a ride back to town. I doubt anyone else would have done the same."

A slight shrug lifted his right shoulder. "He's family, Lucy. Can't say I'm happy about that, but family's family." He grinned slowly. "Truth be told, I just wanted to get him out of here as fast as I could."

She could learn to like this husband of hers. She wouldn't, of course, but she *could*.

"What in blazes was that thing in his hat—a weasel?" Jed asked, shaking his head.

A small laugh escaped Lucy's throat. "It's a ferret."

"A what?"

"A ferret," she repeated. "He's had it about a month now."

"Ugliest thing I ever saw." Jed shook his head slowly. "What kind of animal has red eyes?"

He downed the rest of his coffee, rinsed his mug and set it near the water bucket.

"Wanna help me tend the horses? They're a little restless tonight."

Not restless. Scared.

Lucy took her husband's hand and walked with him to the barn. "I'll just watch," she said. "I'm like Deacon when it comes to big animals."

Jed squeezed her hand slightly as he led her inside. "You, dear Lucy, are *nothing* like your brother."

CHAPTER NINE

Even with his back to her, Jed sensed Lucy's every breath. Something wasn't right. She'd followed him into the barn, but hadn't spoken a single word.

He finished with the horses, set the water bucket outside and closed the door.

"You've been awfully quiet since your brother left." He pressed his hand against the small of her back and gently urged her back toward the dying fire. "Something wrong?"

Lucy shook her head, but Jed wasn't convinced. The moment Deacon arrived, it was like a dark cloud fell over her.

"Don't let him upset you." He tried to smile, but she wouldn't look at him. "If you don't mind my saying so, Lucy, your brother's an ass."

They stopped at the fire, but it was a long moment of silence before she looked up at him. Her green eyes, usually snapping with fire or mischief, were now dull, almost lifeless.

Then it struck him.

"Oh my God." He took her by the shoulders and stared down at her. "You're scared of him, aren't you?"

She didn't answer. She didn't have to.

"Has he hurt you before?"

When she spoke, her voice came out as flat and lifeless as the look in her eyes.

"Not how you think."

"Sweet Jesus, Lucy, why didn't you tell me?"

Again, she didn't answer, just looked at him with that wooden expression.

He pulled her into his arms and breathed softly against her hair. "You're safe here."

Lucy pulled out of his arms and stepped back. "You can't stop him, he's too strong. He has power you can't even imagine."

A direct slap to his face he could have taken. But a slap to his pride—that was completely different.

How could she possibly think a no-account bootlicker like Deacon would be any kind of threat to them? She must think Jed was pathetic. He rubbed his palm across his mouth, smothering a string of curses.

If she thought Deacon was more of a man than him, what chance did he stand of winning her respect?

"Lucy, listen to me." He tossed a few more chips on the fire, then pulled her up so he could sit on the rock with her on his lap. "Deacon doesn't scare me. If he even tries—"

A sad chuckle fell from her lips. "You don't understand. It won't matter who you are, or who *I* am. When Deacon decides to do something, he does it." Her voice lowered to barely a whisper. "There'll be no stopping him."

Jed wondered on that a moment. How strong could a dandy like Deacon possibly be? He couldn't threaten them physically—it might mean his pretty-boy gloves would get dirty.

Light from the stoked fire danced across her pale,

drawn cheeks. She let out a long, weary sigh—something that worried Jed more than anything else.

In the short time he'd known Lucy, she'd never allowed anything to defeat her. Sure, she'd ripped dresses and threatened to throw pots, but she'd never let anything beat her before. She simply buckled down and tried again.

She had a fire inside that refused to be doused. Until tonight. And even though her stubbornness was a challenge Jed hadn't counted on, he much preferred that to this defeated and crushed Lucy.

She obviously wasn't going to say anything further on the matter. He eased her head down to his shoulder and wrapped his arms around her.

"You're safe with me. No one can hurt you now."

A soft sniff was her only answer, but it wasn't long before the neck of his shirt began to feel damp against his skin. He'd never known what to do with a woman when she cried, so he simply sat there, holding her and murmuring reassurances into her hair.

Damn Deacon. Damn him to Hell and back.

No one made Jed Caine's wife cry.

No one.

*   *   *

She was getting weaker. She didn't know why, but she had to do whatever it took to stop it.

Deacon had always been strong, had always been able to douse what little light she had in her soul with minimal effort. But she'd never cried over it before—at least not in front of anyone. Last night she'd done her best to ward him off, to keep him away from her soul, but he'd still managed to weasel his way in somehow.

Her only victory had been Deacon's arrogance. So intent was he on turning Jed, he hadn't noticed his unsettling effect on Lucy—and that was the edge she needed.

She'd made the mistake of letting him surprise her, of letting him overwhelm her with his mere presence last night—a mistake she wouldn't soon repeat. She needed to regain her strength, to focus on her plan, and to prevent Jed's comforting words and touches from fogging her vision again.

In truth, his touch caused an eruption of disturbing sensations. Strong, tender and gentle—his hands left her feeling both safe and vulnerable at the same time. Her heart had physically ached last night when he'd put his arm around her. If he had any idea of who she really was, he never would have touched her.

Anger, frustration and fear boiled out first, followed by desolation and loneliness. These were not new to her, but since when did she feel them for another soul?

Last night, she'd felt everything for Jed. Fear of what Deacon could do to him, and anger at not having the strength to stop it from happening. But it was only when Jed set her on his lap and held her that the loneliness hit her.

If she won her freedom—no, *when* she won it—Jed would no longer be there with her. He'd never force another cup of her coffee down his throat, he'd never again suggest she restock the supply of buffalo chips, and he'd never run his fingers up her arms or over her back as he had last night after Deacon left. She'd never feel Jed's mouth on hers again. And she'd never feel that swirling dive in her stomach when he leaned in for a kiss. Jed would be gone.

Lucy rolled over on the scratchy blanket and stared through the gloom at the barn wall.

What did she care if she never saw Jed Caine again? And what did she care if he never kissed her again? She could have kisses from any man she wanted.

Oddly enough, the thought of kissing any other man was about as appealing as kissing one of those damned chips in the yard.

The sounds of Jed starting the morning fire filtered through the cracks around the door. Any minute now, he'd slip in to get his precious coffeepot as he did every morning.

Lucy squeezed her eyes shut. If she didn't look at him, she'd have a few more minutes to shake the clouds from her head and focus on what needed to be done. And even though the plan seemed less alluring than it had a week ago, it was still the plan.

She needed to get Jed's soul and she wasn't going to do it by falling apart every time Deacon showed his face. Her brother had no idea how determined she was. He'd always thought of her as a weakling and until now, he'd been right.

But not this time.

The barn door creaked open and Jed tiptoed inside. As usual, he was a rumpled mess, with his shirt buttoned wrong, hanging partway out of his waistband and bearing yesterday's sweat stains. Lucy stayed tucked under the blanket, watching and waiting.

In less than a minute, he'd collected his coffee supplies and slipped back outside.

Jed Caine was a handsome man, no question, but for some reason, that fact was multiplied a thousandfold when he first woke up. It might be because he looked so warm and vulnerable, or because she knew that minutes before he'd been lying next to her, all warm and masculine.

Or maybe it was simply because morning was the only time of day he didn't wear that stupid hat.

Jed Caine had amazing hair: wavy, silky and begging to be touched. Yet he insisted on hiding it under that wide-brimmed monstrosity.

She squeezed her eyes shut, forcing his image from her mind.

Be strong. Focus.

After a few long, deep breaths, she slipped out of bed and pulled the blanket around her. It didn't matter how attracted she was to Jed. What mattered was how attracted he was to her and how she would turn that attraction into love.

It would help if she had any idea how to tell the difference between his lust and love. Though many humans believed the two to be the same, Jed obviously did not cotton to that way of thinking.

Until she figured out how to tell the difference, simple desire would have to do.

With teeth chattering and fingers trembling, she dropped the blanket and rid herself of the dress she'd slept in. Then, as quick as she could, she pulled the blanket around her again, leaving it open just enough to bare her shoulder and the thin string holding her chemise in place.

With her boots pulled on but unlaced and her teeth clenched to stop their rattling, she stepped out into the chilly morning air. Cold be damned, she had work to do, and not a great deal of time to do it. Once she was free, she wouldn't have to worry about baring skin. She could dress in as many layers as she liked—as long as they were pretty layers, of course.

"Morning," she mumbled, stepping close to the fire.

Heat. Please give me heat.

"Morning." Jed crouched near the flames, stirring his damned coffee, and didn't look up until he was into his next sentence. "I thought I'd get started on . . ."

His gaze wandered over Lucy, following the blanket up her body until it reached her shoulders. He swallowed hard, blinked, then moved his eyes to her face. His Adam's apple bobbed again.

Lucy tipped her head, waiting for him to finish. So far, so good. He cleared his throat, rubbed both palms across his stubbled cheeks, then rose.

"On the . . . uh," he swallowed again. "On clearing the ground for the new barn."

She forced a smile and nodded. "All right. When I'm done here, maybe I can help."

Jed's features twisted in an odd mixture of desire and frustration. Only a man would get worked up over a woman doing chores.

Good. If she could keep him in that state, maybe she could finish things faster. She slammed her mind shut against the confusion that followed that thought.

Jed's practical side finally won over again. He coughed twice, then motioned toward the far side of the fire. Their last six eggs lay in a basket next to what was left of the ham.

"Thought you might want to try again," he said, a hopeful gleam in his eye.

A groan battled to be released, but Lucy fought it back. If she could manage to cook this one meal—just this one—without burning it, maybe that would win her some regard with Jed.

Yes, the first few attempts to fry eggs had turned them into little more than charred ashes, but maybe this time . . .

"Feeling brave this morning, are you?" she teased.

Color crept over his cheeks, but Jed only shrugged, never taking his hungry gaze from her.

Lucy wiggled her back against the blanket.

"Could you . . . ?" she wiggled again. "This blanket's so itchy."

Jed was beside her in a heartbeat. "Where?" he asked, his voice a tight croak.

"Right . . . there." Lucy dropped the blanket another couple of inches and twisted her arm around to point to the non-itch in the middle of her back.

The second his fingers touched her, she cursed herself like a madwoman. He was magic against her skin; his warmth seeped into her, turning her whole seduction against her—again!

"That's good," she muttered, yanking the blanket back up. "Thank you."

Jed mumbled something incoherent as she ducked back into the barn. She kicked the stable door with the toe of her boot and cursed herself again. There had to be a way to seduce Jed without having him touch her.

Maybe he was right. Maybe she needed to earn his respect to make him love her. But could she do it before Maggie's baby came?

Lucy dressed quickly in the dark, tossed yesterday's dress into the pile near the door, then ran a brush through her hair. As much as Jed liked to look at it when it hung loose, it would only be in the way, so she quickly knotted it at the back of her head.

If he wanted a practical wife, he'd get one. Those kind of women got respect, didn't they?

A minute later, she was back at the fire, determined to cook him a decent meal. Or at least one that didn't disintegrate on his plate.

Crouched as close as she dared, she refused to look

away from the frying pan. At the first signs of the yolks hardening, she flipped each egg with careful precision, then turned the ham slices. So far, so good.

A shifting movement to her right dragged her attention away. Garden snake. Big one, too. She snapped up the axe and chased it down until it was good and dead, lying in pieces behind the house. If only she could rid herself of the snake that was her brother.

By the time she got back to the fire, her perfect breakfast had begun to burn. Using the piece of cloth she'd ripped from her skirt that first day, she yanked the frying pan from the flames and dropped it in the dirt. Thankfully, only one of the smaller pieces of ham bounced out. She lifted it up with the tips of her fingers, brushed the dirt off and set it on her plate.

Jed emerged from the barn a moment later, looking freshly shaven and dressed in his cleaner clothes. His eyes widened the closer he walked.

"Looks great," he beamed at her. "Even smells great."

Lucy shook her head. "The eggs are a little burned on the bottom," she muttered. "Stupid snake."

"Snake?" he frowned. "Where?"

"Behind the house." She dished two of the eggs onto his plate, then loaded it with ham before taking her own. Jed was halfway to the house before she stopped him. "I already got it, but that's why the eggs are burnt."

"You got it?" he repeated. "What kind?"

She shrugged. "Just a garden snake."

"You sure?" He strode back, concern clouding his face.

"Believe me, husband, I know my snakes." Her laugh was brittle, even to her own ears. "Now come and eat before it goes cold."

Jed walked slowly back toward her, his boots leaving clouds of dust in his wake.

"How many were there?" he asked, nodding his thanks as she handed him his plate.

"Just one."

"What did you kill it with?"

"The axe."

Jed gaped. "You took the axe to it?"

With a tip of her head, Lucy smiled slowly. "I couldn't help myself. It reminded me of Deacon."

His laughter rolled between them in warm, rumbling waves. "Well I'll be damned."

The irony of that simple statement . . .

Lucy bit back a chuckle. "It's just a snake, Jed."

He shook his head slowly, then sat on the ground next to the fire and filled his fork with the half-burnt eggs. Lucy held her breath and waited.

Jed's eyes widened, his chewing slowed, then sped up again.

"This is pretty good," he managed over his next forkful of egg. "Really!"

Lucy lifted her fork, doubtful he spoke the truth. But once the egg hit her tongue, she couldn't help smiling.

"This *is* pretty good, isn't it?"

Jed hunkered down over his plate and continued to shovel the food in as fast as he could chew.

"Is there more?" he asked when he'd scraped the last speck from his plate.

Lucy shook her head and swallowed. "Sorry, I'm saving the rest for Berta—and Maggie if she'll eat it."

"Nope, don't be sorry." He set the plate aside and patted his stomach. "Too much of a good thing does a body harm."

"I don't know about that," she murmured with a sly smile. "I'm certain there must be some good things a body can never get enough of."

"Wha . . . ?" Jed stopped, chuckled, then nodded slowly. "I'll go find the shovel and rake. I'll be behind the barn when you're ready."

It was Lucy's turn to laugh. "Behind the barn? Oh yes, dear husband, I'll gladly meet you behind the barn—with or without the shovel and rake."

He started to say something, then stopped. Instead, he reached over and kissed her cheek. It almost seemed a natural thing for him to do, as if he'd begun to enjoy her attempts to seduce him.

"Thank you. That was the best breakfast I've had in too long to remember." He rose to his feet and flashed her that wink, the one that made every cell of her body weaken. "I'm looking forward to more."

Lucy watched him walk away, taking a moment to admire his rear end. He'd get more all right, more than he expected and a hell of a lot more than he would know what to do with.

CHAPTER TEN

Berta kept her eyes averted even as she walked directly toward Lucy.

"Good morning," Lucy said.

Berta nodded.

"How is Maggie this morning?"

With a mournful glance back to the house, Berta sighed, and finally spoke. "She's not well, the poor dear. She needs to eat something other than bread and cheese."

Lucy pointed toward the basket. "I saved some of the eggs and ham. Will she eat that?"

A faint light glimmered in the other woman's pale eyes. "Hopefully."

While Lucy set to cleaning up one set of breakfast dishes, Berta set to dirtying another set. The woman worked with a sure efficiency that both amazed and irritated Lucy. Why couldn't *she* do that?

Perfect eggs and crisp, but not burnt, ham was ready in no time—all cooked in silence.

"Looks good." Ugh. Had Lucy said that out loud?

"Thank you." Berta bobbed her head slightly before scurrying back into the cabin.

Why on earth was the woman so nervous? The woman's

soul was troubled, no question, but for a human, she had a remarkable ability to block soul-seekers from getting too close. How could a human gain that skill?

◊   ◊   ◊

Jed paced off the area to be cleared, then marked the corners with large rocks. By the time he set the final corner, Lucy had arrived, armed with her work gloves and a bucket of water.

"What's wrong?"

She smiled back at him, but it was too late; he'd seen the frown, the tight lines around her mouth and the distant look in her eyes.

"Nothing."

"Lucy." He stepped up, tugged the bucket from her hand and set it on the ground. The gloves followed. "Tell me."

If she chewed that bottom lip any harder, she'd no doubt draw blood.

"Is it Maggie?"

A brief hesitation, then a short shrug. "Berta."

"What?"

Lucy sighed softly and tried to pull her hands from his, but he held her fast.

"There's something not right with her, but I can't put my finger on it."

Jed grinned. "You probably scared the bejeebers out of her at the auction, with the way you walked in and told her how things were going to be."

She didn't look convinced, but nodded anyway. "I'm sure you're right."

"Ready to get started?"

She lifted her brow in answer and tugged on her work

gloves. Using the small chip-cart, Lucy loaded up weeds, brambles and rocks, and wheeled it to the area Jed outlined. Anything useable was piled separately to be retrieved later for the corrals and stalls; the rest would be burned.

Under the piercing July sun, Jed mopped his brow and neck every few minutes, but Lucy didn't seem the least bit bothered by it. Several times she stopped working, but only to rub her hands up and down her arms.

She was working just as hard as Jed, so how could she possibly be cold?

They worked past noon, pulling up the lighter stuff and hauling it away. Conversations were brief, given they'd have to almost yell to hear each other across the area they worked, but Jed did plenty of watching.

She was a helluva lot stronger than he ever would have guessed. In fact, she could probably outwork all of the woman and most of the men at the auction. Maybe he'd made the right decision after all, even if it hadn't seemed very practical at the time.

Every passing day with Lucy surprised him a little more. She didn't enjoy the work, that was evident, but she did it. She often seemed ready to quit, to run screaming down the road as fast as she could, but she never did. She'd simply grind her teeth together, glare fire in Jed's direction, then get back down to work.

She refused to give up on making coffee—wouldn't even let Berta do it for her. It was as though she enjoyed the challenge. And finally, for the first time since she'd arrived, she'd cooked a tasty meal. Hell, it had been more than tasty. A little burned, but damn fine nonetheless.

"What?" Lucy leaned against her rake.

Jed gave his head a quick shake. How long had he been staring at her?

"How do you know this is going to work?" She nodded to the yard around them, then looked directly at him, not with one of her sly smiles or seductive looks, but simple curiosity.

Jed offered her his best smile. "Because we'll damn well make it work, that's how."

When she grinned back, he continued, suddenly desperate to convince her he was right. "Hard work can make pretty much anything happen, Lucy, just so long as we don't back down from it and don't let anyone convince us otherwise."

She nodded slowly. "I understand that," she said. "But given the type of ground we're clearing here, what do you expect the herd to eat when it arrives?"

"Grass, of course." He pointed south, toward the main pasture. "There's plenty of grass out there on the other side of the creek."

"Will you take me there?"

"One day."

He shot her a wink and she smiled back, but as usual, it didn't reach her eyes. After a moment, she ladled him a cup of water, then waited for him to finish before she drank herself.

"Do you have other family besides Maggie?" she asked.

Jed shrugged as nonchalantly as he could. "Ma died about ten years back."

"And your father?" She sliced off another large chunk of the prickly pear she'd been cutting down and tossed it aside.

Jed reached for the water bucket, filled and emptied his mug twice before he managed to chase the bile back down his throat.

"Haven't spoken to him since Ma died." He swiped his

forearm across his mouth before adding, "But didn't speak much before then, either."

"Why?"

"Nothing to say I guess." That was true enough, but for two men who didn't have anything to say, they'd sure done a lot of yelling.

"Does he live around here?" She stopped now, too, her brow furrowed, her eyes watching him ever so carefully.

"Dunno." Jed retrieved the axe and set back to work. "Last I heard he was still living on the farm near Helena."

"Montana?"

He nodded shortly. Montana—big as that damned territory was, it wasn't near big enough for both him and his father.

"My goodness," she said softly. "You're a long way from home, Jed Caine."

"Nope." He brought the axe down in a long swift slice that left the remaining cactus split in two. "I've finally found my home."

❖   ❖   ❖

With the animals fed and watered, Jed washed quickly at the creek, then made his way back out to the fire. Did he dare hope for another meal like he'd had at breakfast?

The fire snapped and sparked, but Lucy was nowhere to be seen. Neither were any pots, pans or other dishes. Fear sliced through him.

Deacon.

He made it to the barn in less time than it took him to think the name. He slammed open the door and charged inside, his blood thrashing through his veins. Fighting to see through the gloom, he finally made out her form after what seemed like forever.

Lucy lay curled up on the straw tick, tucked beneath the gray blanket. Her steady, soft breathing calmed the paralyzing fear that froze Jed inside the door. A wayward piece of straw had worked its way through her hair, and another poked through just below her nose, fluttering back and forth against her breath.

A lifetime passed before Jed's heart slowed to a normal beat. A second lifetime passed before he could pull his gaze away from her. She'd never looked so beautiful as she did then. Her face smudged with dirt and God knew what else, her hair tangled half in, half out of its knot, and her soft, full lips opened slightly in sleep.

Jed wanted to kick himself. Lucy had worked like a dog all day, and still he'd expected her to make supper.

That was no way to treat his woman. She needed her rest. And she needed to eat if she was to keep up her strength.

Despite the fact Jed's hunger had spun from wanting food to wanting Lucy, he couldn't touch her. He wouldn't be that kind of man. Respectable men controlled their urges. And God help him, he'd learn how to control his.

He gathered the things he needed and crept back outside. Wouldn't be a great meal, but it'd be better than nothing.

He dug around in the corner of the barn until he found some dried meat and a few leftover potatoes. Even though most of their food supplies were kept on shelves either in the house or the barn, he'd have to get a proper storage room built soon. They'd been fairly lucky so far, but it was only a matter of time before the mice and other vermin started helping themselves.

Miss Blake was bent over the fire when he stepped outside again.

"Hello, Mr. Caine," she said. "I was just going to make

Maggie some supper. I'd be happy to make yours and Mrs. Caine's as well."

The offer was almost too good to pass up, but Jed forced it out. "That's mighty kind of you, ma'am, but I can manage. It's enough that you're caring for Maggie."

"Poor girl," Berta tsked. "She can't have long to go before that baby comes, yet she's so thin."

Jed nodded. "I was hopin' you could do something about that. Even before Lucy came, I couldn't get Maggie to eat much more than bread and cheese."

The woman's brow puckered. "That's something, but I do wish I could get her to eat more, especially more meat and vegetables."

Jed held up the potatoes he'd brought out of the barn. "Until we get a garden going, I'm afraid this is the best I can offer."

Berta offered a small smile. "She told me she won't eat potatoes. But if you have any meat . . ."

"Only this." He handed her the dried meat, but she shook her head. "Not all of it. She'll never eat that much."

Jed chewed the inside of his cheek for a moment. "Do you think we ought to bring Doc Billings out?"

Berta stirred the pot of beans she'd been warming. "The baby is still active, and that's an excellent sign. I doubt there's anything the doctor can do, but if you think it would make Maggie feel better, then by all means . . ."

"The only thing that'll make her feel better is Sam walking down that road again." He sighed and rubbed the back of his neck. "And you and I both know that's not going to happen."

Berta didn't reply, but set to filling Maggie's plate with beans and the dried meat Jed had given her.

"I'll clean up," he said. "Thank you, again, for coming out to help. I know this isn't what you had in mind."

She looked straight back at him, her eyes steady for the first time since she arrived. "I told you I'd do whatever I could to help Mrs. Caine, and if this is what will help her, I'm happy to do it."

Jed watched Berta disappear back into the cabin. Why the hell would she be so set on helping Lucy? They'd never met until the auction.

Women. Who could understand them?

He scrubbed the potatoes clean, then chopped them into a pot of water and set them to boil. The dried meat might not be very tasty, but it would do for now.

Tomorrow he'd have to go find something fresh.

When the potatoes were done, he filled two plates and carried them back into the barn. Lucy remained exactly as he'd left her. He ducked back out for the water bucket and filled them each a cup.

When he couldn't think of anything else to do to keep away from her, he crouched beside the pile of straw she'd formed into a mattress and pulled the straw from her hair.

"Lucy," he whispered. "Supper's ready."

She didn't move.

"Lucy," he said again, slightly louder. Nothing.

"Hey." He rubbed the back of his hand against her cheek, loving the silkiness of her skin, and amazed at its coolness.

She moved slightly, pressing her cheek against his hand, but her eyes remained closed, her breathing even.

"Wake up," he murmured, then leaned closer and pressed his lips against her cheek, exactly where his hand had been a moment before. "Lucy."

"Mmm." Stretching slightly, she twisted her face around until it lay directly under his, a mere breath separating their noses.

Jed didn't even hesitate. He should have, but he didn't. He couldn't.

His lips brushed hers once, then twice. The third time, she moved beneath him, whimpered softly, and opened up to him.

He couldn't get enough of her taste, her smoothness, and her soft, dizzying moans. He kissed her slowly, savoring each moment, pulling her toward him, in both mind and body.

She woke gradually, as if resisting it, but even half asleep, her response to his kisses drove him to his knees. Her fingers poked out from beneath the blanket and twisted around the front of his shirt, holding him close, as if afraid he'd leave.

He smiled against her mouth. "You're awake."

"No," she breathed. "I'm still dreaming."

He kissed her still-closed eyes, the tip of her nose, and her chin. But when she whimpered again, he cupped her face between his hands and caressed her lips with his, demanding more, begging for more.

His breathing came in ragged gasps, his heart thrashing against his ribs with enough force to break them.

He pulled back enough to look at her; her lips were moist and swollen from his kisses, her fingers clenched in his shirt, her eyes beginning to flutter open.

"I made supper," he whispered.

"Mmm." Finally, her eyes opened. "I'm too tired to eat."

Jed smiled. For a minute there, something washed over his heart that he couldn't be sure about, but it was better than anything he'd felt before.

"Come on." He eased her up to a sitting position, but she immediately slipped over.

"I just want to sleep," she muttered, reaching for the blanket again.

"Okay," he agreed with a sigh. "Keep your blanket."

As gently as he could, he helped Lucy sit up against the wall.

"There." He retrieved the plates from the floor and crawled up onto the bed beside her. With her plate balanced on her lap, he handed her a fork and set to work on his own supper, now almost cold.

Lucy just sat there, watching him through half-closed eyes and smiling softly.

"Eat up," he teased. "Today was nothing. Wait 'til you see what I have planned for tomorrow."

"Can't wait," she mumbled. "But I think I need to spend tomorrow collecting chips."

Jed choked on a mouthful of potato. "Oh no," he laughed. "You're not getting out of work that easily."

"Please?" She started to lean sideways, so he propped her up again.

By the time he'd finished inhaling his supper, she hadn't lifted her fork once. So he did it for her. The dried meat was a waste of time—he should have boiled it, too—but he managed to get a few forkfuls of potatoes into her before finally giving up and moving the plates back to the floor.

Lucy closed her eyes again, but Jed knew she wasn't asleep. Not yet, anyway.

"I'm sorry, sweetheart," he murmured, easing her back down onto the bed. "I didn't mean to work you so hard today."

"Lie with me." Her voice was barely audible, but each word screamed right to Jed's aching conscience. He shouldn't.

In his next breath, he stretched out behind her, and pulled her back against him. Prickly straw be damned—

he'd lie there every night if it meant he could hold her like this.

Lucy snuggled deeper into her blanket and nudged her way against him until he folded her beneath his arm and sighed into her hair.

He kissed the back of her ear and sighed. "Sleep well, Lucy."

"Mmm."

I sure as hell won't.

It didn't matter, though. All that mattered was his woman tucked up in his arms, sleeping soundly without a care in the world. All that mattered was that he'd begun to feel something deeper and definite for his wife.

And all that mattered was hoping someday, somehow, she could feel the same for him.

CHAPTER ELEVEN

By the end of the following week, Jed had made a decision: His wife deserved a day off—and damn it, he was going to give her one.

He'd lain awake most of the night again, battling his wants. Part of him wanted to wake Lucy up and make love to her for a month straight. But the other part of him wanted to stay exactly as he was because she felt so damned good right where she was.

He only hoped there was enough blanket between them that his painfully hard want was well hidden.

Lucy sighed, stretched, and turned to face him.

"Good morning," she smiled lazily.

Didn't seem right that she could look so disgusting and so amazing all at the same time.

"Sleep well?" he asked, between kissing her brow and eyes.

"Mmm." Another stretch. "You?"

"No." He buried his face in her hair and laughed, though it came out more like a ragged cry.

For the first time since he'd met her, Lucy laughed a real laugh, not her usual forced, cynical or disbelieving one. The sound sang in his ears and danced across his heart.

"It's your own fault," she said, tipping her head so he could nuzzle her neck—which he did, gladly.

"My fault?" He kissed the back of her ear. "It wasn't my snoring that nearly collapsed the walls."

"What?" Lucy sat bolt up and shoved him hard. "I don't snore!"

Jed rolled onto his back and laughed. "There was only you and me here, darlin', and since I was awake most of the night, I know it wasn't me making that noise."

In a whoosh of speed, she jumped off the bed and gathered the blanket around her. She was trying hard to look offended, but her eyes sparkled with laughter.

"You, dear husband, deserve every sleepless minute of agony you had to live through last night." She swept the blanket dramatically over one shoulder. "Now get out so I can dress."

The thought of staying to watch glued him to where he lay sprawled on the bed, but the second she moved to drop the blanket, he jumped off like a shot and raced for the safety of outside. A man could only take so much.

"Coward," she called as he slammed the door behind himself.

"Damn right." He rubbed both hands against his face and dragged in half a dozen long breaths before he moved again.

Coffee. Lots of coffee. And the stronger the better.

By the time she emerged from the barn, blanket in tow, he'd just poured his first cup.

Sleep lingered in her movements, her body not fully awake yet, and her eyes blinked hard against the glare of the morning sun.

"Shall we try this again?" she asked with a teasing smile. "Good morning, Jed. How did you sleep?"

She pressed a small kiss against his cheek before wrinkling her nose at his mug of steaming coffee.

Jed resisted the urge to pull her back for a better kiss. No matter how often he looked at her, the desire to touch never lessened—even when she looked like a shapeless lump with that blanket hanging around her.

"Slept like a baby." He grinned back. "Never better."

"Glad to hear it." She laughed again—the same genuine laugh as earlier—and all Jed could do was stare at her.

How the hell did he ever get so lucky? Of all the men she could have chosen, of all the men who would have sold their souls to be her husband, she'd picked him.

It still nettled him that he probably wouldn't be her first, but at least he had the comfort of knowing he'd be her last. No other man would ever touch his Lucy again.

"I made tea," he said when he'd found his tongue again. "Don't know why I didn't think of it sooner."

If he expected her to jump up and down with excitement, he was sorely disappointed. In fact, she almost looked confused.

"You have had tea before, haven't you?"

"No," she laughed softly. "But if it smells anything like that mud you drink, I'll have to decline."

Jed shook his head in mock disappointment.

There was a change in her he couldn't quite pin, but it was good. No, it was amazing. *She* was amazing.

"Try this." He poured a mug of tea, added a spoonful of sugar and handed it to her.

She eyed it warily, then him, but accepted the mug and lifted it to her nose. Her first sniff eased some of the doubt from her frown. After the second sniff, she kept the mug close to her nose. And the third sniff finally convinced her to try a sip.

As she lifted it to her lips, a whippoorwill cried sharply from the roof of the house.

"Caref—" Jed began, but it was too late.

"Yow!" Lucy slopped half the tea into the fire in her haste to get it away from her tongue.

"It's hot," he finished on a lame note.

"Thanks for the warning." Using the corner of the blanket, she wiped the sloshed tea from her chin while carefully balancing the mug in her other hand.

He tried not to laugh, he really did. But how could he not?

"Thought the steam would have been a pretty clear warning," he chuckled over the rim of his mug.

Fire snapped back to life in Lucy's eyes. Her mouth opened, for what Jed was sure would be an angry retort. But instead, she closed it again and smiled.

"Okay," she answered. "You win. But I'm not even half awake yet—how can I think clearly?"

"It's tea. It's supposed to help you wake up."

"It is?"

Jed shook his head slowly, and even as he spoke the words, he regretted each one. "How can you not know these things?"

Lucy's smile faded, and her eyes hardened. "Just stupid, I guess."

"Lucy." He stepped closer. "That's not what I meant."

She didn't answer, but stood with her face turned toward the fire. Jed reached over and plucked a piece of straw from the blanket. He held it a long moment before dropping it into the fire.

"I've just never met anyone who never tasted coffee or tea before." Jed shrugged out his apology. "Doesn't mean you're stupid."

When she finally looked at him, he offered her a small grin, too.

"I reckon it means I'm the stupid one for not thinking before I go and open my big mouth."

Lucy lips twitched. "Now that's something we can finally agree on, husband."

"Am I forgiven?"

A look so odd crossed her face that Jed couldn't even begin to guess what it meant or what she was thinking.

"You want *me* to forgive *you*?"

He shrugged again, grinning. "That's normally how this works. Someone says they're sorry and the other person forgives them."

"Hmm," she mused. "Interesting. I've never forgiven anyone before."

The shock of that simple statement nearly yanked Jed's jaw to the ground. But rather than upset her again, he forced a look that he could only hope was anything but surprised. If he didn't know better, he'd swear Lucy had dropped clean out of the sky or something.

He swallowed the rest of his coffee, tipped her a nod and pointed toward the tea.

"Willing to try it again?" he asked. "I recommend you blow on it a little to cool it down first."

Lucy lifted the mug again, blew a few times and took another tentative sip. Then another. Wonder filled her face as her eyes began to light up again.

"Mmmm," she managed between sips. "It's warming me up from the inside out!"

Jed wanted to be the one warming her up. Hell, with what he wanted to do to her, they'd probably both burst into flames. He shook himself from that train of thought and cleared his throat.

"I was thinking," he said.

"Oh no," she moaned. "Every time you say that, I find myself knee deep in prickly pear and mesquite bushes."

"No," he laughed. "Not this time."

She allowed him to refill her mug, then settled herself on the ground. Jed refilled his own mug, and sat next to her, fighting the urge to crawl inside that damned blanket with her.

"What would you think about going into town today?" he asked.

Lucy started so quickly, she nearly spilled her tea again.

"Into town?" She wiped a drop of tea from her bottom lip, a simple movement that had Jed adjusting his position to find a comfortable spot again.

"Yes," he finally managed. "I need to pick up some supplies, and I figured while we were there, we could go find you a dress you won't want to rip apart. Maybe a coat, too."

Lucy's eyes widened with every word. "Really? A coat?"

"Sure," he laughed. "Unless you want to keep that blanket with you all the time."

"Uh, no," she admitted. "But why would you waste more money on me?"

"Waste?" Jed scratched his head and frowned. "If it makes you happy, Lucy, it's not wasted."

She didn't look impressed with his gallantry. Instead, she looked wary.

"Are you sure you can you afford it? You don't even have the herd yet."

Jed tapped her on the nose. "Yes, *we* can afford it. Don't worry. And while we're in town, I'll go make the final arrangements with George to take over part of his herd."

Lucy carefully sipped her tea and nodded along with him, even as a frown crinkled her forehead. Of course she was worried, thought Jed, Deacon was staying in town somewhere. Maybe this was Jed's chance to prove he could handle Deacon. Maybe Lucy would finally realize there was nothing to worry about from an ass like Deacon.

"It'll be fine, Lucy."

She looked up at him, but Jed would have sworn she didn't actually see him. It was as though she were looking through him.

In a rush of energy, she leapt up, dropping the blanket to her feet, but keeping her tea tight in hand. She filled a large pot with the remaining water from the bucket and set it atop the fire.

"I can't very well go to town looking like this," she announced, then eyed him skeptically. "And neither can you."

Jed couldn't help laughing. This was the Lucy he needed back. The Lucy who would rather die than let others see her looking anything but her best. The Lucy who'd deny it forever, but who had as much pride as Jed himself.

"I'll go clean up at the creek," he said when he'd stopped laughing at her.

"Ooh, the creek," she mused. "A bath *would* be better."

Oh no. The mere thought of Lucy standing naked in his creek was more than Jed could stand. In fact, he couldn't stand at all at the moment.

He needed to keep her away from that creek—it was his sanctuary, the one place he could go to control his urges with the cold water. Granted, it didn't control them completely, but at least it helped manage them a little.

"I don't know," he croaked. "That water's mighty cold. You sure you want to . . . expose . . . yourself to that?"

Lucy didn't seem to notice the strain in his voice or the way his teeth ground together with each word.

"Maybe not." She grinned, then focused back on the pot of water. "I'll wash up here, you go to the creek, and we'll get going as soon as possible."

She pulled the coffeepot from the rocks. "Are you done with this?"

Before Jed could answer, she emptied the pot on the ground with one graceful swing of her arm. But she made sure her mug was filled before she sent the remaining tea in the same direction.

"Guess I'm done now," he muttered, struggling to his feet.

The look of excitement on Lucy's face doused any irritation he had over a stupid pot of coffee.

"I'll tend the horses, then go clean up," he said. "Be ready in an hour?"

"An hour?" Lucy shook her head. "Oh no, dear husband, we'll be well on our way in an hour—so you best get going."

She pulled the mug from his fingers—the still half-full mug—and pushed him toward the barn. He reached back for his coffee but she'd already dumped it out.

Damn. If she weren't so adorable, he'd almost be angry. Almost.

Instead, he trudged off to feed and water the horses, grinning stupidly the entire time. He took his time harnessing them to the wagon. After all, no woman could possibly have her chores done and be dressed within an hour. He had plenty of time to get ready and plenty of time to ponder this woman he'd married.

If someone had told him two weeks ago that he'd be

married to a woman like Lucy, he never would have believed them. And if they told him he'd be happy about it, he'd have thought them completely mad.

Yet there he was, married to a woman so unlike himself it could hardly be believed.

And he liked it.

Actually, truth be told, he *more* than liked it. He couldn't imagine being married to any of those other girls at the auction, and he offered a silent word of thanks for the odd turn of events that got him to where he was.

If he'd followed his plan the way he'd set out to, would he be this happy? Somehow, he doubted it.

The creek did little to wash Lucy out of his mind. In fact, he kept envisioning her standing knee-deep in the water, her eyes laughing back at him, her body dripping with—

"Stop it," he muttered. "Just stop it."

He scrubbed his own body with the hard yellow soap, rinsed quickly, and dressed in his clean set of clothes. Dried soap flaked from his shirt as he buttoned it over his still-damp skin. Hopefully one day Lucy would learn how to rinse better before she hung the clothes to dry.

But he wasn't about to mention it to her. He'd just wear whatever was clean and be damned thankful he wasn't the one who'd had to use that cursed scrub board.

He buttoned his shirt as he walked, checking to make sure he had the buttons in their proper holes. Wouldn't do to let anyone think he was distracted.

What the . . .

Jed stopped next to the huge, hand-shaped cactus. The four yellow blooms were still as vibrant as ever, but now, the fourth 'finger' was pushing a bloom out as well. It was still small compared to the others, but it stood out for no other reason than it wasn't yellow like the others, but red.

By the time he made it back to the house, Lucy was dressed and waiting at the barn door. Her green silk dress was slightly wrinkled, but she still looked beautiful in it. Her face glowed from its fresh scrubbing, and her glossy black hair fell loosely around her shoulders.

It was the way he liked it best. Not very sensible to leave it down like that, but damn if it didn't make him want to slide his hands through it silkiness and—

He squeezed his eyes shut, swallowed back several curses, then forced himself to look back at her.

"Decided against the blanket, did ya?"

"Yes," she answered with a cheeky smile. "I save that particular look just for you, dear husband. Aren't you lucky?"

He deposited his dirty clothes just inside the door, then swept a soft kiss against her cheek.

"Luckiest damn fool in the world." He shot her a wink, then added, "Give me a second."

His knock on the cabin door was answered immediately.

"Lucy and I have to go in to town," he told Berta. "I don't figure Maggie will want to come with us, but if there's anything you think we need—"

Berta murmured her answer, then closed the door. Jed hesitated a moment before returning to Lucy. He lifted her up into the wagon, then climbed up beside her, suddenly feeling like he was, truly, the luckiest man God ever saw fit to put on the earth. And yet, at the same time, he was the most pathetic man ever.

He clicked to the horses and breathed in a deep lungfull of fresh morning air. How could his life be so mixed up? On the one hand, he had a wife who'd begun to settle into his heart, who'd finally made his parched piece of land begin to feel like home.

On the other hand, he had a sister-in-law who was losing her senses, whose baby was due in a few weeks, and who refused to consider herself a widow. Once the baby was born, he'd have to talk to her about putting up a stone for Sam.

In the meantime, he'd trust Maggie's care to Berta and hope the baby was born healthy. He also needed to prove to his wife that he wasn't the weakling she seemed to think he was; that he could—and would—protect both her and Maggie from anything that threatened to hurt them.

Even if it meant protecting Lucy from her own family, and Maggie from herself.

CHAPTER TWELVE

Lucy arranged her skirts neatly around her, then rearranged them. Anything to keep herself occupied. If only she could keep her mind occupied with something other than Jed.

He was going to buy her a coat. And a new dress.

He didn't seem to have any personal reasons for giving her these things. Most humans were selfish by nature, and only did kind things if it meant they would reap some benefit themselves.

That didn't seem to be the case with Jed.

It was as if he honestly wanted her to have these things just because it would make her happy.

How odd.

She felt his concern. He worried over her meeting Deacon while they were in town, and he didn't want her to think he was weak. But she worried over neither of these things.

She could no sooner control Deacon's movements than she could the tide, so it was a waste of energy to think on it. And as for Jed being weak—it was a moot point. No human could withstand the powers Deacon wielded. She didn't doubt her husband's physical strength or ability, but this was a fight he had no hope of winning.

He sat on the bench next to her, his elbows resting on his knees, the reins dangling loosely between his fingers. A new and unsettling fear settled over Lucy as she watched him. It was one thing for *her* to be working against Jed, but she shuddered at the thought of Deacon getting involved.

As though he knew she was staring at him, Jed sat up and turned to face her. "You all right?" he asked, his deep voice carrying in the empty desert.

"Yes," she answered, perhaps a little too fast. After a brief hesitation, she smiled. "Just admiring the scenery."

Jed tipped his hat back slightly and glanced around them. "It sure is pretty, isn't it?" He sighed contentedly. "No crowds, no noise. Just us."

And the tumbleweeds.

Lucy frowned. "I wasn't talking about the land, Jed."

He cocked his brow. "What else is there?"

She slid across the bench until they sat side by side. She didn't tease him as she'd done the first time they'd ridden together, though. Instead, she slipped her hand beneath his elbow and rested her head on his shoulder.

"I was talking about you."

"Me?" Jed snorted. "I think that sun finally got the better of you. Knew you should've been wearing that bonnet."

"I'm fine." Lucy swatted his arm. "But you can be sure I'd welcome sun-addled brains long before I'd agree to wear that horrible bonnet."

She memorized every inch of his face, from the sun-bronzed color to the tiny white scar beneath his right ear. His stubborn streak showed itself in the firmness of his jaw, and his kindness bared itself through his coal-black eyes—the same eyes she'd once considered unreadable.

"You're a very handsome man, Jedidiah. Did you know that?"

Color raced up his neck and face, disappearing at his scalp.

"You are," she insisted. "I'd say you're probably the most handsome man I've ever seen."

"Then you obviously haven't seen many men." He laughed at himself, but Lucy wasn't going to let him off so easily.

"It wouldn't matter how many I had or hadn't seen. You are, in fact, a handsome man." She sat forward a little so she could look directly into his face. "Do you really not know that?"

"It's not something I pay much mind to."

"I know." She smiled at his embarrassment. "That's what adds to it."

Jed licked his lips, blew out a long breath, then licked them again. "Could we talk about something else, please?"

"Better yet," she said, turning his face back to hers. "Let's not talk at all."

She pulled him toward her until their lips touched, briefly, then again, slightly longer. He tasted like sunshine and fresh water, and before she knew it—and before he could stop her—she wiggled herself onto his lap.

She kept his face between her hands and kissed him again, sliding her tongue over his mouth and pulling a low growl from him. His arms shifted beneath her, wrestling with the reins, until the wagon came to a stop.

Lucy clung to Jed. She needed to kiss him. She couldn't explain why, she just knew it was something she had to do. And, all the better, it was something she enjoyed doing.

If he pushed her away, she'd be lost. How would she find her next breath?

The air around them stood still for a very long, tortu-
ous heartbeat. She eased back far enough to look into the
darkness of his eyes and what she saw there nearly ripped
her in two. Need as strong as her own shone back, con-
suming her with its heat.

Jed's hands cupped her bottom and shifted her slightly.
The feel of him, hard against her backside, sent jolts of
excitement racing through her veins to places deep inside
she'd never felt before.

His gaze never wavered, not even so much as a blink.
Lucy licked her lips, swiping her tongue across them
slowly, in the hopes of finding his taste still there.

Jed's mouth found hers with a kiss so hungry, so demanding, Lucy's entire being quaked. He slid his hands
up her sides, brushing his thumbs against her straining
breasts. Heat poured into her, ripping through her veins
and sending shiver after shiver over her skin and up her
spine.

His hands were in her hair, caressing each lock, then
holding her head still while he devoured her.

A soft whimper came from Lucy's throat.

What is wrong with me? This wasn't how it was supposed to be. For Jed, yes, but certainly not for her. She
wasn't meant to crave his touch or to want his kisses so
much. It wasn't right.

But if it wasn't right, she was more than happy to be
wrong; so very, very wrong.

She squeezed closer to Jed, until his chest pressed
against her, his heart pounding out a rhythm fast enough
to cause any other mortal's to explode. The mere thought
made Lucy smile.

Her mortal was so much better than the rest of them:
stronger, better looking, and completely irresistible. Oh
yes, she'd chosen well with him.

Jed moaned against her lips, then pulled back. Not far, just enough to rest his forehead against hers, the tips of their noses brushing each other.

"You're killin' me," he whispered, his voice harsh and raspy.

"Funny," Lucy whispered back. "You feel very much alive to me."

Jed let go a ragged laugh and settled her head against his shoulder.

She wiggled closer and reached for the buttons on Jed's shirt. His breath caught when the first one released. His Adam's apple bobbed hard on the second. But when she started on the third, his hand covered hers and held it tight.

"Not here," he moaned. "Just the thought of it's more than I can handle right now."

Lucy sighed softly, but didn't object. How could she when he held her hand that way? If she'd ever wondered what feeling safe felt like, this would be it, sitting on Jed's lap, with his arms wrapped around her and her hand tucked in his. There couldn't be a safer place in all the world.

"Should we go then?" She closed her eyes and held her breath. *Please say no.*

"Give me a minute, will you?" Jed's chuckle came out as more of a choke.

They sat in silence for much longer than a minute. Lucy curled against his shoulder, while Jed traced circles across her back with his huge, gentle fingers. She'd expected his desire to soften after a time, but it didn't.

Not even a little.

"Would it be better if I got off your lap?" she asked softly.

"Lord no," he moaned. "I'm afraid of what'll happen if you move."

Lucy tried to stifle her laughter against his neck, but it was no use.

"I'm glad you're finding this so amusing," he said, and even though she couldn't see his face, she knew he was smiling, too.

"I'm sorry," she laughed. "What can I do?"

"I think you've done enough." His lips smiled against her forehead. After another minute, he inhaled a long, slow breath. "On three, I'm going to lift you straight up and off. But God help me, Lucy, don't you so much as twitch. Just let me do it, okay?"

She nodded against his neck, fighting back another snort of laughter.

"One." He wrapped his hands around her waist. "Two." Lucy tensed slightly.

"Don't move," he growled.

Laugher ripped from her throat before she could stop it. "I'm sorry," she said again.

"No, you're not." His jaw tightened, and in one swoop, he lifted her straight off his lap and plopped her on the bench beside him.

The horses tossed their heads at the disturbance, but stayed where they were. Jed didn't move. He didn't look at her, and for a second, she thought he'd stopped breathing all together.

"Well," she said, not even attempting to hide her smile. "Shall we carry on then?"

She shifted on the bench, arranged her skirts, and looked up at him with her best wide-eyed innocent look.

Jed shot her a glare that might have unnerved her if he hadn't been grinning at the same time.

"Just one second. Can't very well go to town looking like this, can I?" He stood up, adjusted his trousers, then sat back down. "*Now* we can carry on."

Lucy laughed all the way to town. And though she knew it embarrassed him terribly, Jed let out a few chuckles, too.

*   *   *

The mid-morning sun shone brilliantly against the cloudless sky. Up ahead, the town of Redemption bustled with its daily business.

Jed hated coming into town. He hated the crowds, hated the smell and especially hated knowing that his presence would send every gossip's jaw wagging about his family again. If it wasn't enough that Sam was presumed dead and Maggie's fragile state got worse by the day, now the gossips had new fodder.

Of all the men at the auction, he'd been the one Lucy had chosen. Him—the man who worked so hard to maintain his reputation as practical and sensible. The man who had never been swayed by a girl in frills or lace.

But swayed he'd been. And he'd never been so dizzy in all his life.

Lucy sat tall in the wagon, her chin lifted and her hands folded neatly in her lap. Aside from the few wrinkles in her dress, and her kiss-swollen lips, she looked exactly as she had when he'd walked out of the auction with her.

Damn the gossips—they could think or say whatever they wanted about him and Lucy. He'd made a fine choice in his new wife and he could only hope she'd eventually come to feel the same way about him.

"Where to first?" he asked, sitting up straight.

A flash of hope covered her face, then faded. "We should go talk to George first. Take care of business and then we'll worry about . . . other things."

Other things. Jed didn't know whether to laugh or not.

The minute he'd mentioned a new dress and coat, her eyes had lit up like the North Star. Yet there she sat pretending it didn't matter a hoot. What an odd creature she was.

"The mercantile's closer," he answered, holding in his grin. "And Miss Celia's dress shop is right over there."

He pointed down the street, but Lucy shook her head.

"No. Business first." She bobbed her head in a definite nod. "After all, we're not sure how much the herd will cost, so it only makes sense to do that first, then we'll know where we stand."

Was this *his* Lucy being practical? Couldn't be.

But as much as he'd love to see her in a fancy new dress right away, what she said made sense.

Jed pulled the wagon up to the livery and set the brake. Herd or no herd, he was going to spoil his wife silly today.

"Here." He set his hands around her narrow waist and lifted her from the seat, realizing she wasn't wearing a corset. What *did* she have on underneath that dress?

Lucy smiled wickedly at him, as though she'd read his thoughts. "Thank you, husband."

He cleared his throat and grinned stupidly. "Be back in a minute."

After arranging care for the horses and wagon, he took Lucy's elbow and steered her toward town. "Last chance to do the mercantile first," he teased as they approached the huge glass window. "Dresses, earbobs, maybe that pretty little feather bonnet right there."

He pointed to a ridiculous-looking yellow hat in the corner of the window display. Barely large enough to fit the crown of a woman's head, it seemed to be sprouting feathers of every color from the side.

Lucy snorted softly and smiled. "If you like it so much," she said, "buy it for yourself."

Jed pretended to consider the idea. "It's not really my color, is it?"

"Yellow?" Lucy's smile faded, her face now serious. "Definitely not."

He'd have sworn his heart swelled a little with those two words.

"Where do we find this George person?" Lucy asked, leaving the mercantile behind them without another glance.

"He's the bank manager." When Lucy raised a brow, he continued. "Seems he came into an inheritance from his uncle, I believe, which included a sizeable herd and a ranch down south a ways."

"Why doesn't he keep the herd then?"

Jed laughed. "George isn't much for ranching. Once you see him, you'll understand—he's better suited to banking."

He led her up the two steps into the bank, then took a moment to let his eyes adjust from the glare of outside to the cooler, dim interior of the bank.

"Good morning, Jed." The bank manager stepped out from his office, a small room tucked off to the side of the bank, and offered Lucy a slight bow.

"George McTaggert," Jed began. "Like you to meet my wife, Lucy."

Lucy tipped her head in a perfect, ladylike gesture and allowed George to shake her hand.

"It's nice to meet you," she said. "Jed tells me you're very good at your job."

George seemed to grow two feet all at once. His wiry frame puffed out and the blush that started at his neck raced over his face and nearly bald head. He pushed his half-moon glasses up on his nose and smiled modestly.

"Thank you," he said. "That's very kind."

He led them back into the quiet of his tiny office, a room barely big enough for the three of them, his desk and the chairs.

"Please, have a seat." He waited until Lucy was comfortable before he took his own chair. "You've come about the cattle, is that right?"

"That's right." Jed settled his hat on his lap and held his breath, hoping George's price wouldn't be too outrageous. George chewed the inside of his cheek, his gaze flicking from his folded hands to Jed and back. This couldn't be a good sign.

"Can I be frank with you, Jed?"

"Wish you would." His fingers tightened around his hat.

"I've taken a liberty on your behalf that I hope won't be too upsetting to you. Or the misses."

Dread began to pool in Jed's stomach. If George wanted more for the cattle than Jed could afford, he might have to forgo buying Lucy that pretty new dress, or worse, the number of head he'd hoped for.

Dammit.

George cleared his throat. "I had a buyer in San Antonio who wanted the whole herd."

Jed forced his tongue still. If George had sold the whole herd . . .

"But I told him you'd already bought half."

It took a second for George's words to sink in. "You what?"

Color deepened George's cheeks. "I'm sorry, Jed, but he wanted an answer immediately, and I had no idea when you'd be in town next, so I told him you'd already bought half the herd."

"Half?" Jed's brain twisted and flipped, mentally calculating how much this was going to cost.

"Yes." The other man ran a finger between his neck and collar. "I'm sorry, but I had no idea you'd been in town for the auction. If I'd have known, I would have talked to you then, even though I'd already given him my answer."

Jed stared at the banker, dumbfounded.

"I'm not sure what I'll do with them if you say you don't want them now," George went on, "because they're already on their way."

Jed's expression must have unnerved the poor man more, for a sheen of sweat broke out on his brow, and he couldn't seem to look at either Jed or Lucy.

"Hold on a minute," Jed finally said. "You saved me half your herd even though you had a buyer lined up in San Antonio?"

George nodded briefly.

"Wouldn't it have been easier to let your buyer take the whole herd?" Lucy asked.

"Undoubtedly," George said.

"Then why . . . ?"

George held Jed's gaze for a few seconds. "Because I gave your husband my word."

He'd done that, sure enough, yet still, something felt off.

"And you already arranged to have them driven up here?" he asked.

Another nod.

Jed blew out a long breath and slumped a little in his chair. The idea of buying Lucy that new dress was floating away like a feather on a spring breeze.

Lucy's foot slid over and nudged him. When he glanced up at her, she tipped her head ever so slightly toward George, who looked as though he was going to be sick.

Jed rested his elbows on his knees and forced his hands to relax their grip on his hat. He even twirled it a few times for good measure.

"I sure appreciate you thinking of me that way, George," he said. "But to be honest—" he glanced at Lucy, swallowed, then continued. "I don't know if I can afford half the herd and the cost of driving it up here."

For the first time, a small smile found George's face.

"I'm certain we can work something out, Jed." When Jed made to object, George held up a hand. "I'm not talking about credit or charity, so get that out of your head this second."

Jed sat back in his chair, unconvinced, but ready to listen. He didn't dare look at Lucy for fear of seeing disappointment.

George pushed his neatly stacked papers across the desk toward Jed. "This tells you how many head are on their way. There's another bull, but he'll be sent by train."

"Why's that?" Lucy asked, inching forward to read the numbers, too.

George and Jed both chuckled, then Jed answered.

"It's not a good idea to have more than one bull around all the cows. They get a little territorial."

All told, the herd numbered about one hundred and thirty, mostly young heifers, yearlings and a good number of steer.

"What are you asking?" Jed dreaded the answer, but sat up straight and waited. Whatever it was, he'd have to find a way to pay it.

George looked him straight in the eye before answering. "Eighty-seven for each of the bulls, twenty-three for the cows, and twelve for the yearlings."

Jed frowned. George's prices were lower than average.

"Wait just a minute—" he began, but again, George cut him off.

"Let me finish." He nodded toward the papers again. "I've listed what I'd want for the heifers and the steer, and I'd also ask you to cover half the cost of the drive."

"Sounds a little too good to be true if you ask me," Jed said. "What's wrong with them?"

Again, color raced up George's face. "Nothing. I swear. They're perfectly healthy."

"Then why the low prices?" Jed gestured toward the papers. "You know the average cost of a good bull is probably ninety dollars these days. And a heifer prob'ly goes for close to twenty."

"Yes," George nodded. "Of course I know that."

"So then why . . ."

"You pay the price I've asked, including your half of the drive costs. In return, you get however much of the herd you want, including the other bull. But I also have one small request."

Jed gripped the arms of his chair. He should have known there'd be a *but* coming.

"What?" he ground out. Lucy laid her hand on his arm, but he still didn't look at her.

"Any of the herd you don't want, I'd like to . . . well . . ." George glanced down at his desk top, then back at Jed. "I'd like to keep on your land for my own use."

Silence filled the space between them for a long breath-held minute.

"You want to do what?" Jed frowned. George McTaggert wanted to be a rancher? Since when?

"I know it sounds odd." George nodded through a nervous chuckle. "My whole life I've been too small for this, not strong enough for that, so I've holed up inside this bank since I was old enough to count coins.

"Look at me, Jed." George waved a hand the length of his torso. "I'm not built for ranching, but I've always wanted to do it."

Jed studied the banker carefully. He never would have pegged McTaggert for anything other than a numbers man.

"Have you ever been around a herd, George?"

"No."

"Ever ridden a horse?"

"Of course," he answered a little indignantly.

"Do you get sick easily?"

"I beg your pardon." George's mouth tightened into a thin line.

"Sorry," Jed said quickly. "No offense intended, but working with the herd can make even the hardiest of men sick—especially when it comes time to castrate them." He cast a glace at Lucy. "Sorry."

She nodded, a small grin tugging at her lips.

"I'd be fine," George replied. "I swear."

George was a businessman, first and foremost. And regardless of how much they respected each other, his first priority would be to make money on this deal with Jed, so charity wasn't a concern.

If all he wanted was to graze a few head on Jed's land and ride along once in a while, that was easily done. Jed pulled the papers from the desk again, worked a few more calculations, scribbled some numbers beside the list, then looked at Lucy. Her smile nearly knocked him out of his chair.

"Well, George," he finally said. "Looks like we've got us a deal here."

A look of such relief washed over George's face that for a minute, Jed thought the man would cry. But he pushed out of his chair and shoved his hand over the desk toward Jed.

"Excellent. I was hoping you'd agree." He pulled a ledger from his desk drawer.

"How long 'til the herd arrives?"

"I'm told they'll be here the end of next week."

"Next week?" Lucy gasped. "That soon?"

George nodded. "Is that going to be a problem?"

"Not at all." Jed laughed. "Just means we'll need to work a little faster is all, ain't that right, Lucy?"

She didn't answer, just stared back at him with wide, disbelieving eyes.

"Very well." George collected the papers and rose from his chair. "I'll have the official paperwork drawn up and you can sign it and pay the next time you come in to town."

"Why don't you take the money now while I'm here?"

George shook his head. "No, sir. We'll leave your money right where it is, collecting interest, until it's needed. Besides, you'll need to check over the herd before you pay for it."

Jed rose from his chair, too. "Pleasure doing business with you, George. Whenever you've got time to spare, you're more than welcome to come out and help. Can't promise the work'll be any fun, though."

George grinned like a little kid. "Anything's more fun than sitting behind this desk day after day."

"You got me there."

"I'll be in touch." George straightened his suit jacket and once again shook Jed's hand, then Lucy's. "Mrs. Caine."

Jed led Lucy out of the bank, his head high, a smile on his face and his pride intact.

"Now that that's over," he said with a grin, "let's go see about your new dress."

CHAPTER THIRTEEN

·

Lucy slipped her arm beneath Jed's elbow and fell into step beside him, smiling. The herd was on its way, soon they'd have the barn finished, and then they could start on their house and . . .

Wait! What was she thinking?

She shook herself hard, trying to rid herself of such ridiculous thoughts.

They weren't going to have anything.

She was going to have it all.

They had no future.

She had a future—and as much as it unsettled her, that future did not include Jedidiah Caine.

How had she let herself slip so easily into the role of his wife? She had to stop thinking that they were partners—because eventually Jed would be gone.

Her heart stuttered in her chest.

Jed would be gone.

Forever.

A pain began in her heart, slow at first, then spreading quickly. She didn't get sick, so this must be one of Deacon's tricks. But her brother was nowhere in sight.

"You okay?" Jed's worried face studied hers.

"Yes, of course." She forced a smile, but he didn't look convinced.

"You got real pale all of a sudden." He stopped in the middle of the boardwalk and turned her to face him. "D'you want to sit down?"

"No." She waved away his concern. "I'm fine. Really."

He shook his head and changed direction, leading her toward the restaurant.

"You need something to eat."

Lucy almost laughed. She didn't need food; she needed someone to stop this searing pain in her heart. Before she could object, Jed ushered her inside the half-full restaurant and held her chair while she settled herself.

The air around her seemed thick, almost suffocating.

"Order whatever you like." He grinned. "We're celebrating."

Celebrating. Yes, of course. They—no, *she*—had plenty to celebrate.

"I'll have coffee," Jed said to a gray-haired woman in an apron who came to take their order. "And tea for my wife, please."

Lucy didn't want anything to eat. She didn't even want the tea when it arrived. But she couldn't very well let Jed know there was anything wrong. He didn't want a weak wife; he wanted a strong woman who'd help him work.

And if that's what Jed wanted, that's what she would give him.

Jed ordered their food, then sat sipping his coffee and staring at her over the rim of his mug.

"Have you given any thought to what kind of dress you want?" he asked.

"Dress?" Lucy frowned.

"You've probably got the color and style already picked out in that pretty little head of your, haven't you?"

What was he . . .

A faint light of memory glimmered in her mind. That's right—he was going to buy her a new dress. And a coat.

She forced another smile, which oddly caused him to frown, before she nodded.

The gray-haired lady arrived with their food then, giving Lucy a moment to find her wits again. The soup was hot and salty, the bread soft and covered in far too much butter for Lucy's liking. Jed all but inhaled it.

Several people nodded toward them, whispered to their fellow diners, then went back to their meals. Lucy seared a glare at one particularly loud whisperer, then froze when the door opened next.

The proprietress offered the newcomers a broad smile and said, "Good day to you, Reverend. Mrs. Conroy."

A spoonful of soup lay on Lucy's tongue. She could neither swallow nor spit it out. All she could do was stare in complete terror.

"Lucy?"

She could feel Jed's eyes on her, could hear the concern in his voice, but she couldn't take her eyes off the man. Men of the cloth were sneaky. The truly spiritual ones could blast a soul to Hell with little or no warning.

The man and his wife moved closer, following the gray-haired lady to a table nearby.

"Lucy?" Jed's voice was like a whisper in a fog.

All she heard was the crunch of the man's boots against the wood floor. All she felt was the icy cold fingers of Hell closing in on her again. And all she saw was the clouded look that fell over the man's narrow face when he looked back at her.

His pace slowed as he neared their table. Lucy averted her gaze and lifted her teacup to her lips.

She needed to get away from him. *Far away*. If he so much as suspected who she was . . .

The preacher's wife wrapped her beefy hand around his elbow and tugged him forward. "Come along, dear, I'm about famished."

The preacher frowned, blinked, then stumbled after his wife. Lucy was on her feet before the couple settled at their table.

"Can we leave, please?"

By the time Jed had scrambled to pull some money from his pocket, Lucy was outside, taking in great gulps of air.

"Lucy." Jed's arms wrapped around her, pulling her into his embrace. "What's wrong?"

She shook her head against his chest.

"Don't tell me 'nothing.' You look like a ghost."

Again, she shook her head, her fingers scrunched in fists around his shirt front. It seemed like forever before she was calm enough to speak.

"I'm sorry, Jed," she managed. "I don't know what came over me. I-I just had to get out of there."

He stroked the back of her head, ever so gently, and whispered softly against her hair. "It's okay, you're safe now."

He brushed his lips across her cheek, bringing several gasps from a group of women nearby, but Lucy didn't care. In fact, she wished he'd do it again.

"Come on," he said with a grin. "Let's go see what Miss Celia has for you to buy."

She offered a feeble smile, one she didn't feel at all, and let him lead her toward the dress shop.

*   *   *

Jed had never been inside the fancy dress shop before. It was as though he'd walked into a whole new world.

Long narrow rods hung against each wall, weighed down by dresses of every style and color imaginable. Plain cotton day dresses hung on one rod, riding habits on another, and the longest rod held the fancy ones: silks, satins and all sorts of lacy frocks trimmed in pearls and other finery.

Yessir, that's the rack they wanted.

Rectangular wooden tables filled the middle of the huge room. Two were covered in bolts of fabric, one held a good supply of shoes and slippers, and the last one, smaller than the others, displayed an assortment of earbobs and pins.

A man could easily get lost in such a place with so many choices.

"Good afternoon, Mr. Caine." Miss Celia appeared from a back room, a tape measure around her neck and a bolt of bright blue fabric tucked under her arm.

In her advanced age, Miss Celia was plenty fair enough to look at, with her soft blue eyes and piles of white hair twisted on top of her head.

"Hullo, Miss Celia." Jed twisted his hat between his hands. "I'd like you to meet my wife, Lucy. Lucy, this here's Miss Celia, best dressmaker in town."

"I heard you'd finally married." Miss Celia smiled, then extended her hand toward Lucy. "It's lovely to meet you, Mrs. Caine."

"Please," Lucy said, smiling back, "call me Lucy."

"Lucy it is." She set the bolt of fabric on the counter and folded her hands in front. "What can I help you with today?"

"Lucy's in need of a pretty new dress," Jed answered. "She'll need a coat, too."

"Very well." Miss Celia nodded slightly, then cleared her throat. "Did you have a price in mind? We have a fairly wide range to choose from."

"Not much," Lucy started, but Jed interrupted.

"I want something pretty." He nodded toward the long rack at the back of the store. "But not outrageous."

"Jed, I don't think that's—" Lucy began, but again, he interrupted with a raised hand.

"Nothing plain, nothing boring, and . . ." he hesitated. He risked offending Lucy if she had her mind set, but he knew what he wanted. And what he *didn't*. "Nothing pink."

Both women's eyes widened.

"No pink?" Miss Celia repeated with a nod, eyeing Lucy thoughtfully. "Yes, I do believe you're right."

"About what?" Lucy glanced down at her dress, worry puckering her brow.

"You're not a pink kind of woman," Miss Celia answered matter-of-factly. "You need bold colors. Pink is for unassuming women who don't want to stand out."

A slow smile spread across Lucy's full mouth.

"And you, Mrs. Caine, are a woman of distinction. You must stand out." Miss Celia didn't say it to flatter. It was the truth.

"Is that why you don't want me in pink?" Lucy asked, turning to Jed.

He grinned broadly and nodded. "I was just going to say you look good in bright colors, but what Miss Celia said sounds better, so let's use that."

The women laughed and set to looking through the dresses hanging nearby. Jed wandered aimlessly around the store, fingering the various silks and earbobs. How did a woman ever decide? Being a man was a helluva lot easier.

"Mr. Caine?"

"Hmm?" He turned to find both women watching him, each fighting back a smile.

"We'll be a while here. Is there something else you'd like to do in the meantime?"

Thank God.

"'Course." He exhaled his relief. "How long?"

Miss Celia shrugged, glanced at Lucy, then back at Jed. "An hour?"

An hour! He could buy himself four sets of clothes and enough supplies to last a month in less time it took Lucy to buy a single dress.

"Fine." He shot Lucy a wink, grinned at her blush, then nodded to Miss Celia. "Be back in an hour."

He was almost out the door when he poked his head back inside.

"And maybe throw in one of these pretty feather bonnets you have here in the window, too."

"Good bye, Jed!" Lucy laughed over her warning glare as he ducked outside.

Grinning like a fool, he jammed his hat down on his head and started toward the mill. With his herd arriving next week, that barn was going to need to be up and ready sooner than he'd thought. And he'd need a couple good sturdy pens to keep the bulls in.

He'd been over the plan in his head enough times that he knew the measurements by heart, even down to how many nails he'd need. But he'd have to replan the house. Simple would never do for Lucy. She needed better, fancier. Might take a little longer to build, but once the herd was tended and some of it sold off, he'd be able to give her that.

And more. So much more.

This wasn't practical. He should be thinking of ways to save money, not spend it. He should be happy to get along with what they needed, not what they wanted. But hell if he could help himself.

His wife had bewitched him, simple as that. She'd walked into his life and in a matter of days had turned it upside down. How had he let that happen?

He had intended to live a quiet life, a practical life, with a quiet and practical woman. A modest life in a modest house.

But somehow in the short time he'd been married, he'd changed his plans. He wanted more. So much more.

And he'd do whatever it took to get it. He'd sell his soul to the devil if it made Lucy happy.

"Good day to you, Jedidiah."

Jed blinked through his haze to find Deacon blocking the boardwalk. He looked as fresh and clean as he had the other night, dressed head to toe in another fancy suit, this one gray with a black vest. His animal—whatever Lucy had called it—lay curled around his neck, its long, twitchy nose sniffing the air.

"Deacon." He bobbed his head in a short nod, but didn't offer his hand.

"Are you here alone?" Deacon asked, glancing over Jed's shoulder.

"No." He forced his tone to remain civil. "Lucy's at the dress shop."

"Of course." Deacon gave a short, icy laugh. "Spending all your money, no doubt."

"It's not my money, Deacon. It's *our* money."

"Of course," he repeated. His blue eyes flashed, much the same as Lucy's. "It's just odd that you do all the work and she does all the spending."

Jed bit his tongue until he was sure it would bleed. Deacon couldn't know anything about him and Lucy. And he sure as hell couldn't know what they did with their money or how hard either of them worked.

But he was Lucy's brother. He was . . . family.

Jed forced an even breath. "I'm on my way to the mill right now to spend a bundle. Care to join me?"

Deacon glanced back over his shoulder toward the mill at the end of town. Even at this distance, the squeal of saws and banging of hammers could be heard over the sounds of the bustling town.

A cloud of dust hung in the air around the mill, as it did every day. No way in hell Deacon would risk his fancy clothes in that.

"No," Deacon answered. "I think not, but perhaps we'll see each other again before you leave."

Not if I can help it.

"We'll see." Jed started past, then stopped. "You'll not be bothering Lucy while we're here."

"Bother her?" Deacon adjusted his stupid bowler hat. "Wouldn't dream of it."

"I hope not." Jed leveled a pointed glare at his brother-in-law. "I won't have her upset again."

A cocked brow was Deacon's only response, and the whole way to the mine, Jed fought the urge to go back and smack it off his face.

Something about that man got under Jed's skin. No question they disliked each other, and even though Jed was willing to look past it for Lucy's sake, he wasn't near stupid enough to believe Deacon would do the same.

But God help that man if he upset Lucy again.

"Whoa up there, Caine."

Jed looked up from his wool-gathering to find himself charging through the open workspace of the mill, right toward its owner, Charlie White.

He chuckled softly and threw a silent curse back at Deacon.

"Hiya, Charlie," he said. "Was wondering if we could do a little business today."

The crashing hammers made him yell it a second time before Charlie nodded and pointed toward his office. Even inside with the door closed, the noise level was ear-splitting.

"Heard you up 'n married a gal at that auction the other week."

"That's true." The mention of Lucy made him grin again.

Charlie chuckled. "An' I heard she ain't like no woman we ever seen 'round these parts, neither."

"Also true," he answered, taking the seat Charlie indicated and tossing his hat on the one in the corner.

"Good for you." The other man took a long sip from his coffee mug, then promptly spat it in a bucket near his feet. "Guh—hate cold coffee."

"Nothing worse," Jed agreed.

Charlie wiped his mouth, then propped his feet up on his desk. "What can I do for you, Caine?"

"We'd talked before about me bringing you the trees off my spread to plane into boards for the barn and house, but I need to change that. Seems my herd's on its way already, and I'd like to have the barn ready by the time they get here in case there's some that need tending and such."

"How much d'you need?"

Jed rattled off the measurements of the barn he'd planned. "And I'll be needing more for another pen. Seems George saved me two bulls instead of one."

Charlie nodded, his eyes narrowed slightly in thought. "You know my prices, Caine. And if you want it delivered, that's another two dollars."

Jed nodded. "Fair enough. How soon can I get it?"

"Well, that depends." He pulled his feet down and leaned across his desk, a wave of embarrassment crossing his eyes. "Your . . . well . . . oh hell. Here's the thing."

He chewed his cheek before continuing.

"Sam put in a fair-sized order a while back, and it's been sitting here for over a week."

Jed swallowed hard.

"I'm sorry as hell 'bout what happened to him," Charlie went on, "but I can't hold that lumber much longer, Jed. If you don't want it, I'll have to sell it to someone else."

Sam's lumber. He'd ordered it the day he disappeared, and had planned to build his wife and baby a proper home. Now that plan sat in ruin, along with Maggie's hopes for a happy life with her husband.

Dammit.

"I'll take it, but I'll need my order as well." He'd use Sam's lumber to build Maggie a home, a place for her to raise her baby and still give her a connection—albeit small—to Sam.

Charlie gave an abrupt nod as he dug through the papers on his desk. "Here's the amount owing. Is tomorrow too soon to deliver it?"

"Nope. Tomorrow's just fine." He pushed up from his chair and retrieved his hat. "I'll get you the money and be back shortly."

He shook Charlie's hand and left the way he came in. Jesus, Mary and Joseph, but he'd never spent so much money in all his life. What with the herd and the lumber, there'd be hardly anything left in the bank.

And how could he forget Lucy's new dress? The idea of her being happy swelled his heart. The idea of her in a fancy new dress swelled a whole different part of him.

CHAPTER FOURTEEN

Lucy stepped out of Miss Celia's dress shop and shaded her eyes against the sun's glare. While Miss Celia took care to wrap the new purchases properly, Lucy pulled her new black wool coat closed and fastened the buttons up to her neck.

She could have stayed inside the shop, where it was warmer, but Jed had been gone too long. What if he'd met up with Deacon when Lucy wasn't there to intercede? Or worse—what if Deacon had . . . ?

No. She wouldn't think about that.

Where could he—

Jed. He stepped up on the boardwalk way down at the end of the street, but Lucy could pick him out of a crowd without hesitation. He had a certain way of holding himself straight when he walked, his head high, his eyes straight ahead.

Deacon hadn't hurt him.

Lucy brushed the thought aside. Deacon didn't matter. All that mattered was that her husband was still very much alive and walking the earth. In fact, he was walking directly toward her, a huge grin on his face.

"Nice coat," he said, then leaned in to kiss her cheek.

"Thank you." She grinned. "I like it."

He stepped aside to let her back into the store, then paid Miss Celia in full before leading Lucy back outside.

"I rather thought you'd be wearing your new dress," he teased.

"Oh no," Lucy shot back. "That one's for your eyes only, husband."

Color shot up Jed's neck. He licked his lips twice and blinked hard.

"Then I guess we should be on our way."

Lucy looped her hand beneath his elbow, ever watchful for any sign of Deacon. Her brush with the reverend had been enough of a fright for one day; the last thing she needed was to meet up with her brother before she'd fully recovered.

She held her breath while Jed settled the bill at the livery, then helped her up into the wagon. It wasn't until they were well out of town that she began to relax again.

"Did you get your business taken care of?" she asked.

"Even more than I'd planned."

"How do you mean?" she asked, scooting closer to him.

Jed moved the reins into his left hand so he could wrap his right arm around her shoulders.

"The lumber for the barn'll be delivered tomorrow, so we can get to work on that right away."

"Good news," she muttered, then laughed and rested her head against his shoulder. "I'm looking forward to it."

"That's my girl." He kissed the top of her head. "It's all going to work out, Lucy. Just you wait."

Oh, she was waiting all right. Waiting and worrying—two thing she didn't have time for.

"So we'd best get to work as soon as we get home then," she said. The thought of clearing more cacti and bushes made her want to cry, but she didn't.

She couldn't.

Weak women cried, and she didn't have time to be weak.

"Well," Jed answered, his voice low. "Not as soon as we get home." When she looked up, he smiled and shrugged. "Seems there's a dress I need to see first."

Maybe tonight would be the night Jed finally gave in to her. Maybe tonight she'd finally get what she wanted.

What was it that she wanted again?

Freedom.

Freedom from an eternity in the deepest, darkest depths of Hell.

She bit her tongue just as the word began to slip from it. Oh yes, she wanted her freedom. And regardless of how warm and wonderful Jed made her feel, regardless of how much she'd miss him when he was gone, and regardless of how much she'd grown to . . .

This was madness.

Nothing made sense anymore. All the emotions she was used to feeling—impatience, fear, anger and hatred— disappeared when she was with Jed. Instead, she felt . . .

It didn't matter what she felt. All she cared about was her freedom. Once she had escaped for good, she could take the time to try to understand these new feelings.

But between now and then, she'd stay right where she was, in Jed's warm embrace, and hope she'd be able to remember it when she was free.

Free and alone.

She'd been alone in her life thus far; she could certainly remain that way once this was over. How hard could it be?

Lucy closed her eyes and inhaled slowly, trying to loosen the knots from her stomach and shoulders. But no matter how hard she tried to block them, disturbing images crashed and crowded through her mind: *Deacon hovering over Jed's lifeless body, then setting his evil sights on Maggie and her baby. Then Lucy.*

A nudge on her shoulder brought her back to reality.

"Hey," Jed murmured. "We're home."

"What?" Lucy sat up slowly, glancing around. Sure enough, the wagon had come to a stop just outside the lean-to barn.

"You slept almost the whole way." Jed smiled at her. "All that shopping must have worn you out."

"Yes," she fumbled to answer. "I guess it did."

The memory of her dream wouldn't leave her alone. She tried to shake it off, but threads of the image lingered in her mind even as Jed lifted her down from the wagon seat.

He handed her the large package Miss Celia had wrapped and turned her toward the barn.

"Go."

"But what about . . ." she faltered.

This was no time to hesitate. She'd spent all this time trying to get Jed to show interest and now that he finally was, she was gripped by a fear so deep she wasn't even sure she could walk.

"I'll take care of this." Jed shrugged toward the supplies in the back of the wagon, then pointed at the package in her hands. "You go take care of that."

She swallowed hard and forced a smile, one that showed no signs of convincing Jed of anything. Ugh—she was so stupid. This was not the time to be afraid. This was the time to finish things. If she didn't, Deacon certainly would.

Lucy hurried inside the barn, back to the far corner where they slept, but took several minutes to catch her breath before she moved a step farther. She could do this. She *had* to do this.

Breathe.

What if Jed didn't react the way she wanted him to—or the way she needed him to?

What if, once he realized she wasn't as experienced as she'd led him to believe, he'd be so furious at yet another lie that he refused to have anything to do with her?

Jed Caine was a man of truth, and even though this wasn't a big lie—or even a bad lie—he'd no doubt consider it a lie nonetheless.

Breathe.

She'd have to deal with that when the time came. Right now, she had to focus on getting him to that point. And that meant she'd have to shake off these fears and finish the job she came here to do.

A rush of warmth pooled in her belly, the same warmth that came with every thought of Jed touching her. No one else had ever caused that odd rush inside her. What did it mean?

Trouble, that's what it meant.

Outside the horses whinnied and snorted while Jed released them from the harness and led them inside the lean-to. A few minutes later, the sounds of the wagon bed creaking beneath his weight hurried Lucy into action. She had to be ready by the time he'd finished.

With careful fingers, she removed the string around the package and laid it open on the blanket. The deep purple silk appeared almost black in the dimness of the barn. No lace, no ribbons, no . . . what was the word Jed had used that first day? Frippery. No frippery.

It was everything she knew it should be, and nothing Jed would be expecting.

She pulled off her green dress, shook it out, and hung it on one of the nails she'd hammered up. Shivering against the cool air, she hastened to rid herself of drawers, stockings and chemise, too.

Poor Jed. He had no idea what was coming.

When he'd sent her into the store for a new dress, he hadn't been overly specific about what kind of dress she was to purchase.

He no doubt expected a fancy supper gown, much like the green one now hanging on the nail. Originally, Lucy had thought the same thing, but then Miss Celia had shown her this amazing garment instead.

A nightgown was still a gown.

Fingers trembling, she shook the silky fabric out gently before slipping it over her head and letting it slide down her body. The only thing better than the feel of silk against her skin was Jed's hands, but she wouldn't think of that.

She *wouldn't*.

She'd think about the silk. Beautiful, plum-colored silk.

It had been a long time since the last creak of the wagon—surely he hadn't finished so soon. Lucy hurried into the matching silk robe and fastened the tie at her throat, her fingers trembling harder with each movement.

No bustle, no hoops, no frippery. Just plain and simple. Almost practical. She glanced down at the neckline and grinned. Maybe not so practical.

She pulled her brush and hairpins from the shelf and set to work. Miss Celia had suggested she wear her hair up in a soft knot, and if anyone knew style, it was Miss Celia. So up it went.

With her neck bare to the wind, and the thin silk doing nothing to keep her warm, she was cold. But one more night of cold certainly beat an eternity of hellfire.

Her stomach fluttered and pitched with every breath, and her hands trembled incessantly. With a final, deep and shuddering breath, she opened the barn door and peeked out into the last light of day.

At first she didn't see him. Perhaps he'd gone into the house . . .

There he was. A hundred yards down the path to the creek, he'd stopped cold and was staring at her. Even with the distance separating them, she could sense his clean shirt prickling against his chest and arms, could feel his fingers aching to scratch it. But he didn't.

Maybe because his hands were full of dirty clothes.

Lucy swallowed hard, but remained where she was. She could do this. She could. Couldn't she?

After a long, earth-tilting moment, he finally took a step, then another, each faster than the last, until he stopped two arms-lengths away. The dirty clothes tumbled from his arms as he walked—first his shirt, then his other pair of pants and underthings. He tripped over them as he walked, but didn't slow down or move to retrieve them.

Water dripped from his tousled hair. A tiny drop of blood caked the curve of his freshly shaven jaw, and he smelled of fresh water and sunshine. The smell of Jed.

"I . . . um . . ." he breathed. "Wow."

Lucy forced herself to move. She spread her arms and turned in a slow, deliberate circle.

"What do you think?" she asked, struggling to find her voice.

He took another half-step, tripped over his hat as it landed at his feet, then stopped again. "I . . . uh . . ."

That amazing smile of his finally found his lips.

"I think that's the best money we ever spent." He blew a long breath across his bottom lip, then found her gaze. He blushed a little, his smile faltering. "I'm almost scared to touch you."

Lucy's skin screamed for his touch. Her mouth ached for his, and the warmth inside her ignited into a massive wildfire.

YES! ☐

Sign me up for the **Historical Romance Book Club** and send my TWO FREE BOOKS! If I choose to stay in the club, I will pay only $8.50* each month, a savings of $5.48!

YES! ☐

Sign me up for the **Love Spell Book Club** and send my TWO FREE BOOKS! If I choose to stay in the club, I will pay only $8.50* each month, a savings of $5.48!

NAME: _____

ADDRESS: _____

_____

TELEPHONE: _____

E-MAIL: _____

☐ **I WANT TO PAY BY CREDIT CARD.**

☐ VISA   ☐ MasterCard   ☐ DISCOVER

ACCOUNT #: _____

EXPIRATION DATE: _____

SIGNATURE: _____

Send this card along with $2.00 shipping & handling for each club you wish to join, to:

Romance Book Clubs
1 Mechanic Street
Norwalk, CT 06850-3431

Or fax (must include credit card information!) to: 610.995.9274.
You can also sign up online at www.dorchesterpub.com.

*Plus $2.00 for shipping. Offer open to residents of the U.S. and Canada only.
Canadian residents please call 1.800.481.9191 for pricing information.

If under 18, a parent or guardian must sign. Terms, prices and conditions subject to change. Subscription subject
to acceptance. Dorchester Publishing reserves the right to reject any order or cancel any subscription.

JOIN NOW!

"Jed." His name was a mere whisper against her lips, but it spurred him toward her. He kicked his hat aside, took her hands and just stood there, staring.

"Sweet Jesus." His dark, stormy eyes roamed the length of her, slowly inching their way back up to her face. "You're beautiful."

Heat rushed over her skin, but she wouldn't look away. How many times had she been told she was beautiful? Too many to count. Tonight, this very minute, was the first time she dared believe it. The first time she dared to let it matter.

He lifted his hand toward her face, then paused, gazing down at her. Each passing second was an eternity.

Lucy's lids slipped closed, and her lips opened, waiting, waiting. But instead of touching her or kissing her, he simply reached up and pulled the pins from her hair. It fell in soft waves around her shoulders and down her back, bringing her eyes open again.

Jed slid his fingers through its length, rubbing it gently between his fingers as he went.

"Down," he murmured. "I like it down."

She couldn't help smiling at him. "Not very practical of you, Jedidiah."

He didn't smile back. Instead, his eyes darkened more, his fingers continuing to stroke every inch of her hair.

"To Hell with being practical."

He moved his right hand to cup the side of her face, gently at first until Lucy leaned into his touch. His left hand caressed her other cheek, his thumb moving over her skin with such tenderness it left a deepening ache inside her. Breath caught in her throat, the air frozen within her lungs.

Warm fingers breathed across her throat to where she'd tied the robe, and slowly pulled the strings apart. Slowly, inch by inch, he slid the silk off one shoulder, then the other, until the robe slipped from her arms to pool at her feet.

"I . . . I can't—" Before she could finish, Jed lowered his mouth to hers and swallowed the rest of her words. She trembled against his touch, frightened of feeling any more, terrified of feeling any less.

Unable to think straight, she simply let him think for both of them, to lead her wherever he wanted. He took his time, feathering light kisses against her lips, tasting, teasing, begging, until she returned his kisses with equal need.

A frightening weakness buckled her knees. She leaned into him, desperate for his strength. Jed wrapped one arm around her waist, bringing her up hard against him. His kiss deepened, as did her need. And her fear.

She slipped her arms around him, desperate to be closer, then closer still, until there wasn't a breath of air between them. Jed dragged his mouth away from hers, then pressed his lips against the skin of her neck.

"Inside," he rasped between kisses against her ear and throat. He lifted her off the ground and moved back inside the barn, out of the chilly air, and out of view of the house.

Lucy couldn't look at him. Couldn't stand to see the emotion burning in his eyes. If only she could close off every other part of her, too.

"Look at me, Lucy."

She couldn't. Every time their eyes met, her resistance took another hit. Many more and it would crash down around her.

Where was a snake when you really needed a distraction?

"I sure as hell didn't expect this to happen so soon," he whispered, brushing his thumb across her bottom lip.

Fire burned behind Lucy's eyes. She couldn't let him

see it, couldn't allow herself even a single tear. So why were her eyes filling up so fast?

He held her face in his hands, forcing her to look into his eyes, where the ugly truth lay open to the world.

"I l—"

Before he could say it, Lucy kissed him. She couldn't let him say it out loud. Not yet. Once he said it out loud, she would be forced to finish her mission. If she didn't, Deacon would.

Selfish, yes, but she needed more time with Jed, more moments like this where she could try to put his touch, his taste and his words to memory, so that when she was alone . . .

Tears coursed down her cheeks, but she no longer cared. She'd let Jed lighten her darkened soul, and that was the worst thing she could have possibly done. He'd somehow made her feel . . . what? If only she knew.

She wasn't capable of love, that much she knew. But that didn't explain why she ached so deeply for him or why it felt as though her heart were bleeding.

"Lucy?" Jed pulled away, frowning at her tears. "What's this about?"

She shook her head, dashing tears away with the back of her hand. "Nothing," she lied.

"It's not nothing." Worry clouded the depths of his eyes—those same eyes that had begged for her lips just seconds before. He took her hand and led her back to their corner of the barn where he sat on the straw pile and pulled her onto his lap. "What is it?"

What could she say? It was so simple, yet it couldn't have been more complicated. She wanted nothing more than to stay where she was right at that moment, wrapped in his arms, safe from everything—and everyone. But that was the one thing she couldn't have.

Would an eternity in Hell be any worse than a future without Jed Caine?

Jed tipped her chin up. His touch, so gentle, so tender, nearly killed her. She closed her eyes again, and tried to focus.

She'd come here for a reason. She'd picked up buffalo chips and worn ugly, ragged dresses. She'd even learned how to cook. Sort of. All because she wanted her freedom.

No, she couldn't go back to Hell. She'd never survive. But she couldn't explain any of this to Jed. Jed cared for her and probably loved her, though she'd not given him the chance to say so. Not yet.

No, not yet.

"Lucy." How could a man of his size speak so softly?

Lucy chewed her bottom lip, blinking back more tears. She had to do this. Jed would make love to her, he'd tell her he loved her, and it would be done. She'd have memories of him to get her through the rest of her mortal life. Memories of his touch, his smell, and the way he looked at her with such . . . Lucy swallowed hard . . . such passion.

The memories would have to be enough.

"There's something I need to tell you," she whispered.

His only response was a slight nod.

"I'm, um . . ." She caught his eye briefly, then looked away. She didn't want to see his face when she told him. "I'm not who you think I am."

He shifted her slightly in his lap, but only so he could tuck her hair away from her face.

"Then tell me who you are."

The tiny corner closed in around them. The air felt more like smoke as it entered her lungs and smelled of . . . fear. Her fear.

She swallowed hard and forced herself to look at him. "I may have misled you."

His expression hardened slightly, and his fingers froze against her hair, but after a second, he nodded for her to continue.

Breathe.

"I . . . I'm not sure . . ." She stopped, chewed her lip again, then cast a glance down at the straw tick. "I mean I've not . . ." The heat that raced over her skin would surely explode out of her any second.

Jed frowned in confusion, glanced at the tick, then gaped. His eyes flew wide and his mouth fell open.

"You—but—you—" He blinked hard, then licked his lips. "Oh my God. *You're a virgin?*"

CHAPTER FIFTEEN

"No," Lucy released a long breath. "But you probably believe I've had more . . . experience . . . than I actually have."

Jed shook his head slowly. "But you . . . I mean, you made me think—" His frown deepened, his hand stilled against her back. "Why?"

"Does it matter?" She twisted her fingers in her lap, wishing he'd kiss her again—or at least stop looking at her like that.

"No." He shook his head. "I mean yes, dammit, it matters."

She dared to glance up at him, and the confusion on his face brought more tears to her eyes.

"Why does it matter?" she asked. "You said it yourself— that lust and passion wouldn't be a problem between us." Lucy lifted her shoulder in a small shrug. "I'm sure I can learn whatever it takes to make you happy."

Jed's chin fell to his chest as a long growl erupted from within him.

"Good God, Lucy." He jammed his fingers through his hair. "You scared the hell out of me."

"I'm sorry." She'd never been sorry before. She'd said it plenty of times, but she'd never meant it until now.

"How many men?" The vein in his temple throbbed menacingly.

"One. One horrible time with one horrible man."

Was that relief she saw? Too soon, it was gone.

"You lied to me again." His voice was raw, and when he looked at her, his eyes were like summer storm clouds.

"No, I didn't." She shook her head and twisted on his lap, which drew another ragged groan from him. "I never said I'd been with other men. You just assumed."

"I—" Jed's mouth fell open. "You're the one who . . . I mean, the things you said . . . the way you—"

Lucy slid her fingers through his and held them in her lap. "I wanted you from the minute I saw you, Jed, that's the truth."

"Why didn't you just tell me?" He stilled her trembling hands in his. "Why make me believe something about you that isn't true? Especially something like this!"

Lucy shrugged. Lie upon lie had gotten her to this point. She didn't dare add another to the pile.

"I was scared."

"Of what?" Jed rasped. "Good God, Lucy—do you know what I've been thinking all this time? Wondering how many men you've been with, what they did to you, where they touched you." He growled again, lower this time, and clenched his jaw until every muscle in his face was taut and rigid.

"I'm sorry," she whispered again. "But you'd already told me I wasn't what you wanted in a wife."

He opened his mouth to interrupt, but she silenced him with a shake of her head. "I was too skinny, too pretty, and not nearly strong enough for what you wanted."

A wave of shame washed over Jed's face, then disappeared.

"That doesn't make it okay to lie to me."

"I know." She looked down at their hands, still tangled in her lap, then back up at him. "But we're working through everything else, the cooking and cleaning and such. Surely we can work through this, too."

"Lucy."

"Shh." She pressed her finger against his lips. "I know it'll take some time for me to learn how to do this, just like with making coffee, but I want to make you happy, Jed. That's all I want."

A tortured chuckle escaped his mouth. "This ain't nothing like making coffee," he muttered. "And I can't imagine you'll need any lessons here."

"But I don't know what to do." Lucy sighed. Why did this have to be so damned frustrating? "I don't know how to touch you or make you feel like . . ."

She couldn't say it. It was too confusing even to her.

"Like what?" Jed's voice was barely audible.

She shook her head, her gaze fixed on her lap, but when Jed lifted her chin, she knew she had to answer. She shouldn't—it would just show how weak she truly was—but she had no choice.

"I'm afraid I won't be able to make you feel the way I do when I'm with you." She tried to look away again, but he held her firm.

"How do you feel?"

His voice was going to kill her. Soft and husky, it melted her fear, turning it to pure, molten lust.

She swallowed. "As if I'll die if you don't touch me. And even when you do, it's never enough."

"Lucy." He breathed a kiss against her forehead. "I already feel that way, sweetheart."

Now who was the liar? He couldn't possibly have any idea what kind of torture he put her through with every touch, every look, every smile.

"Oh really?" she asked, sharper than she'd meant. "And do you feel as though you'll never be able to stand up again because I've turned every one of your muscles to mush?"

He laughed, but it was a choked, harsh sound. "Look where we are, Lucy."

She pursed her lips and frowned. Okay, so they were sitting down, but that didn't prove anything.

"I'll bet you've never lain awake at night wondering how long it would be before we could be together. And I'll bet you've never felt like your heart was going to beat out of your chest and wither on the ground." Tears began again, but Lucy didn't care. How dare he pretend he felt anything near to what she did?

"And," she continued, "I'll bet you never lay here wondering what I'm dreaming about."

"No," he chuckled again. "I've never lain awake wondering what you were dreaming."

"There you have it." She nodded, and crossed her arms tightly over her chest. Maybe that would help ease the ache in her heart.

"Let me finish." He eased her arms down and took her hands in his. "But I do lie awake nights wondering why I haven't taken what you've offered so freely. I stare at this damned ceiling night after night cursing my stupid self and wishing you could feel half of what I do."

It took a moment for his words to settle into her brain.

"But you could have had me any time you wanted." He was so infuriating! "You're the one who said—"

"I know what I said," he murmured. "And I still think we were right to wait."

"Because you enjoyed torturing me?"

"No." He traced his finger down the curve of her face. "Because I wanted to be sure."

"Of what?"

"Of you. Of me." He paused. "Of us."

"Us?"

He nodded, his gaze fixed on her mouth. "Mm-hmm." His lips brushed hers gently. Lucy's body melted against his. "Us."

One simple word brought everything crashing down on her. There was no "us." There couldn't be. There could only be a "her."

Even so, she wasn't ready to give him up. Not yet. Maybe never. Pain knotted her insides until she wanted to cry out. A few more days wasn't too much to ask, was it? As long as Maggie's baby didn't come too soon and as long as Deacon didn't do anything first, Lucy would have enough time to store as many memories of Jed as she could.

But tonight was not the night to end it.

"Jed?" she whispered against his neck, breathing in his scent, his strength and his need.

"Mmm?"

How long would the memory of his touch stay with her? Would she eventually forget the way he could heat her through by simply running his fingers up her arm?

"Could we just lie together without . . . ?"

His breath caught, his fingers stilled. "You mean . . ."

Lucy nodded slowly. "I want to, really, I do."

"But?"

Tell him the truth.

"I'm scared." She swallowed back another rush of tears. "Is that bad?"

"No," he moaned. "Of course not."

He tipped her face up to his and smiled. "Can't say I'll get much sleep, but if that's what you want . . ."

"I'm sorry."

"Don't be." He kissed her again, a tender sweep that would have driven her to her knees had she been standing. "As long as I'm with you, it'll all be fine. Besides," he grinned sheepishly, "there's plenty of cold water in the creek."

They sat in silence for a while longer, Jed tangling his fingers through her hair and running them down her arms, and Lucy toying with the buttons on his shirt, all the while filling her lungs with Jed-scented air.

She would need enough to last her a lifetime.

"Lucy." His voice, soft against her ear, sent goose bumps racing down her arms. "I think I best go visit that creek now."

* * *

Outside, Jed leaned back against the barn wall and let himself slide to the ground. The wife he'd spent too many hours wondering about—about how many men she'd been with and how he could possibly measure up—was afraid to let him bed her.

So, instead of enjoying the evening the way he'd hoped, he was outside sitting in the dirt. Meanwhile she was fighting to keep warm in that nightdress.

And what a dress. Sweet Jesus, he couldn't believe his legs actually held him upright after seeing her in that thing. And all he wanted was to see her *out* of it.

Wasn't going to happen tonight. But how was he supposed to lie beside her all night knowing she wanted him as much as he wanted her?

From the minute they'd met, all she did was try to get

him to take her to bed. Now that he was willing to do just that, she was the one who refused.

What the hell was going on?

Jed ground the heels of his hands into his eyes. How could he control himself all night, next to her in that bed? He'd done it before, but this was different. Tonight, she'd purposely set out to seduce him with that gown, with those lips, and with looks that could set his soul on fire. And he'd set out to let her seduce him.

Then she'd brought it all to a screaming halt.

Damn him to hell if he'd ever figure out his wife. Maybe it was better if they waited a little while longer. If she truly was afraid, and if her only other time with a man had been horrible, then everything needed to be perfect their first time together. Last thing he wanted to do was scare the poor girl more.

Or disappoint her.

"Shit shit shit!" Jed hurled a tin bucket across the yard, sending it crashing and rolling toward the house. Berta peeked through the window, but Jed ignored her.

Tonight was the only night in the near future he and Lucy wouldn't be exhausted by the time evening came. Starting tomorrow, they'd be neck deep in getting the barn built, then working with the herd. They'd be lucky to have enough strength left at the end of the day to eat, never mind anything else.

He let go a loud groan. This was a helluva predicament he'd gotten himself in. For all his plans, all his practical ideas and persistence, he'd ended up right where he never expected to be.

He was in love with his wife.

How that happened so quickly, he couldn't begin to guess. But there it was. And because of that, he had to do as she asked and not touch her tonight. It might very well kill him, but he had to do it. Somehow, he had to try and forget how soft her skin was, how willing her lips were, and how her simple breath against his neck could make him hard as a rock.

And somehow he had to do this while she lay beside him.

Not even a saint should be tested this way.

With another loud curse, he pushed to his feet and stormed toward the creek. There wasn't near enough cold water down there to cool him off, but he'd have to make do.

All his plans to marry a practical girl had been shot to hell when he married Lucy. And his stupid idea of moving slowly, of taking time to get to know his wife, was all a waste of time, too. He knew everything he needed to know about Lucy.

She was strong, funny and smarter than she gave herself credit for. She was also vulnerable, frustrating and sexier than any woman had a right to be. It was a combination he hadn't counted on. Hell, he hadn't even imagined that combination could exist.

He made it to the creek without remembering a single step. Fully clothed, he waded waist-high into the chilly water, then plunged headfirst beneath its rippling current. Maybe he could wash the thoughts of Lucy away.

And maybe tomorrow the sun would rise in the west.

He stayed under as long as he could, pushing his lungs to their absolute limit, then burst up, gasping for air and cursing himself the fool.

Now he had no clothes for tomorrow. This set was soaking wet, and his others were filthy. But at least he'd cooled off a little. Not much, but a little.

And once he got settled on the bed with the blanket positioned between them, Lucy wouldn't know how hot he still was.

Jed stumbled out of the creek and swiped his hair back from his face. Maybe he'd build a fire and dry off before going back in the house. That would give Lucy time to fall asleep.

"Shit." He kicked a broken piece of brush and headed home. Wouldn't make a spit of difference if she was awake or not.

The house and barn were both dark when he got back, and not even the mockingbirds dared break the night's silence. Jed tossed a few chips into the fire pit, added a handful of the twigs and sticks Lucy had stacked nearby, then threw a match on top. In a few minutes, the fire was big enough to draw warmth from. Not that he needed any, but maybe he could dry his clothes.

He pulled off his boots first, dumping the water from each and setting them against the rocks. His socks and shirt soon followed, each laid out as flat as possible without getting too close to the flames. He had just unbuttoned his trousers when the creaking of the barn door froze his fingers against his groin.

No. Go back to bed.

"Jed?" Lucy's sleepy voice whispered through the air, and against his skin. "What are you doing?"

The ugly gray blanket hung around her shoulders; her hair tumbled over it in long dark streaks, and the look on her face almost sent him running for the safety of the creek again.

Her eyes—those bottomless green eyes—widened, smoldered, then blinked hard. She stared straight at his chest, then moved her gaze lower to where his trousers lay open.

God help him.

"I'm, uh, drying off." He turned away, cursing his fumbling fingers. Why couldn't he get those damned buttons refastened?

"Why—" She stepped closer, then smiled. "Oh, I see."

"I'm hoping you don't," he muttered. Before he could fasten the last button, Lucy was beside him, looking up at him.

"I'm sorry," she whispered. "I know it's unfair of me to ask this of you."

"It's fine," he ground out, then chuckled dryly. "There's that word again."

Lucy didn't laugh. In fact, if he wasn't mistaken, it looked as though she was ready to cry again.

"Come here." He pulled her into his embrace and held her close, wishing more than anything that he could climb inside that blanket with her. "It's okay, Lucy. Don't fret over this."

She sniffed against his chest. "I wish I could explain it to you," she whimpered. "I really do."

"Shh." He pressed a kiss against her head. "There's nothing to explain. Besides"—he turned her face up to his— "it'll happen when you're ready for it to happen."

Tears teetered against her lashes, then fell. Jed wiped them away with his thumbs, then kissed her nose.

"No more tears, Lucy. I promise you it's all okay."

She tucked her head back against his chest and nodded, but Jed wasn't stupid enough to think she believed him. He'd have to prove it to her.

Though it pained him, he released her and moved to the other side of the fire. Using what was left in the water bucket and then handfuls of dirt, he doused the flames. Too bad he couldn't douse the raging fire inside himself.

Without a word, he lifted Lucy into his arms and carried

her back into the barn. He laid her on the bed, tucked the blanket around her, then stepped into the darkest corner of the miserable little corner to remove his trousers.

Wouldn't do either of them any good if Lucy saw how much he wanted her. And hot damn, but he wanted her. But he also wanted to get out of his wet trousers.

With no clean clothes to speak of, and with Lucy wrapped in the only blanket, Jed's only option was the towel Lucy used for her sponge baths. He fought back the groan that crept up his throat at the thought of her bathing.

He held the towel in front of him, then hurried out of the corner and climbed onto the bed next to Lucy. The straw poked him in every place imaginable, but it didn't matter. All that mattered was Lucy and making sure she felt safe.

He bunched the towel between himself and Lucy, hoping to hell it did the job he needed it to do.

"Here," he turned her so her back was against his chest, then wrapped his arms around her, inching her closer. Then closer still. Didn't matter how much it killed him to have her close, he just couldn't get her close enough.

Lucy snuggled into his embrace and sighed softly.

"But you don't have a blanket," she whispered. "You'll freeze."

Jed laughed into her hair. "Believe me, sweetheart, I'm plenty warm."

Even with his entire body bared to the room's cool air, he'd probably burn alive.

"Jed?"

"Mmm?" Damn, she smelled good.

"Thank you." She wiggled against him until she could free one arm from her blanket and rest it on top of his.

"Don't mention it." He grinned. "It's not *all* bad for me, you know."

"Will you lay with me tomorrow night, too?"

"And every night after that," he murmured into her hair.

She sniffed again, then fell silent, her fingers moving in small, soft circles over the top of his hand.

He should tell her he loved her. He started to earlier, but then she'd kissed him and he'd lost every thread of sense he ever had. If he told her now, it might help relieve her worries.

Or maybe she'd think he was just saying it to make her feel better.

Was anything easy with Lucy? He loved her, that was true enough, but he didn't want to scare her any more than she already was.

If he told her he loved her, she might feel obligated to say it, too, even if she didn't feel it. Jed's heart pinched. She might never feel it. And if that was the case, they would simply go on the way they were—with him aching for all of her, body and soul, and Lucy simply aching for his touch and nothing more.

Not too long ago, he could have lived with that. But now he wanted more. He wanted the whole deal: a wife who wanted his touch, who respected him, and who loved him.

That wasn't too much to ask, was it?

CHAPTER SIXTEEN

H ullo in the house!"
  Jed sat bolt upright in bed. *What the . . . ?*
Lucy stretched beside him, her eyes opening slowly.

"Caine, you in there?" The gravelly old voice bellowed
again from outside.

"Oh, shit." Jed tried to step off the bed, got tangled in
his towel and the corner of Lucy's blanket, and went
down hard on his face.

"What's going on?" Lucy rolled over and laughed.
"Oh my."

"Caine!"

"Yeah," Jed called back, struggling to get to his feet.
"Be out in a second."

Of all the days to oversleep.

"Who's out there?" Lucy asked, still laughing. "You really should get dressed before you go out."

Jed twisted in circles looking for something to put on.
Nothing. His wet trousers were still hanging on the nail,
and every other stitch of clothing he owned was outside,
some draped by the fire, some scattered in the dirt.

Shit.

"Gimme the blanket."

"Oh no," Lucy said, gathering it up and scurrying to the far corner of the bed.

"Everything I own is wet or outside in the dirt." He made to grab for the blanket, but she ducked out of the way.

"You're a big strong man." Lines crinkled around her eyes, and though she appeared to try and hold it, she was soon laughing all over again. "You'll survive."

Jed stood straight in front of her, stark naked, and hard with need already. "It'll be embarrassing for both of us if I have to go out there like this."

Lucy's gaze raked the length of him, her eyes widening at the exact length of him. She sputtered a few times, then nearly fell off the bed in her haste to hand over the blanket.

He took a minute to admire her in her new gown. Even wrinkled, it looked better on her this morning than it had last night. In fact, if Charlie's man, Dwight, wasn't waiting outside with his load of lumber, he'd take more than a minute to admire her. Hell, he'd take his own sweet time in . . .

"Caine!"

"Thank you." He shot her a quick wink and ducked out the door. He'd never live this down with Dwight—or Charlie—but there was nothing worse than wet clothes. Dirty ones he could deal with—as soon as he gathered them all up again.

"Mornin', Dwight." He walked barefoot through the yard to face the man, only to have his embarrassment double.

Berta stood by the fire, staring open-mouthed.

"Berta," he stammered. "I wasn't expecting you out here so early."

Dwight's laughter split the air between them. "We can see that, Caine. Don't look like you was expectin' anyone."

He couldn't stop the heat that raced over his cheeks, so he shrugged and tried to laugh it off.

"Seems we overslept," he said.

"Overslept," Dwight repeated, glancing from one piece of strewn laundry to the next. "Right."

"Sorry," Jed said to Berta, who'd finally turned her face away, then grinned back at Dwight. "Could you pull it over by the lean-to there? I'll go find some clothes and be back in a minute."

He didn't wait for an answer, just scrambled to pick up his scattered clothes, gave them a hard shake, then raced back inside the barn. Lucy had just slipped her blue day dress over her head when he walked in.

He almost wished he was buttoned into his trousers—at least then his desire wouldn't be so damned obvious.

"Lumber's here," he said when he'd found his voice again. "Here, let me help."

He covered her hands with his until she released the buttons on the back of her dress and let him take over. The blanket pooled at his feet, but he didn't care. He couldn't help himself. Every time his fingers brushed against her back, Lucy shivered. And so did he.

Every time she took a breath, it shook on release.

"There," he murmured. "All done."

"Thank you." She kept her face averted and set to work on tying back her hair.

Jed inhaled deeply, then hurried into his dirty, smelly clothes.

"Lucy."

She'd finished with her hair and was busying herself

with her boots. She hesitated when he spoke, but finally turned to face him.

"I just, uh—" *Ah, hell*. He took her in his arms and kissed her, over and over again until she relaxed. Her lips moved against his, searching for everything his did, her fingers weaving through his hair until he moaned against her.

She smiled against his mouth and leaned into him.

"Find this funny, do you?" He smiled back, his mouth still pressed against hers.

Lucy shrugged slightly and kissed him again.

"Oh, God." He groaned again. "You're killing me."

"I'm sorry." Her whisper brushed over his skin.

"I'm not," he whispered back. He kissed her cheek, her eyes, and the tip of her nose. There were so many other places he wanted to kiss, to taste. Like that spot right under her ear, and that tiny hollow at the base of her neck. And that valley between her breasts, and—

"I better go." After one more kiss, of course.

Lucy cupped the side of his face in her hand and let his kiss linger before she lowered her hand and released him.

"That's a nice way to start the day," she sighed.

Jed laughed and stepped back toward the door. "That part, sure. The part where I fell out of bed stark naked and then ran outside wrapped in a blanket . . ." He rolled his eyes. "Not so nice."

Lucy laughed softly. "I enjoyed it."

"Is that right?" He moved back to her and yanked her against him. "Let me show you what I'd enjoy."

She pushed against his chest, laughing all the while. It was a soft, feminine sound that made him want to forget all about Dwight and the load of lumber.

And Berta.

Dammit. Of all the bad luck.

But he had to have one more taste. Just one. Maybe two.

Lucy met his kiss with waiting open lips and a sigh. If he didn't get out of the barn right then . . .

"I'm really leaving now," he muttered.

"Then why are you still here?" She kissed his chin, his jaw line, then his Adam's apple. Desire ripped through him hotter and faster than ever.

"I'm not," he answered. "I'm gone."

"Hmmm." She kissed his earlobe, then his neck—in that same spot he wanted to kiss her. "Bye, then."

"Yeah." He yanked the pins from her hair and filled both hands with its length. God but he loved her hair. "See ya later."

"Mm-hmm." She found his mouth again, her lips pressing softly against his, her tongue dancing with his.

"Caine!"

Lucy's lips froze against his, then curled into another smile.

"Dammit." Jed sighed. Maybe later, they could . . . no, they couldn't. Not yet.

He leaned in for one last kiss, then jerked the door open. Before he could leave, though, Lucy touched his arm, bringing him to a dead halt.

"Thank you, Jed." She almost looked embarrassed, but Jed would have none of that.

"Hold the thanks 'til I've done something you'll be truly thankful for." He wiggled his brow at her. "And believe me, the things I have planned for you—"

"Come on, Caine, I ain't got all day."

He blew her a final kiss and ran outside. It was going to be a long, miserable day unloading that lumber and getting the barn going.

The only saving grace was knowing Lucy would be by his side again tonight. That thought alone was enough to get a man through Hell and back.

⁕   ⁕   ⁕

Tremors continued to rock Lucy after Jed disappeared outside. How could something feel so wonderful when she knew it was so wrong? So horribly, horribly wrong.

Her fingers trembled against her lips where Jed had kissed her only moments before. For a man who claimed to be so practical and sensible, he certainly knew how to leave a girl out of sorts.

A smile eased up beneath her fingers. Last night had been amazing. From what she knew of human men, they weren't apt to get that close to bedding a woman, then have to stop. But that's what Jed had done for her.

Could it be that he really did love her? It had to be more than lust, that was for certain. Otherwise, he would have insisted she lay with him.

Instead, he'd tucked in behind her and held her all night. It was definitely a feeling she could get used to. One she'd like to get used to.

If only there was a way . . .

CHAPTER SEVENTEEN

"Too much." Berta smiled her nervous little smile and took the spoon away from Lucy—again.

"But it's not completely mixed."

"I know," she answered patiently. "With biscuits, you only want to stir enough so the ingredients are slightly mixed, and no more than that. Otherwise, you'll end up with rocks."

"Again."

Berta coughed over a laugh, but her eyes never met Lucy's. They'd moved the table outside and had been mixing, folding and stirring for almost an hour while Maggie slept, yet Berta had not once looked directly at Lucy, at least not when she thought Lucy would notice.

"Why don't you go stir the stew, and I'll take care of the biscuits for now?" She handed Lucy a large spoon and practically shooed her toward the fire. "You can try this again tomorrow."

Lucy shrugged and did as she was directed. For the first time in weeks, she and Jed were going to eat something other than beans—she'd lick Berta's boots if that's what the woman told her to do.

Jed walked around the freshly stacked lumber just as Lucy reached the fire.

"Is that . . . no." He stepped closer, his nose lifted to the wind. "Miss Blake's stew?"

Lucy forced a hurt look. "You don't think it smells better than my beans, do you?"

"I . . . uh . . . well—"

"No lying, remember?"

A guilty smile played across Jed's face. "Okay, well, then how about this: it smells *different* from your beans."

"Excellent answer, husband." She pointed the spoon at him and grinned. "I suppose I should warn you that she's been trying to teach me how to make biscuits."

Jed tipped his head to the right. "What do you mean *trying?*"

"Apparently, among my other cooking faults, I don't stir properly." She whipped the spoon around the stew for good measure. "Imagine my surprise."

"I dunno about that." He sidled up beside her until their hips pressed together. With a quick glance in Berta's direction, he tipped his head closer to Lucy and whispered, "You stir me up pretty good."

Lucy rolled her eyes. "Not even a little bit funny, Jed."

"Sure it was." He winked and shrugged. "True, too."

She snuggled against him until he wrapped his arm around her shoulders.

"She always looks at me with such an odd expression." Lucy frowned at the stew pot. "And she's always so nervous."

"Nervous?" He shook his head. "She seems okay to me."

"Maybe," Lucy mused. "But in all the time she's been here, she won't look at me. Most of the time, she won't even talk to me."

"Maybe she's shy."

Lucy quirked her brow. "Doubtful. You don't think she believes what Maggie says about me, do you?"

He didn't answer, but he didn't have to. Maggie had held firm to her beliefs and steadfastly refused to set foot outside the house—at least not while Lucy was anywhere nearby.

Berta had forced her outside the day Lucy and Jed went into town, but Maggie refused to stay out long, in case Lucy surprised them by coming back earlier than expected.

The closest Maggie got to fresh air was sitting by the open window in the early morning and late evening, when Lucy was still inside the barn. The second she stepped foot outside, Maggie returned to the farthest corner of the house and stayed there.

After downing two mugs of water, Jed kissed Lucy's cheek and returned to his stack of lumber. It all needed to be sorted and divided into piles: one for the barn, one for the house, and the leftovers for the corrals. And Dwight still had at least two more loads to deliver.

"How's the stew?" Berta's voice startled Lucy.

"Good." She watched the other woman for a minute, noting every time she flinched, twitched, or cast another nervous glace Lucy's way.

She couldn't stand it another minute.

"What's wrong?" She stood over the fire, spoon in hand, watching Berta's profile for any clue. "Have I done something?"

"No," Berta hurried to answer. "You've done nothing to me."

"Then what is it?"

Berta took a long moment to wipe her hands before she turned. When she finally faced Lucy, her eyes were red and swollen with unshed tears. Her chin trembled and she licked her lips several times.

"Sit down," Lucy said. "Please." A nervous knot began to coil in her belly, warning her to get out. To run down to the creek and forget she'd ever asked her stupid question. Why should she care if this woman was afraid of her?

But something else, an unfamiliar and much stronger pull, rooted her to the spot.

Using the dish towel as a handkerchief, Berta dabbed her eyes and nose. Then finally she looked straight at Lucy. The longer she stared, the more Lucy began to see a strange familiarity in Berta's face. She fought the urge to run.

Berta looked more than just familiar. It was almost familial. No.

No.

"Lucy," she began. "I'm . . ."

No. Lucy's head shook of its own volition. It couldn't be.

"I'm your mother."

Lucy stumbled back a step, staring at this woman . . . this horrid *horrid* woman.

"I felt it the moment you appeared at the auction," Berta continued, "but I . . . I wasn't sure and w-was too frightened to say anything." Tears streamed down the woman's chubby cheeks, but she didn't wipe them away. "I didn't want to believe it."

"But how—" Lucy stopped, took a deep breath, and swallowed. "What about . . . why?"

"I was weak," Berta sobbed. Her shoulders shook with each ragged breath. "And I let Sa—your father seduce me. He promised me everything I ever wanted."

"And what you wanted," Lucy said, holding her own tears in check, "didn't include me."

"That's not true," Berta sniffled. She reached for Lucy's hands, but Lucy drew back. "Please try to understand."

"Understand?" she cried, then lowered her voice. The last thing she needed was Jed—or Maggie, for that matter—running out to hear. "How can you expect me to understand? You left me with him! Do you have any idea what that was like?"

Berta shook her head, then let her chin drop to her chest. "I'm so sorry."

"You're sorry?" Anger propelled Lucy in a large circle around the fire. "Sorry?"

She paced the ground in front of Berta, clenching and unclenching her fists, wishing more than anything she could throw something.

"Yes," Berta said between sobs. "I'm so ashamed of what I did. But he didn't give me any choice."

Lucy froze in the middle of her next step and glared at the woman who'd given her birth, the *human* woman. "We all have choices, Berta. You obviously made yours."

"It's not what you think."

"No?" Lucy seethed. "Then what is it? Explain to me how a mother gives up her baby daughter to a life like that. If you didn't want me, there must have been someone who did."

Berta blew her nose into the towel and stood up to face Lucy. "My father was a church minister," she started. "I was afraid if he discovered my secret, I'd be condemned on the spot."

"Oh, I see," Lucy said, wringing her hands to keep them from wringing Berta's neck. "You didn't want to spend eternity in Hell, but it was all right to send your child there."

"No," she cried, wiping her nose again. "It wasn't me."

Lucy waited for Berta to continue.

"Pregnancy isn't something a woman can hide for too long," she said. "When my father learned of my condition, he beat the truth out of me."

For a second, Lucy almost felt for the woman. Almost.

"He threatened to kill me and my child for shaming him so badly." She sniffed again. "That's when your father came back."

Lucy's patience teetered on snapping. "And what did he do?"

Berta took a breath. "He told my father if he let us live, he'd take the child and Father would never have to see it."

"Or?"

"Or Father would condemn himself to Hell for murdering me and my child."

"Choices," Lucy muttered. "Always choices."

"Yes," Berta nodded, wiped her eyes, and continued. "I was sent to live with my aunt until . . ."

"Until you handed me over."

Tears fell in a steady stream from Berta's eyes. "You were six months old when he took you from me. I loved you more than you can ever imagine, Lucy."

"Just not enough to keep me."

"I tried."

Lucy snorted.

"No, I did," Berta hurried on. "I ran away from my aunt's house after you were born. I thought if I could get far enough away from there, he wouldn't be able to find me."

"Did you honestly think you could hide from him?" Even as the words spilled from her lips, Lucy wanted to take them back. How many times had she tried to hide, knowing full well it was impossible?

"I was fifteen." Berta nodded and sniffed. "You can't imagine how awful it was."

"Yes, I can." Lucy stared at this woman who claimed to be her mother. "You never came back for me."

"I was so scared." Berta's voice trembled, her head shook slowly. "I had no one left to help me. No way of knowing how to get to you."

Lucy narrowed her glare at the woman. Her mother. There was only one way to retrieve a soul from Hell, and no human had that kind of strength.

"Why didn't you say something at the auction?"

Berta blew a long breath and slumped back on the boulder again. "All this time I didn't dare hope to see you again until I was dead. And then suddenly you were there, standing in front of me, looking more beautiful than I ever imagined."

Berta's smile sparkled in her eyes, even as more tears poured out. There was something in that smile—but what? A spark ignited in the woman's soul and began to push the darkness away.

"Right then, I knew I had to do something to protect you. Something to keep you safe and away from him."

"Is that why you pushed Jed into marrying me?"

"You seemed set on having him." Guilt and shame crowded Berta's features, but her voice was firm and determined. "I didn't have time to think of anything else, Lucy. All I knew was that of all the men there, you wanted him."

When Lucy didn't answer, Berta shrugged slightly. "Jed's a good man. I knew if anyone could keep you safe, it'd be him. Those other men only wanted you for . . . well, you know what I mean."

Oh yes, Lucy knew exactly what Berta meant. They'd all wanted her for one thing, just as she'd wanted Jed for one thing.

They fell silent for a moment. If Berta knew who Lucy

was, did she know why she'd come to Redemption? Lucy had to be sure her mother wasn't lying—or worse, in cahoots with Deacon.

She lifted the stew off the fire and set it on the ground next to the pit. If they dared let it burn, Jed would surely suspect something was up. According to him, Berta never burned anything.

"Do you know why I'm here?" she asked quietly, with a furtive glance toward the barn, then the house.

Berta hesitated a moment, then nodded. "I think so."

The nervous knot that had started in Lucy's stomach tightened until she could no longer breathe. Berta knew. And Berta was human. Humans were cursed with consciences. If Berta let her conscience get the better of her, there was no telling what she'd do.

She might even tell Jed what Lucy was doing.

"You're after his soul, aren't you?"

Any hope Lucy had of her plan working began to slip away.

"And Maggie's?" Berta's tears flowed again. "The baby's?"

"What if I am?"

A long moment passed before Berta spoke, and when she did, it was little more than a guilty whisper.

"I want to help you."

"Help me?" Lucy's laughter was anything but funny. "You just stood there and told me what a good man he is." She hesitated, tried to swallow against her parched mouth, then lowered her voice even more. "You know he'll go straight to Hell once I've taken his soul."

Berta nodded slowly and wiped her eyes.

"And Maggie."

Another nod.

"And . . . the baby."

Her nod was shorter, briefer, and followed by a choking sob. "You are my only concern."

"Me?" Lucy scoffed. "You gave up your right to be concerned for me when you abandoned me. You left me to be raised in a place so awful, no mortal can even begin to imagine." She fought back the knot in her throat. "Why would I believe you're suddenly concerned about me after all these years?"

The woman's shoulders slumped. "I'm so sorry, Lucy. I begged him not to take you. I offered to go in your place, but he didn't want me. He only wanted you." She paused, took a breath. "I was so scared. And it seemed the more frightened I became, the stronger he was."

The backs of Lucy's eyes prickled slightly, but she blinked it away. That was how her father worked; he preyed on human fear and hatred.

"I begged God and any saint I thought might listen to bring you back," Berta said. "No one did."

"You should have tried harder." Lucy could not feel anything for this woman. She *wouldn't*. "I was your child."

"Yes," Berta sobbed. "You were. You *are*. And there's nothing I can do now to change what I did. Saying I'm sorry won't make anything better."

"You're right." Lucy stiffened. "It won't."

Berta took a moment to compose herself before she spoke. Once she did, her words came out over hiccupped sobs and sniffles.

"I can't pretend to know what you've been through, but if I can help keep you from going back, I'll do whatever it takes."

Jed came around the corner of the barn with a long board balanced on his shoulder. Berta scurried back to the table and busied herself with the bowl of batter she'd abandoned. When Jed raised his brow in question, Lucy simply shrugged and pretended to check the cooling pot of stew.

"Should be ready in just a while," she called out, surprised at the calmness in her voice.

He grinned, set the board against the north wall of the barn and headed back where he came from.

Berta waited another moment, paused near the door of the house, listened, then headed back to the fire.

"If you want out," she whispered, "you need a baby's soul. Am I right?"

Lucy nodded hesitantly. Could she really trust this woman?

Berta's face scrunched. "Let me help you."

There was no mistaking the pain in the woman's voice. And though Lucy would have willingly handed her over to Satan right then and there, something pulled at her.

"Berta." She took a small step closer, then stopped. She did not want this woman to touch her. "Do you have any idea what that would mean for you?"

"I won't lose you again."

For a moment, Lucy thought Berta might be sick, but the woman struggled through a few long, choking breaths, then continued. "I'm going to Hell anyway," she sniveled. "There's nothing I can do about that. But I won't let it happen to you again. Not if there's anything I can do to prevent it."

Lucy chewed her lip raw. Her mother, of all people, wanted to help her, and was willing to do anything it took.

Before she could move away, Berta grabbed her hands and squeezed them tight.

"Jedidiah Caine is the last person on earth who deserves Hell, but if he has to be sacrificed to save my own child, then so be it."

Lucy fought through the fog in her brain. None of this made sense. This had to be Deacon's doing.

Jed came around the barn with another piece of lumber, smiled brightly at Lucy and disappeared again. Had she smiled back? And what would he think if he saw Berta holding her hands?

"Lucy." Berta's gentle tug pulled her back to their conversation. "You're half human."

Human.

A glint of hope shone in her mother's eyes. Hope for what? All her life, she'd believed her mother was just another dark soul her father had claimed. Never had she suspected her mother was human!

It certainly explained why Lucy was weaker than Deacon, but that's all it explained. Berta's smile brightened.

"You have the capacity to love. And you have the capacity to *be* loved."

"No." She shook her head, even as the truth of Berta's words ripped through her heart.

"Yes." Berta's fingers tightened around Lucy's. "Your husband is crazy in love with you already. And I'd wager you feel the same way for him."

"What?" Lucy gasped. "Have you lost your mind? How can you even suggest such a thing?"

"Deny it all you like, Lucy, but it's there. And it could save you."

Poor Berta. Like all humans, she held on to the slightest glimmer of hope any time it presented itself.

"No, Berta. It can't." She pulled out of her mother's grasp and stepped back. "It doesn't matter if I l . . . feel anything for him or not. The fact is simple: once he learns the truth—and he will learn the truth eventually—he'll despise me."

"No," Berta protested. "He can't hate you—he loves you!"

Lucy didn't answer. Sure, Jed might think he loved her, he might even want to say it out loud, but no human loved enough to take on the devil.

"Miss Blake!" Maggie's cry carried through the closed door and out into the yard.

"Oh dear," she muttered. "Think about what I said, Lucy. We can do this. I can help."

CHAPTER EIGHTEEN

M aggie's resting again." Berta carried the two chairs outside and set them next to the fire. "I suggested her time might be very close, so she should get as much rest as she possibly could."

Lucy tried to steady her breathing, but it wasn't working very well. How could she stay calm with both Berta and Jed sitting there around the fire? Knowing her luck, Deacon would show up, too.

"You'll join us for supper, then?" Jed asked with a smile. "Seems only fair."

Lucy looked back at Berta and felt Jed's gaze follow hers. He took in a sharp breath, but neither woman turned to look at him again. They simply sat staring at each other, Berta's red, puffy eyes begging forgiveness, and Lucy trying desperately to make sense of everything.

"Is there something going on?" Jed asked. His voice, low and full of concern, seemed to fill the air around them.

Lucy watched Berta for another moment. If her mother was lying to her or working with Deacon, Lucy was in a great deal of trouble. But there was something in

Berta's eyes, something deeper than fear, deeper than shame. It was like a fire burned there, but not the fires Lucy was used to.

She leveled a pointed, warning glare at Berta, then turned to Jed and smiled.

"It's fine."

Jed shuffled on his feet, his hat twisting between his hands. "Fine like supper was fine or fine like fine?"

Lucy laughed softly. Jed Caine really was a funny creature.

"Fine like fine," she answered, then rose from her chair to take Jed's arm. "In fact, Berta and I have some, um, surprising news."

Jed's brow shot up, his gaze flipping between the women. "What's that?"

Lucy reached her other hand toward Berta, urging her out of her chair. The other woman mopped her face before rising to her feet and facing Jed.

"We've just discovered Berta is my mother."

Shocked silence stretched between them until Jed finally found his tongue again.

"Your mother?" He blinked hard and stared first at Berta, then Lucy, then back at Berta. "How the hell . . . I mean . . . how'd you figure that out?"

Berta's expression froze.

"It's a long story," Lucy said.

Jed's expression hardened, his jaw tightened. "Did you find Lucy through Deacon?" he asked.

"Deacon?" Berta frowned, her head shaking hard enough to fall off. "He's no child of mine."

"Deacon is my, um, half-brother," Lucy explained, turning back to Jed. "My . . . father . . . wasn't exactly an honorable man."

"There's an understatement." Berta snorted, chuckled, then covered her face with the towel and cried through her laughter.

"Wha . . . ?" Panic shot across Jed's face, then confusion. "So Deacon's not your son?"

"No," Berta choked out. "Lucy's my only child."

"And her father . . ."

"Is the devil himself," Lucy answered. Berta glanced up from her towel, her mouth open in shock, then she started laughing all over again.

"That he is," she muttered into her towel. "That he is."

"What?" Jed squinted at Lucy.

Poor Jed. Even though he was hearing the truth, he would never believe it. Most humans didn't.

"It's fine," Lucy laughed. "Really. We just need a little time to get used to this is all. It's all a bit of a shock."

Jed blew a breath over his bottom lip. "A bit."

"How about some stew?" Lucy dipped the spoon into the pot, and began dishing out the delicious-smelling concoction. She would *have* to learn how to make this!

She could feel Jed's eyes on her as he peered over the rim of his bowl. She could feel the confusion clouding his mind and the worry he felt about Lucy finding her mother after all these years.

Thankfully, though, Berta's stew was too delicious to give him time to talk or ask questions. He finished two full bowls, shamelessly accepted a third after some was set aside for Maggie, then waited until the ladies were good and full before he lifted the pot from the rocks and licked it clean.

"How long can you stay, Berta?" Jed winked at Lucy then ducked out her reach as she stabbed her fork toward him.

"Don't you have chores, husband?"

"Not if there's pie for dessert . . ."

"No such luck," Lucy answered.

He nodded his thanks to Berta, then Lucy, and headed off to the barn. Lucy and Berta wouldn't have a lot of time to talk, so she needed to get things sorted out quickly.

"How is Maggie doing?"

Berta frowned. "Does it matter?"

How could Lucy explain it? She'd seen so very little of the woman since arriving as Jed's wife. Yet, somehow, Jed's worry had become her own. And that worry was one more thing to wear on Lucy's strength.

"She's as healthy as a woman can be in her state," Berta said with a sad smile. "That baby's a feisty one, I'll tell you that. Reminds me of when I carried you."

Two fat tears slid down Berta's cheeks. The last thing Lucy expected was to feel tears of her own for Maggie or her baby, yet there they were. And more surprising was how many fell. The faster she wiped them away, the faster they sprang up.

What the hell was wrong with her?

*　*　*

The fire snapped and danced in the still evening air. Red and pink streaks faded from the sky as darkness crept in, easing the last remnants of daylight beyond the horizon.

Jed settled on the blanket behind Lucy and eased her back against him. She fit perfectly, as though she were meant to be there. It was probably not the most gentlemanly thing he could do, given that her mother was sitting with them, but that hardly mattered anymore. Wasn't so long ago Berta had seen him in nothing but a blanket.

Besides, he wanted her to know her daughter was cared for. Hell, he more than just cared for her.

He loved her. And no mother could ask for more than that.

Berta watched them for a second, a sad smile on her face. What was there to be sad about? By no small miracle, she'd been reunited with her daughter. And by yet another miracle, that daughter was married to a man who loved her and wanted nothing more than to spend the rest of his days making her happy and giving her children.

Lots and lots of children.

Neither Lucy nor Berta had offered any details as to how they became separated in the first place, and Jed wasn't about to ask. He'd seen enough tears in the last few days to last him a lifetime. He wasn't about to do or say anything to cause more.

"I think I'll tuck in for the night." Berta rose to her feet, brushing the dirt and pebbles from her dress.

"G'night, Miss Blake." Jed rose to his feet and nodded briefly. "Much obliged for the stew tonight."

An odd look washed across Berta's face, but she smiled her sad smile again and nodded. "Good night then."

"Good night." Lucy stepped up to Jed, her back resting against his stomach.

He wrapped his arms around her and rested his chin on the top of her head, but Lucy wanted more. Always more. She pulled his arms tighter around her, then rested her own arms atop his.

"Quite a day, huh?" he asked quietly.

"Hmmm." She yawned.

"Come on, then," he said. "Let's get you tucked in, too."

He doused the fire as quickly as he could, then wrapped his arm around her shoulders and headed toward the barn. Lucy's teeth chattered the whole time.

Jed snickered and pressed a kiss against her head. She'd never survive winter.

"I need to tend the horses. And you"—he tapped her on the tip of the nose—"need to tend to you."

Lucy nodded sleepily and wandered over to their corner in search of her beloved blanket.

The irony of Jed's life hit him like a brick.

He'd wanted to earn her respect before he took her to bed. She'd wanted to get straight to bed, respect be damned. Now he was dying to make love to her, and she wasn't ready. And if that wasn't torture enough, he was going to have to sleep next to her all night without touching her.

Again.

It was the most exquisite kind of torture.

With the speed of a demon, he had the horses fed and watered, and the tack stored out of the way. He turned down the lantern and crept toward the last stall, aching to crawl in with Lucy—even if it meant he had to keep his hands to himself.

It took a moment for his eyes to adjust to the dimness, but there she was, curled up in a tight ball, the blanket wrapped around her like a cocoon. Still her teeth rattled. What was wrong with that girl?

"Lucy."

"Yes?"

He swallowed his laughter. "I'm going to make a suggestion, but before I do, I promise you it's completely innocent." *Well, mostly*. "It'll help keep you warm."

"I'll do anything."

Jed wiped his palm across his mouth. "Take off your clothes."

Lucy snorted over a shiver. "How is that supposed to warm me up?" she asked.

Jed started on his own buttons. "Our body heat will keep each other warmer than our clothes will."

"Nice t-try, Jed."

He finished with his buttons and yanked his arms out of the sleeves. "I know it sounds strange." He tugged one boot off and tossed it aside. "But it works." The other boot followed. "Trust me."

She peeked out from beneath the blanket, her eyes suspicious. "This isn't your way of . . ."

Jed's fingers froze against the top button of his trousers.

"No." He must be crazy. He couldn't lie next to her, skin to skin, and not do anything. Maybe it wasn't such a good idea after all. "If you'd rather—"

Lucy stopped him before he could reach for his shirt.

"Wait." She stared up at the ceiling for a long moment. "Do you really think it'll work?"

His tongue wouldn't move, so Jed simply nodded.

"Okay. But just wait there a minute." She ducked under the blanket and squirmed around for several minutes before poking her head back out. One hand held the blanket around her chest, while the other reached back under and brought out her nightgown.

Jed's eyes blinked about a hundred times. Why the hell couldn't he breathe? When she was done, she snuggled deeper into the straw and smiled shyly.

Sweet Jesus.

She'd done it. She'd taken off all her clothes and now she lay there—completely naked—under one ridiculously thin blanket. And all because he promised her she'd be warmer.

When he hesitated, Lucy clicked her tongue at him.

"I'm f-freezing here, Jed. Could you hurry up, please?"

He shucked his trousers in less time than it took him to find his breath. He could do this. He was a practical man.

His wife was cold and he needed to warm her up—without causing himself too much embarrassment.

Jed took a deep, steadying breath, then slid in beside her. He could do this.

He could.

They tucked the blanket around them and lay side-by-side, both staring up at the ceiling.

"Okay," he struggled to say. "You're going to have to slide up against me, like last night."

Even in the dimness of the darkened corner, he could see the color fill her cheeks.

"Maybe this isn't such a good idea," she murmured. "It's going to be too hard."

"It's already too hard," he muttered, then released a harsh breath. "Never mind, just come on."

He propped himself on his side and waited while Lucy did the same. When she was settled, he ground his teeth together and moved up against her, biting back every curse he could think of.

"Is that—" she squeaked.

"Yes." He wrapped her in his arms and pulled her in as tight as he could. "Now for God's sake, don't move."

She straightened her legs and pressed their length against his. Blood crashed through his veins.

At least last night he had the bulk of the blanket between them. Tonight there was nothing. Just skin against skin.

"You . . ." God, if she didn't stop moving like that. "Your legs . . ."

"Sorry," she mumbled. "I just can't get comfortable."

She twisted her foot slightly until it rested on top of his, and he groaned.

"Are you okay?" Lucy whispered. "Are you comfortable?"

"No," he grunted.

"D'you want me to move?"

"No!" He hissed out a breath against her hair. "For God's sake, just be still."

"Sorry."

Jed closed his eyes and tried to focus on anything else: the straw poking into his ears, the way the blanket scratched his skin, anything. Nothing worked.

"Jed?" Lucy whispered. "Can I ask you something?"

"Mm-hmm. As long as it doesn't involve movement."

"It's not very ladylike."

He snorted softly and tightened his arms around her belly. "D'you really think that matters at this point?"

"Right. Well, um . . ." She rested her hands on top of his, then moved her fingers in circles over his skin. "Is it always . . . um, that hard?"

Jed choked out a laugh. "Only since you came along, sweetheart."

He waited for her to say something else—to make a joke at his painful expense, but she didn't. Instead, she twined her fingers through his and squeezed gently.

His heart swelled until he thought it'd burst from his chest. She'd never hinted at it before, but that one touch sparked what he'd been afraid to hope until now.

Maybe Lucy could grow to love him. And maybe—just maybe—she was already beginning to.

Jed tucked her head under his chin and sighed. One small touch made his night of agony all worth it.

*　*　*

Lucy lay as still as she could, eyes closed, forcing her breathing to go in and out in a steady rhythm. Maybe if Jed thought she was asleep, he'd sleep, too. The last thing she wanted—or needed—was for him to see her cry again.

As soon as he'd wrapped his arms around her, the all-too-familiar sensation began prickling her eyes, and every passing second wrapped in his arms made it worse.

She wasn't supposed to cry over a human, especially one who'd made her work as hard as Jed had. She wasn't supposed to want to be there lying in a smelly, old, pathetic excuse for a barn and thinking there couldn't possibly be a better place.

How would she live without him? And why would she want to? Life without him would be Hell itself.

No, it would be worse. Much, much worse.

Her whole life she'd been told she'd never feel anything but hate, loathing and shame. And that's all she'd ever felt for anyone—human or otherwise.

Until Jedidiah Caine walked into her life.

What she felt for him was too confusing to sort out. While she was supposed to hate him and his practical ideas, she found herself understanding and agreeing with them. When she was supposed to loathe him for making her work, she found herself wanting to work harder just to have him smile and wink at her with that look that made her stand taller.

And when she was supposed to shame him for not giving her everything she wanted the very moment she wanted it, she had learned to respect him for not doing just that.

If she respected him, was it possible that she might actually—

No. She was the devil's daughter. She wasn't capable of such feelings, was she?

According to her father, no. According to her mother . . .

Lucy opened her eyes and stared down at Jed's arms

wrapped around her, sharing his warmth with her. It didn't feel hateful. And there was no shame, either. It just felt right. It felt . . . good.

Her pulse quickened, her breath came in short gasps. Her father had drilled into her that no child of his could ever be loved, and no child of his could ever feel anything but hate for anyone else.

But he'd also told her he wouldn't interfere in her plans.

Angry tears coursed down her cheeks in blazing hot streaks. Of course Satan lied to her—it's all he ever did. How could she have been so stupid?

Simple, stupid Lucy.

And that's why he'd sent Deacon. Not just to see her fail, but to step in if she ever realized the truth. Well, she realized it now.

This was love, this warmth, this pride, this need to protect Jed from her father and her brother . . . and herself.

She loved her husband. She loved his practical ways, the way he worked and the way he made *her* work. She loved his hands, his arms and especially his eyes. She could get lost in those eyes.

And what made it so much better was knowing he loved her, too. It wasn't just lust he felt, though the evidence of that was still pressed against her.

He loved her.

Her. Lucille Firr, the devil's daughter.

The pain of that sudden knowledge sent piercing spasms through her chest. She had to protect him somehow, had to find a way to shield him from Deacon. And she had to do it soon, before Maggie gave birth and Hell literally broke loose.

Her tears doubled, leaking out the corner of her eyes and falling to Jed's shirt bunched beneath her head.

There was, of course, only one way to save Jed. It didn't matter how many tears she cried or how long she tried to come up with another plan, there was no other choice.

She had to go back.

If Jed ever discovered the truth about Lucy, he'd never forgive her. His soul would be darkened toward her forever. And if he let that hatred turn on himself—or anyone else—Deacon would surely win.

Lucy couldn't let that happen. Now that she finally understood what she felt, and how deeply she felt it, there was no question. Jed's happiness had to come before her own, and to Hell with Deacon and anyone else who tried to stop her.

She'd lived in Hell; she knew what to expect. Jed had no idea.

Anger, frustration and fear swirled in her until she thought she'd be sick. *So stupid*. At least Deacon had been right about that.

But Jed didn't think she was stupid. Even though she still couldn't make coffee, or biscuits, or even wash a shirt properly. Jed loved her and she loved him. Nothing else mattered.

At least not out here in the barn.

Tomorrow, in the light of day, she'd find a way to save him from the horrors she'd brought with her. But tonight she was going to stay in his arms, secure in the fact that she could love. And she could *be* loved. If only she could tell him.

Of course she didn't dare, and she had to keep him from uttering the words, too. It was the last thread keeping him safe. If he kept the words to himself, his soul would never fully be opened to her. But once he spoke them aloud, he'd be vulnerable to Deacon and any other devil spawn. It was the words themselves, spoken out loud to another, that humbled a human in the most defenseless way.

Humans risked everything by saying it out loud. In that moment, a human's soul was at its weakest, desperate for the other person's love.

She could have let him say the words, could have finished all this days ago, but hadn't. Her selfish need to be with him a few more moments, a few more days and a few more nights had stopped her. And now it was too late.

She couldn't go through with it.

Lucy forced her eyes shut, trying to dam the tears that refused to stop. Even so, they squeezed out and trickled down her face. She sniffled softly, not daring to move.

"You okay?" Jed's voice, soft in her hair, made her jump. He hadn't been asleep after all.

"Mm-hmm." Damn her weakness. Even her mumble trembled.

"No, you're not." He leaned up on his elbow and stared down at her. "What's wrong?"

"Nothing." She sniffed over her forced smile and dashed the back of her hand across her eyes.

Jed eased her down until she lay flat on her back, looking up at him. He truly was a beautiful man. Everything about him made her love him more, from his tousled, dark hair to those melting eyes that he nearly consumed her with.

"Lucy." Her name was a ragged breath from his lips. He hadn't moved an inch; he just leaned over her, watching, staring. "What is it?"

Damn these tears. She moved to wipe them again, but Jed caught her wrist and moved it down.

"Let me make it better," he said, brushing his thumb against her tears.

"You c-can't." A sob caught in her throat. No one could make this better.

"How do you know?" He wiped her other cheek slowly, his eyes following his thumb's slow movements.

She had to touch him. She shouldn't. She'd asked him not to touch her, but she couldn't stop herself. If she could put every inch of him to memory, maybe she could survive Hell again.

Her fingertips trembled against his chest, moving slowly, finding more strength with each passing second.

His breath hissed. "Lucy—"

"Shh." She pressed her palms flat, moving over him with the barest of touches, pausing over his left breast to memorize his heartbeat. "I just want to—"

"Oh God, don't," he pleaded. "Whatever it is, please don't."

"But it's—" She slid her hands around his waist, then lower to his backside.

He sucked in a sharp breath. "Lucy. I can't . . . stand . . . this."

Lucy reached to kiss his chin, his cheek, and his nose. As her mouth searched his out, found it and pulled another low guttural groan from him, she whispered softly.

"Touch me, Jed."

She'd barely finished his name when he hauled her up against him, then rolled so she lay on top of him, the length of her body pressed against him.

She shouldn't do this, shouldn't give in to her need.

Just once and then she could go back.

Just once and maybe then she could find the strength to live without him. She pushed the ridiculous thought from her head. Once would never be enough. She'd always want more.

But once was all she'd ever have, so she'd have to savor every moment.

Jed's hands were everywhere: in her hair, on her back, her hips, and then her backside. A jolt of lightning shot through her, sending her mind reeling, her heart pounding and her hands searching.

Lucy sat up, her legs straddling his hips, his erection pushing against her, but Jed held still.

"Make me your wife," she said, staring down into the depths of his dark eyes. She pressed her hands against his chest, loving the way the hair tickled her palms.

His own hands stilled on her hips. "Are you sure?" he rasped. "'Cuz once this starts . . . stopping . . ."

She leaned toward him and kissed him full on the mouth. "I won't want you to stop."

Before she could blink, Jed had flipped them so he now straddled her, his beautiful face hovering above hers, his smile promising things she couldn't even imagine.

"God, but I l—"

She pressed her hand against his mouth. "Don't tell me," she whispered. "Show me."

CHAPTER NINETEEN

Fire trailed behind Jed's touch. He held her wrists at the sides of her head, then leaned down to kiss her, but not on the mouth.

He started beside her eyes and moved slowly over her face, coming close but never close enough to her waiting lips. She wiggled beneath his grasp, but he only smiled and tightened his grip.

"Jed, please," she whimpered.

"Oh no, sweetheart." He ran his tongue with feather-like softness across her bottom lip. "You're not getting off that easy. I've had a long time to think about what I want to do to you, and it's going to take all night—maybe into the morning."

He kissed all around her mouth, over her chin, then moved up to nibble her jaw.

She whimpered again, afraid he'd never kiss her, and yet afraid he *would*, thereby ending this exquisite torture.

When his mouth finally found hers, she couldn't get enough. He teased her, tempted her and caressed her until she began to wiggle beneath him. She needed more than this. She needed him—all of him. It was as though she were on fire and only Jed could douse her flames.

"Hold on," he murmured. "We haven't even started yet."

"I can't," she gasped. "I . . ."

"Shh, just hold on." He moved lower, kissing his way down her neck, over the hollow in her throat, and then over each collar bone. Lucy sucked in a breath. Surely he didn't mean to . . .

He did. With great tenderness, he kissed his way over one breast, then the other. She arched toward him, needing more, always more. He smiled against her skin a second before his tongue darted out and flicked against her hardened nipple.

Lucy gasped sharply once, then again when he set to work on the other nipple. He released her wrists and cupped her breast in his warm palm.

She couldn't have caught her breath if she tried.

"Please, Jed." That couldn't be *her* voice—it sounded too desperate, too weak.

"Hmm?" he murmured against her belly. He kissed her rib cage, then moved to the other side. Then lower.

"I—I—oh my!"

He moved his hands down her body, over her hips and thighs.

Someone moaned, but she didn't know who.

"Jed," she pleaded.

"Shh." His fingers inched up her leg, near to the ache that would not be sated. She had no idea what he had planned, but if he didn't do something quick, she'd surely die right there.

His fingers moved closer, closer, until they found it— the place that begged to be touched. He slid a finger inside, just enough to drive her toward the edge of sanity. She bucked against his touch, then cried out when he pulled back.

"No," she moaned.

"More?" he whispered even as he slid his finger back inside. "More of that?"

"Yes," she rasped. "More."

He slid out again, then slid in two fingers. She arched again. *More*. Would she ever get enough? Jed pushed into her deeper, his mouth pressing soft kisses against the inside of her thigh.

"I, oh, I . . ." Lucy arched again, pressing herself into his hand, toward his mouth. She could feel herself teetering on an edge she couldn't even begin to describe. But the second Jed's lips found her, she spiraled off that edge and crashed into a fire so deep, so hot, she was sure she'd died and gone to . . . Heaven.

Jed pressed his hand against her gently, easing her through the fire.

"Let it go," he murmured. "That's it."

Her fingers tightened in his hair, holding on for dear life—fearing she'd never make it back to him. But back she came as Jed slid up her body, pressing himself against her, keeping them skin to skin.

"I . . ." Lucy swallowed a huge gulp of air, then pulled him down for a long, slow kiss. "That was . . ."

Jed grinned wickedly and kissed her again. "That was nothin'."

He rained more kisses over her face and neck, nibbled her ear, then kissed her neck right below her earlobe. That deep ache started again, low in her belly.

No. She'd never survive another one. She couldn't.

He *wouldn't*.

"Hold on," he moaned in her ear.

"Again?" She wanted to whimper, but was already reaching for him, arching against his touch.

"Oh yeah," he chuckled softly. "At least once more."

He settled over her, his eyes fixed on her, his hands set

on either side of her head, keeping his weight from crushing her.

He pushed against her once, then slipped just inside. Lucy lifted herself off the blanket—that couldn't be it—she needed a helluva lot more than that.

Jed smiled, pulled out, then slid in again—a little farther. The vein on his forehead throbbed, his teeth ground together, but he never took his eyes away from hers.

"Jed," she whispered, reaching to touch him. His body tensed as she trailed her fingers across his chest and down his belly. "Can I . . . ?"

"God, yes."

She slid her hand between them, and tentatively ran her fingers around him. A low growl started in his throat. *Interesting.* She closed her fingers around him and squeezed ever so gently, then moved her hand over the length of him, until his growl ripped free, and he pushed all the way into her, then stilled, watching, waiting.

He was inside her, and it was better than Heaven could possibly be.

Lucy couldn't stand the stillness. She shifted beneath him, reached her arms around and pulled him closer. Her hips moved in small circles. She had to have more, had to find that cliff again.

Jed moved slowly. With long purposeful strokes, he slid in and out until Lucy was right back there, teetering, and crying out his name. He moved one hand beneath her backside and lifted, at the same time pushing into her until they became one.

Lucy gasped, crashed into the fire again, and gave in to whatever forces were coming to claim her. There was no way in Heaven or Hell a mortal could survive such a thing twice.

"Lucy," Jed breathed out her name as his whole body

went rigid. A second later, the arm supporting him gave out. Before he crushed her, he swept her up and rolled so she lay on top of him.

She settled tight against him, afraid he'd pull away. They lay that way for long minutes, Jed pulsing inside her, and Lucy counting his heartbeats as they thundered beneath her ear.

He reached for the blanket and began to tuck it in around her.

"Jed?" she whispered against his chest.

"Hmm?"

"Leave the blanket. I've never been so hot in all my life."

Laughter rumbled in his chest. "Thank God, 'cuz I'm about to burst into flames here."

She couldn't stop touching him. His chest had the most amazing feel to it, with its smooth skin, rough hair and tight nipples.

"Is it always like this?" she asked, then wished she hadn't.

"I imagine it will be with you," he whispered back, as his fingers drew circles over her back. "Are you okay? I didn't hurt you, did I?"

"No." She kissed the underside of his chin. "I'm fine."

"Fine?" His fingers stopped and before she could protest, he had her on her back again and was grinning down at her. "What we did here was more than just fine."

She started to laugh, but he caught her mouth against his and kissed her until she couldn't breathe.

"Say it." He kissed her jaw, then her collar bone. "Say it was more than fine."

"And if I don't?" Lucy squirmed beneath him. "What then?"

Jed's fingers trailed a line from one breast to the other. "Then we're going to have to keep going until you do."

She wound her fingers through his hair and finally found enough breath to answer him.

"Oh, but it *was* fine, Jed. Most certainly fine."

His hands were already touching her everywhere, stoking the fire deep inside her and making her reach for him again. As she closed her hand around him, squeezing gently, he pressed his face into her neck and sighed.

"Anything more than *fine* is gonna kill me," he moaned.

❖ ❖ ❖

The morning sun peeked in beneath the door and through the cracks in the lean-to when Jed woke up—alone.

Damn—he'd rather hoped for a little *fine-ness* to get him started. The horses nickered on the other side of the barn.

"Yeah, okay," he muttered. "Gimme a minute."

He could have spent the whole night loving Lucy, and it wouldn't have been nearly enough. For a girl who had such limited experience, it didn't take her long to figure things out.

Jed grunted and pushed himself to his feet. He'd only drive himself crazy lying there thinking about her. Besides, he had the rest of his life to get his fill of her, if that was even possible.

He dressed quickly, threw some oats to the horses, then grabbed the buckets and headed outside. The animals would have to wait for water—he needed to kiss his wife first.

Low, harsh voices whispered near the house. *What the . . . ?*

"I have to do this," Lucy was saying.

"No you don't," came Berta's furious response. "And I'm not about to let you—"

Jed stormed toward them. "Let her what?"

Both women started, their faces red with anger. Lucy was the first to recover. Her smile was big, but not real.

"Good morning." She kissed his cheek and indicated a nearby chair. "Berta made coffee."

Jed didn't move. "Let you what?" he repeated.

"Oh, it's nothing," Lucy tried to wave it away.

"Lucy." He held her arm until she looked up at him. "It's not nothing."

Her mouth opened, but Berta's voice came first.

"She thinks she's ready to make a pie all by herself." She cleared her throat, then lifted her chin, as if daring him to argue. "And I was just saying that I wasn't about to let her ruin perfectly good pastry."

Jed's blood began to simmer. "Lucy doesn't ruin things. And you'll watch how you speak to her."

Berta looked crushed, and Lucy couldn't have looked guiltier. Something wasn't right—and it had nothing to do with pastry.

He looked down at Lucy, who seemed less agitated than she'd been a minute ago.

"Really," she said. "It's just silliness. Nothing to worry about."

He didn't believe that for a second, but he didn't want to accuse Lucy of lying in front of her mother. He hesitated, then spoke pointedly, first to Lucy: "I'll be back for the coffee and a proper good morning." Then he addressed Berta: "Let her make whatever the hell she wants."

Berta nodded stiffly but kept silent. *Women*. Maybe it was a good thing she spent most of her time in the house with Maggie. Seemed no one in Lucy's family treated her right.

He walked to the creek, filled the buckets, and went back to tend the horses. When they'd been fed and watered, he let them loose in the corral. They wouldn't be needed today. As he closed the gate, he heard the creaking of a wagon coming toward the house.

"Good to see you up and dressed, Caine." Dwight grinned.

"Mornin', Dwight." Jed stood by the first pile of lumber until Dwight had set the brake on the wagon. "Just gonna go grab us some coffee. Be right back."

"Want it stacked in the same place?" Dwight asked, nodding toward the far corner of the yard.

"Yup." Jed left the other man to start unloading while he hurried back toward the fire, and the tension between mother and daughter.

The two women had dragged the table out of the cabin and were now stooped over it, both up to their elbows in a bowl of dough.

"Lucy."

She whirled to face him, sending pieces of dough flying. Flour dusted her nose and chin, and her apron was covered in splotches of gooey pastry.

"A quick word please?" He pointed toward the barn, letting her scurry off ahead of him, and leaving Berta to look after them with a troubled expression.

Once inside, Lucy turned to face him.

"What is—"

Jed swallowed her last words with the kiss he'd been aching to give her since he opened his eyes. He held her face in his hands and dragged the kiss on until she melted against him, her doughy hands fisted in his shirt.

"*That's* how you should say good morning to me," he breathed against her flushed cheek.

"But—"

"No buts." He kissed her again, nipped at her lip, and brushed the flour from her face.

"No buts," she repeated, her voice soft and whispery.

"Good." He held her an arm's length away and grinned. "Now get back over there and make that damned pie. Hell, make beans again if that's what you want."

Her smile warmed him through.

"Just promise me one thing," he added, taking a large step back.

"What's that?"

"As long as Berta's here, let her make the coffee."

Lucy lunged at him, but he ducked out the door.

"Berta won't be here forever," she called after him. "If you think my coffee's been bad up 'til now . . ."

Jed laughed as he filled mugs for himself and Dwight. He hated to tell her he was almost getting used to the swill she called coffee.

Almost.

CHAPTER TWENTY

Lucy leaned back against the cabin door and exhaled slowly. Berta sat slumped in a chair, her face buried in her hands.

"You can't do this," she said, her voice a mixture of anger and anguish.

Maggie murmured in her sleep, but didn't wake.

"I have to." Lucy walked to the window and stood staring out after Jed. "There's no other way."

"Yes, there is." Berta lifted her reddened face. "Finish this. That man loves you, and he'll do anything for you."

"I know." It was what she had planned. It was what she needed. And now she had to walk away from her dream.

Berta watched her for long minutes. "You can always fall in love again . . . after . . . with someone else." Her voice cracked and shook. "There are plenty of men out there who'd be happy—"

Lucy whirled on her. "I don't want plenty of other men. I want Jed."

"It's impossible." Berta's voice broke on a sob. "Please, Lucy, don't do this."

"I have to." She had to stay strong. If she started crying

again, she might never stop, and she might never have the strength to do this. "You said it yourself—Jed doesn't deserve to go to Hell."

"I don't care what I said," Berta cried. "I can't lose you again. Not now."

Lucy cast a quick glance at the sleeping Maggie, then took her mother's hands in hers. "You want me to be happy, isn't that what you said?"

Berta nodded miserably.

"I've *been* happy." The warmth in Lucy's heart spread through her veins until her whole body basked in it. "For the first time in my life, I've learned what it's like to be happy, to love someone and to be loved. And it's . . . it's . . ."

There were no words to describe it.

"I want you to stay here and keep being happy," Berta mumbled. "Is that so wrong?"

"It's not wrong, Berta," Lucy smiled. "It's just not possible."

"Of course it's possible." She yanked her hands away from Lucy and swiped them across her eyes. "All you have to do is finish this. Take his soul, Lucy. Please. Take Maggie's. Take the baby's."

"I can't."

"But—"

"No." *No buts.* Lucy swallowed the fear creeping up her throat. "I won't do it."

"Lucy." Berta's sobs became increasingly louder. If she didn't hush, she'd wake up Maggie and then the wailing would really begin.

"Berta." When the other woman didn't respond, Lucy took her hands. "Mother. Remember how you felt when you gave me to him."

A harsh snort.

"Can you really do that to another mother? Can you put Maggie through that kind of pain?"

Berta hesitated a long time. Finally, she shook her head slowly.

A sense of urgency crept through Lucy. This was right. This was good.

"I need you to do something for me."

The other woman grunted and sniffed.

"I want you to take Maggie into town. Take her straight to the church and leave her with Reverend Conroy. He's her only hope."

Lucy's gaze bore into Berta, until she finally looked up. "You can't be here when I tell Jed."

"And what are you going to tell him?" Berta choked on another sniff. "That you were born from the Devil's seed and you came here to claim his soul? Or that you came to steal the soul of an innocent newborn? No man in his right mind is going to believe that."

"It doesn't matter if he believes it or not. All that matters is he'll be safe."

Lucy frowned. Regardless of what happened, Jed was going to hate Lucy by the time this was over. Her only hope was that if *she* told him the truth—every ugly detail—he might not hate her as much as he would if he heard it from someone else, someone like Deacon.

"There is no good answer for any of this," she muttered. "All I know for certain is I have to do this before Deacon comes back."

"Deacon is no threat to you." Berta sniffed, her voice stronger, "He doesn't know what it means to love another soul. You do. That's a strength no son of Satan can ever imagine."

A lone tear slipped down Lucy's face. "Deacon will do

anything to please Father, especially if it means bringing me down again."

"But he's your brother."

"It doesn't matter." She stared blankly at the table. "My fear is that he'll go after Jed's soul, too, unless I can find a way to protect him somehow." Her voice lowered. "The only way we can protect Maggie and the baby is to get her to the church. If this goes the way I hope, Deacon will be so focused on me, he'll forget about Jed long enough for him to get away, too."

Hope? Is that what Lucy was left with? She'd seen enough in her life to know hope meant nothing.

"We should all go to the church," Berta said. "We'll all be safe there."

Lucy shook her head. "The preacher will never let me inside. And Jed will never leave me without an explanation, and even then . . ." She sighed. "We need to protect that baby first and foremost."

Berta's chin fell to her chest again. "I don't understand any of this."

"I know," Lucy said. "It's impossible to understand because there are no rules. My father will do whatever he must to get what—or who—he wants. I can only hope Jed's strong enough to get through this."

"There must be some way to stop him."

Lucy shook her head slowly, blinking back more tears. "Nothing that will work here." There was only one thing her father feared, only one thing that might stop him: love.

He recoiled at the mere idea of love, and if anyone dared show the slightest hint of it near him, his wrath was unbearable.

But Lucy didn't have to worry about that. Once Jed knew the truth, he'd feel nothing but anger and hatred toward her. He'd been mad enough when she'd lied about being able to cook, but this—this couldn't even compare.

If he could forgive her, if he could hold on to his love for her, then maybe . . .

No. No human could forgive a betrayal like this. It was too much to ask. She knew it, Berta knew it, and pretty soon, Jed would know it, too. All Lucy could do was hope her love would be enough to save him.

As the minutes ticked by, the pain in Lucy's heart sliced deeper. Sitting with Berta, she'd been able to focus on what needed to be done without giving in to her anguish. But now, as the time to tell Jed grew nearer, she was overcome by surges of fear, helplessness and nausea. She no longer feared Hell, no longer feared the wrath of her father when she returned. Her greatest fear was the way Jed would look at her when he learned the truth.

He'd be furious, repulsed and maybe a little frightened. She'd never again see those deep, dark eyes full of love turned her way. He'd never send tingles over her skin with the simple touch of his finger. And he'd never love her as he had last night.

She would never actually hear him say he loved her.

An eternity seemed to pass in each second, and yet suddenly, it was time.

∘   ∘   ∘

They finished stacking the lumber, and Dwight was ready to head back to town. All they needed to do was get Maggie into the wagon.

"Jedidiah," she cried, clutching her stomach. "They're going to take your soul! Don't make me go!"

"Maggie," Jed said soothingly. "Miss Blake is taking you in to see the doctor. We just want to make sure the baby is okay, and then you'll come right back."

"No," she pleaded, groping for his hands, but Berta continued moving her forward, toward Dwight and the waiting wagon. "They're after your soul! If you make me leave, they'll kill all of us!"

"Maggie—" Lucy stepped forward, but Maggie screeched and jumped behind Dwight.

"Stay back," she warned. "Devil woman."

"Come now, Mrs. Caine." Dwight took her arm gently and steered her toward the wagon. "It ain't good for you or that baby to get all worked up like this."

"No." She continued to sob, but her strength was visibly draining.

"Are you sure she'll be okay?" Jed asked Berta. "It's a long ride into town, and in her condition . . ."

Berta glanced at Lucy before answering. "Let me get her into town and she'll be fine."

Jed took Maggie's other arm as he and Dwight helped the distraught woman up to the bench.

"It's fine, Maggie," he said, trying his best to offer even a little bit of comfort. She wouldn't look at him, but sat in her spot, shoulders sagging, as she continued to sob.

He considered giving in and letting her stay. What could the doctor do for her at this point that Berta wasn't already doing?

As Lucy's hand slid into his, he knew he had to let Maggie go. She was working herself up into a lather, and getting worse by the moment. Maybe the doctor could get her to calm down a bit.

"If Doc decides to keep you in town," he said, "we'll drive in every day to check on you. I promise."

Lucy kept looking at Berta with a strange, strained

plea, but the other woman seemed to be avoiding her. Jed scratched his head. Women were too confusing.

"Thank you." Lucy pulled Berta into a tight hug and whispered something too low for Jed to hear.

Berta sobbed against her shoulder, but whatever she was trying to say kept getting stuck on sobs and sniffles.

Enough already—if Jed didn't get Berta and her sobs loaded into the wagon, she'd flood the whole damn place with all those tears.

"It'll be fine." Lucy smoothed her hand over Berta's hair and forced a smile. "Don't worry."

She caught Jed's eye and motioned for him to help. He eased the women apart and helped Berta up into the wagon beside Maggie.

"We sure appreciate all your help, Berta." He draped his arm casually around Lucy's shoulders. Instead of snuggling into his embrace as he'd grown used to, Lucy seemed to stiffen.

He was going to enjoy making her relax.

What the hell was taking Dwight so long to leave? All he had to do was take hold of the reins and turn the horses around. He fussed with his hat, took his sweet damn time putting his gloves on, then he sat there for what felt like four days just smiling down at Jed and Lucy.

Didn't he know Jed had work to do? He had a barn to build for cryin' out loud. 'Course he also had a wife who needed tending, and that would have to come first.

With a final salute, Dwight clicked to the horses and turned toward the road. As they pulled away, Berta twisted around in her seat and waved.

"Good-bye, Lucy," she called out. It looked as though she had more to say but didn't. The wagon bumped and rocked, knocking Berta sideways. She righted herself, waved and yelled even louder. "She loves you, Jedidiah. Believe in that!"

Lucy stiffened. So did Jed. The way Berta carried on, you'd think she wasn't coming back in a few short hours, hours Jed would much rather spend exploring his wife than wondering about his mother-in-law.

"So my wife loves me." He turned Lucy in his arms and gazed down into her amazing green eyes. "That's good because I l—"

"Don't say it." Lucy slapped her hand over his mouth.

Her hand was warm. Her hands were never warm. Even when the sun pounded down as it did then, she'd never been warm.

"Okay," Jed murmured against her palm. After a long moment, he eased her hand away and bent to nuzzle her neck. Lucy released a slow sigh as she tipped her head to the side, giving him better access to that soft, sensitive spot behind her ear.

"I reckon the new barn can wait a while longer, don't you?"

"The barn?" She tried to pull away, but he held her fast.

"Oh, no you don't." He slid his fingers through her hair, then down its length. "I've finally got you alone for a few hours, and we're going to make good use of it."

Lucy didn't move. She stared back at him intently, almost as if she was putting his face to memory.

He tucked her hands between his and pressed them against his chest. "It's true, isn't it?" he asked.

"True?"

"What Berta said." He lifted her hands to his lips and pressed slow kisses against each knuckle. "Do you love me?"

The clouds lifted from her eyes, until all that was left

was the same love Jed felt for her. He tipped her chin up and gazed down at her. "Say it. Tell me you love me."

Two tears slid out of the corners of her eyes. What the hell? Hadn't she run out of them by now? His mother had never been a crier. A yeller, yes, but never a crier.

If it was the last thing he did, he'd prove to Lucy that she had nothing to cry about. Their life was going to be perfect.

"No need for these," he murmured as he caught the tears on his finger. "Everything's going to be fine, Lucy. You love me and I lo—"

"Stop." She pushed against him, but there was no strength behind it.

"Why?" He frowned. Why couldn't she just say it? Why did she have to be so damned stubborn? "Just say it."

"Not yet." She clamped her mouth shut and swiped the tears from her cheeks. "I need to tell you something first."

"Tell me you love me. Nothing else matters."

"No, Jed, please, you have to hear this." Lucy licked her lips and hesitated. That was her first mistake.

"What?" He watched her mouth, the way her lips trembled, the way she moistened them with the tip of her tongue.

Hot damn, but he wanted to kiss her. And he would—after she told him she loved him.

"Tell me, Lucy." He leaned closer until his cheek brushed hers; his kisses grazed her jaw, then the tip of her nose. "Tell me you love me."

She turned her face, searching for his lips, but instead of kissing her, he covered her mouth with his left hand, while holding her fast around the waist with his other arm.

She struggled against him, her eyes wide, panicked. She didn't think he'd harm her, did she?

"I love you, Lucy." For a second, he thought he might

cry, too, but that was ridiculous. Instead, he grinned what must have been the stupidest looking grin, and kissed her nose again. "Plain and simple, I just love you."

She sagged against his hand, her hot tears searing his skin where they landed. After a moment, he lowered his hand and stepped back, waiting.

Lucy shook her head slowly, as her tears continued to fall. A giant knot twisted in Jed's gut. Maybe she *didn't* love him. Maybe he'd been wrong about what he felt— about what he thought *she* felt.

She continued to shake her head. "I'm sorry," she croaked. "I love you, too, and I'm so, so sorry."

"You're sorry?" he cried, pulling her into his arms, relief washing over him like a giant wave. "God, Lucy, you scared the hell out of me."

She pushed away again and stepped out of his reach. "You have to listen to me, Jed."

"I'm done listening, and you're done talking." He grinned as he reached for her. She ducked out of the way, then held up a hand to ward him off.

"No!" She moved around the big rock by the fire pit and crossed her arms over her chest. Then she let them fall to her sides. Twice more she crossed them, then let them fall. "You have to listen, to try and understand what I've done."

Jed stepped closer, every inch of him aching to touch her again; to slide his fingers through her silky hair, to feel the warmth of her bare skin against his, and to taste every inch of her.

"I've made a horrible mess." She circled around the rock, keeping one step ahead of him.

Jed shrugged. "So we'll clean it up later."

"N-no," she stammered. "We can't. I need to fix it right now."

She stopped moving and stood facing him. Something

wasn't right, something was obviously upsetting her, but if she'd only let him, he could make her forget her worries. He would take care of her.

He closed the distance between them, ready to take her in his arms.

"I've put you in terrible danger." Incredible anguish, plus a shot of relief, filled her voice. "And Maggie, too."

Jed stopped cold. "What?"

"I'm sorry," she went on, her words tumbling faster and faster. "When I first came here, to you, I didn't know you, I didn't know Maggie and I certainly didn't know myself."

"What are you talking about?" Jed stumbled slightly. Unease gurgled through his stomach.

Lucy took half a step toward him, then stopped. "I didn't come here to be your wife." Her words hung in the air between them. "I came here to save myself, and the only way to do that was to . . ."

She stopped, took a long breath, and stared at the toe of her boot. Fingers of ice crept up Jed's spine; fear, confusion and disbelief swirled in his blood.

"What have you done with Maggie?"

It took a long time for Lucy to look at him. Every passing second was another rip in his heart, every breath an agonizing chore.

"Maggie's fine. Berta is taking her to the preacher."

"The preacher? What about Doc Billings . . . ?" Jed frowned.

Lucy swallowed slowly. "The preacher's the only hope her baby has."

"What?" He stumbled back a step, reaching for the top rung of the corral.

"I came for the baby." Lucy's face had gone from pale to a sickly greenish color. Her mouth pinched against each word, and thick tears flowed steadily down her cheeks.

"The baby?" Jed's voice was drowned out by the sound of a wagon crashing down the road toward the ranch.

Maggie.

"Caine!" Dwight's terrified voice reached Jed's ears before the wagon rounded the corner into the yard. "Caine!"

With a sideways glance at Lucy, he raced toward the wagon. The horses foamed at their mouths, their eyes wide with fear, but Dwight's terror shadowed theirs. His arms shook, his breath came in shallow spurts, and his voice quaked uncontrollably.

"He took 'em," he said, looking left and right. "Took 'em, I tell ya."

"Who?" Jed reached for the bridle of the nearest horse, but it pulled away.

"M-Maggie," Dwight stuttered. "And M-Miss Blake. He took 'em."

"Who took them?"

"And Maggie . . ." Dwight's jittery gaze seemed to look everywhere at once, but seeing nothing. "Her baby . . . it's comin'."

"Dwight!" Jed shouted, bringing the other man's eyes back into focus. "Who took them?"

"Never seen him b'fore," Dwight answered, "but he's like the devil, I tell ya."

It felt as though an avalanche of rock had fallen inside Jed's stomach. "Deacon."

Lucy gasped behind him, then fell into deep gut-wrenching sobs.

"Where are they?" He had to yell it twice before Dwight answered.

"Couple m-miles back." Dwight's body shivered uncontrollably. "Th-that stable near Doc's."

"Take me." Jed moved toward the wagon seat, but Dwight slapped the reins against the horses and they shot off in the opposite direction.

Gravel sputtered from beneath the wheels as he raced back toward the road.

"I ain't goin' back," Dwight called over his shoulder. "He's the devil, I tell ya!"

"Dwight!"

But he was already gone, leaving behind a huge cloud of dust.

Without so much as a glance at Lucy, Jed raced toward the barn, pulling the tack down as he moved.

"Jed," Lucy's sob followed him inside. "You can't win against Deacon. I'll go."

His hands stilled against the saddle, as words dried on his tongue. Maggie had been right all this time, and he'd been too blind to see the truth.

He flipped down the stirrups, took up the reins and moved toward the door. He refused to look at her, refused to be taken in by the green of her eyes or the trembling of her lips.

"Why did he take them?" Lucy moved toward him, but he flinched and pushed past her. "Why?" he repeated as he hurled himself up into the saddle.

"He wants the baby's soul."

"He what?" Jed shook his head to settle the confusion.

He didn't have time to try to understand what she meant by *he wants the baby's soul*. All Jed could think about—all he *must* think about—was Maggie and her baby. He'd deal with Lucy afterward.

Jed spurred the horse into a run and didn't look back.

CHAPTER TWENTY-ONE

J ed was gone.

He knew the truth—at least the beginnings of it—and now would never look at her again. He would never touch her, never kiss her, and never again would he warm her with the heat from his smile or the burning desire in his dark, beautiful eyes.

Lucy mopped her eyes and ran her arm under her nose. She'd never get Jed back; no human could forgive something like this. All she could do was focus on Maggie and the baby. If she was in labor already, then they were rapidly running out of time.

As she fought to think clearly, Lucy moved back inside the barn. She couldn't stay there, doing nothing.

Jed's anger and confusion would only add fuel to Deacon's powers. The only hope Maggie and her baby had was with Lucy.

And the only hope Lucy had of making any of this right was to find the preacher.

The only horse in the barn, a huge black beast with white feet, snorted and side-stepped away when Lucy neared him. She reached for its bridle, but the horse jerked out of reach, then reared slightly.

Damned animal! Lucy didn't have time to calm it; she needed to get to the preacher. She hurried from the stall and stood outside, calling on powers she hated.

Deacon could appear and disappear whenever he liked, and today, so would she. She closed her eyes and forced herself to concentrate on the small church she'd seen at the edge of town.

Nothing.

She tried again, and again, but nothing worked. She couldn't even move herself across the yard.

Damn Deacon. And damn her father. This was their doing.

Lifting her skirt, she ran back inside the barn and jerked the stall door open. The huge horse side-stepped again, nostrils flaring, eyes huge.

"I'm going to ride you," Lucy stated. "Saddle or no, it's going to happen."

Before the animal could rear at her again, she grabbed its mane and jerked its head toward her own.

"I *will* ride you."

The horse tried to pull out of her grasp, but Lucy yanked harder. With both hands now fisted in the thick mane, she led the animal closer to the stall gate. Using its rungs as a ladder, she scrambled up and threw her leg over the horse's back.

"Run!"

It didn't need to be told twice. With Lucy bent over its shoulders, the horse raced out of the barn toward the road, trying to get away from the thing that spooked it so badly. Lucy dug her knees into the horse's sides, kept her hands fisted in its mane and her cheek pressed against its neck.

As they sped past the side road to Doc's, Lucy didn't

dare look. She needed to focus on the preacher and how she was going to convince him to come with her.

❖ ❖ ❖

Jed reined in his horse and leapt from the saddle before it had even stopped. The animal reared back, snorted and ran back the way they'd come, but Jed charged forward.

"Get away from her!"

Maggie lay in the shade of the towering pecan tree, her face contorted in pain, her hair matted with dirt and sweat. Berta, who'd been hovering beside her, bounced up at the first sight of Jed. Deacon simply lounged against the side of the dilapidated, open stable, petting his stupid weasel.

"Where's Lucy?" Berta flung herself toward Jed, her face awash with guilt and fear.

She'd known.

She'd known, and he'd let her care for Maggie. Jed shrugged past her and headed straight for the tree.

"Maggie." He knelt beside her, taking her hand in his and smoothing her hair back from her face. "I'm so sorry."

"I told you," she whispered weakly. "I told you they wanted my baby."

"Hello, Jedidiah." Deacon sneered over the rodent's head. "So good to see you again."

Jed lunged at him, but caught empty air. Deacon now stood on the other side of the stable, at least three feet away, completely unaffected by Jed's attack.

"Tut, tut. Such violent behavior."

"Son of a bitch," Jed growled. "I swear to God—"

Deacon's laughter was like ice through his veins.

"Your god does not frighten me, human." Even as

he spoke, fear flicked across his face, then vanished. "You can't save them, no matter what Lucille might have told you."

Maggie whimpered softly behind him.

Jed twisted between Maggie and Deacon, trying to keep Berta in his sights, too.

"What do you want?" he asked, fighting to keep his voice calm.

"Surely Lucille has explained all that by now." Deacon lifted his bowler hat from his head, brushed a glove over it, and set it back in place. "I'm here for the child."

Maggie cried out, and Berta was right there to comfort her.

"It's okay now, Maggie," she said softly. "Jedidiah won't let anything happen to you or your baby."

Deacon tipped his head toward the women. "Miss Blake is mistaken. Jedidiah can no sooner prevent this from happening than he can prevent the sun from rising."

"Shut the hell up." Jed's voice was dangerously low.

"Can't do that," Deacon said plainly. "Hell is wide open and waiting."

A door swung open in Jed's brain. *No. It couldn't be. There wasn't really fire in Deacon's eyes; it had to be a reflection—except there was no fire. The sun maybe . . . ?*

Jed didn't know where to look, so he continued to shift his gaze between everyone.

"What did your wife tell you?" Deacon asked. He looked so calm, so cool, that it was all Jed could do not to lunge at him again.

"That's none of your business," he ground out.

"Actually, it is," Deacon countered. "It's a family business." Very slowly, he stepped out from behind the railing and began to walk in wide circles around the tree.

An overwhelming sense of dread filled Jed, begging him to shut his ears to everything Deacon said, to shut his heart to everything Lucy hadn't said.

And she obviously hadn't said a helluva lot.

Deacon clicked his tongue in disgust. "Your wife is not who you think she is."

Jed reached for the closest post for support. "Who . . . ?" He didn't want to know. He didn't. Lucy was his wife and that's all that mattered. She'd put them all in some sort of danger, but Jed would fix it.

Deacon came around the back of the tree, then paused close to Berta's back. "Lucille's mother is this wretched creature you've kept as a guest, the one who offered to help you." He rolled his eyes and snorted softly. "But she was of no help to *you*, human."

Jed stood in the blasting heat of the sun, but it was a cold sweat that trickled down his neck.

"Did Lucille ever tell you about our father?"

"Deacon, no." Berta reached a hand toward him, as though she could stop his words with a simple gesture, but the look Deacon shot her momentarily froze her in mid-movement.

Jed released a breath. "A little."

"A little," Deacon repeated over a snort. He crossed his arms over his chest and tsked. "Did that 'little' include the fact he's Satan?"

"Who?" No. *No!* Fire burned Jed's throat. A vise gripped his lungs, making breathing near to impossible.

Satan? The *devil*? As in—

"Lucifer." The word slipped from his tongue and he watched in horror as Berta shuddered at its sound.

Lucy Firr.

*   *   *

Lucy stood at the bottom of the steps and stared up at the church door. Reverend Conroy was their only hope. She had to go inside, consequences be damned.

The small chapel was a place of hope, a place where humans gathered to find comfort and peace from life's torment. It was too much to hope she'd find any peace inside, but she wasn't asking for herself, she was asking for Maggie. And for Maggie's baby.

"Stay here," she spoke low, hoping against hope the horse would do as instructed. Without another thought, Lucy hurried up the steps and pushed open the door. She took a moment to let her eyes adjust, fought past the tightness in her chest, and stepped toward the man hunched over the pulpit.

"Reverend Conroy?"

His head jerked up, his eyes widened, and his knuckles whitened around the edge of the pulpit.

"You—" His grainy voice was a mere whisper.

Lucy moved closer, but stopped when he recoiled. Reverend Conroy's mouth twisted around each word he spoke.

"Away from me, Satan! For it is written: Worship the Lord your God, and serve Him only."

"Reverend, please." Lucy took another step toward him.

"You dare set foot in the House of the Lord." His eyes rolled upward for a moment, as though expecting God to send a bolt of lightening down upon her. To both of their surprise, nothing happened.

"I need your help."

"You are beyond any help I can give." He held a well-worn Bible at arm's length and stepped down from the pulpit. But instead of moving away from Lucy, he advanced toward her, forcing her back toward the door.

"Well, it's not actually for me," she hurried to explain.

She bumped into the pew behind her, righted herself, and continued to back up. "It's Maggie Caine. She needs your protection."

"From what?"

A sudden lump in Lucy's throat made her stop, swallow hard, and blink back fresh tears.

"From me. From my brother. And from my . . . my father."

Reverend Conroy stopped walking, but continued to hold the Bible at chest level. "Your . . . f-father?"

Lucy nodded. "There's no time to talk about this now. Maggie is in grave danger and if you don't come with me, she's going to lose her baby."

Reverend Conroy hesitated, uncertainty making him balk. "Maggie has been ill for quite some time. How do I know this isn't some kind of trick? How do I know you're not here for me?"

"Reverend." Lucy inhaled a long slow breath. "If I were here for myself, or for anything my father wanted, do you honestly believe I would have made it through that door?"

He shot a glance toward the door, then back at Lucy. She watched as realization fell over him. It was the truth. The God he served would have struck her down before she made it to the top step.

"Please, Reverend. They're after Maggie's baby."

The man's thin face paled, then flushed. He closed his eyes, steepled his fingers in front of his face and murmured, "Strengthen me, Father. Fill me with your Spirit." With a short nod at Lucy, he added quietly, "Take me to her."

"Do you ride?" Lucy asked, leading him outside. The black horse stood where she'd left it, nibbling the dry weeds at its feet.

"No," Reverend Conroy answered, not bothering to close the door behind him. "I have a carriage."

"Today you ride." She led the horse over to the church stairs and nodded. "Climb on."

Without a second glance, he handed Lucy his Bible and scrambled up onto the animal's back. The book felt odd in Lucy's hands, warm and smooth, almost comforting. Yet at the same time, the weight of it terrified her.

He took the Bible from her, wrapped his hand around her forearm and helped pull her up behind him.

"Go!"

* * *

Jed couldn't move. Not because that sonuvabitch had done his freezing thing on him, but because he barely had the strength to remain upright, never mind anything else.

Deacon scanned the ground around him, then took a hesitant step. "Lucille and I are both children of the devil, but her mother is this human woman. So unlike myself, Lucille is half mortal, half demon. So much strength and so much weakness in one being."

Jed wanted to fall to the ground, to cover his ears and refuse to listen. But Deacon went on as calmly as if he were discussing the color of the sky.

"We were raised in Hell alongside the rest of the damned, and considering her obvious shortcomings, I think Lucille managed fairly well." His evil gaze flicked between Jed and the two women on the ground. "But, being who she is, being *what* she is, she's always held on to the unfortunate hope that she would somehow get out. Of course, she knew she'd never be able to live a completely mortal life, but as long as she thought she could get out of Hell, she was going to try."

Maggie's cries brought Jed around. She needed his help, but what the hell could he do? He searched around frantically for something—anything—he could use to protect her.

Nothing.

Deacon's voice rattled in Jed's brain.

"Our father offered her a deal: Bring him a newborn soul, or be cast down to the darkest corner of Hell where she would never again have a chance at freedom." He shook his head slowly, almost as though he couldn't believe what he was saying. "It couldn't have been an easier job. I already had a deal in the works with Sam, and Sam's wife had a baby on the way, so it was simply a matter of securing its soul."

Jed fought the urge to wretch. If this were true, if Lucy were the devil's daughter and after the baby's soul, that meant Maggie wasn't crazy. She knew what had been going on all the time, but Jed had been too stupid to believe her.

He'd been so distracted by his lust that he didn't give Maggie the attention she deserved. The attention Sam would have wanted her to have.

Sam.

Jed forced himself to look at Deacon. "What did you do with Sam?"

Deacon frowned in confusion, but only for a second. "Oh, yes, Sam." He tipped his head to the side a little, and smiled. "It's because of him that you're all here."

"No," Maggie sobbed. "Sam loves me. He'd never do anything to hurt our baby."

"Shhh." Berta's worried face gazed down at Maggie, who struggled to sit up. "You mustn't get up."

Jed spied a mound of hay in the corner of the stable and moved toward it. "Please, Maggie, listen to Berta."

"Don't talk to me, Jed," Maggie screamed. "You brought

that devil-woman here! You did this! Sam would never have done anything to—"

"Sam is dead." Deacon's emotionless words hung in the air for what felt like an eternity before they settled in Jed's heart.

"No!" Maggie's cry echoed across the sky as she curled her arms over her belly, and turned her back on Deacon. "No," she sobbed.

Jed scrambled to arrange the pile of hay as some kind of cushion. Then he ripped his shirt off and laid it on top.

While Deacon continued to talk and circle them, Jed and Berta moved Maggie over to the hay and tried to make her comfortable.

"Your Sam was such a worrier. Worried this child would turn out the same as the others and never draw breath, worried his wife wouldn't survive the birth—"

"You sonuvabitch!" Jed rose to his feet and lunged toward Deacon, who once again vanished and appeared a few feet away.

"So when I made him an offer," Deacon went on, as carefree as the wind, "he took it."

"What offer?" Jed's teeth clenched tight, his fists tighter.

"Nothing difficult," Deacon answered. "His soul would be mine in exchange for a healthy baby."

Jed started. "His soul . . . but . . ." He stopped and inhaled until his lungs threatened to burst. This was too much. Too crazy.

Too real.

His rage grew hotter and deeper. "If you already have Sam, you have no claim to this child."

"Humans." Deacon chuckled softly. "You're so gullible." He pulled the ferret out of his pocket and stroked it gently. "Remember who you're dealing with here, Jedidiah. Integrity is not something we're known for."

Jed blinked hard. This whole thing was just wrong.

"It's not that difficult to understand." Deacon rolled his eyes impatiently. "The newborn soul is the purest soul, unaffected by the trials and tribulations of life, and ripe for us to take. When our father sets his sights on one, he does whatever it takes to get it."

Jed choked back bile. "But why Maggie? Why Sam?""

Deacon shrugged. "The opportunity presented itself." He stopped to watch Maggie fight through an increasingly painful contraction. "Sam started it all with the deal he made. He may have done it with good intentions, but we all know where that road leads."

He chuckled at his own joke, then continued, "With his soul at our disposal, we had access to his child and the child's mother. Lucille assumed the child was hers to take but, of course, our father saw things differently."

Jed fought to make sense of this. "You killed Sam."

"I'm many things," Deacon said, outraged, "but not a murderer. Sam did that himself. I just took his soul."

"*Just?*" Jed choked. "And then you used his disappearance to make Maggie crazy."

"Yes."

"And Lucy came here thinking she could get the baby's soul to trade for her own."

"Very good, Jedidiah."

Jed swallowed hard. "But that's not what's happening here."

"No." A patronizing smile lifted Deacon's lips. "I knew you'd catch on sooner or later."

"So—" Jed tried to steady his breathing. "What do you want with us?"

Deacon cocked his brow slightly and smirked. "You are all simply a means to an end," he said. "The baby is what's important."

A strange darkness began to build inside Jed. He frowned against the pounding in his head. It was as though someone had stuffed his brain full of dirt and no matter how hard he dug, he couldn't find his way out.

Deacon nuzzled his ferret for another moment before tucking it back in his pocket. Maggie fought her way through another pain; her teeth ground hard together, her right hand fisted around Berta's skirt.

"To get to the baby, Lucy first needed to get to the man protecting it. She needed to make you love her so much you'd be willing to give her anything—including your own soul." He stopped, hands clasped behind his back. "Of course that meant you would be condemned to Hell in her stead, but that's a small price to pay to keep herself out."

Deacon might as well have reached in and ripped Jed's heart straight out of his chest. He *would* have given Lucy his soul if she'd asked him for it. He'd have done anything for her.

Now . . .

Reacting on impulse alone, Jed dove at Deacon, but he'd vanished again.

"You think you can hurt me, human?" Deacon snorted from a few feet away. "You have no idea who you're dealing with, do you?" He shook his head pitifully. "Think, Jedidiah—she gave you enough clues."

The darkness inside Jed grew deeper. What clues? Her name, of course, but what else? He started to walk, then crashed against the tree trunk.

"Reverend Conroy."

"Very good, human," Deacon sneered. "No being with Satan's blood would dare stand before a man of the cloth."

"Jed." Berta's worried voice pulled him back. "We don't have much time."

Maggie's whole body heaved with uncontrollable sobs and almost constant pain—the pain that would soon push the baby from her womb. What could he do? How could he possibly protect Maggie from something like Deacon?

"It'll be over soon," Deacon said. "Nothing to do now but wait."

"No." Berta pushed to her feet and stormed toward both men. They each started, found their balance, and stepped out of reach of her jabbing finger.

"You," she barked at Deacon, "are nothing but a spineless coward. There is no hope for someone like you."

He simply cocked his brow at her and flicked his hand as though to wave away her words.

"But you." She turned on Jed and jabbed her finger into the middle of his chest. "You are better than this, Jed. You know what needs to be done."

"Berta—"

"No." She stopped him with her raised hand. Deacon snickered, but Jed and Berta ignored him. "I've listened to you and him"—she indicated Deacon with a nod of her head—"go on about things that can no longer be helped. God bless him, but Sam is dead. We can't do anything about that."

"But—" Jed tried to interrupt.

"Lucy came here to win her freedom," Berta continued, "and she was bent on doing whatever it took to get it." Berta stepped closer and jabbed him in the chest with her finger. "But even you can't be stupid enough not to notice she's changed."

Jed didn't answer, just stood there, staring down at this half-crazed woman who kept poking him.

"She could have taken you down long before today." Her voice rose with each word until she was on tiptoe, yelling in his face. "She could have been done with all of this, and she could have been the one sitting here waiting on that baby."

Maggie cried out as another pain ripped through her. Jed and Berta both cast anxious glances back to the stable, even as Berta continued yelling.

"But she didn't, did she?"

"She's always been weak," Deacon interjected.

Berta ignored him and pushed her glasses up her nose. "It has nothing to do with weakness, Jed. It has to do with strength."

He shook his head and made to move away from her, but she gripped his arm with the strength of a woman possessed.

"She loves you, Jed." When he shook his head, she nodded harder. "Yes she does. She loves you. And you love her."

Deacon let go a loud snort. "Lucille is the devil's daughter, incapable of love."

"No, Deacon." Berta spun to face him, a bundle of fire yelling loud enough to wake the dead. "*You* forget who she is. Lucy is my daughter—part human and fully capable of every emotion possible."

That shut him up for a second.

"B-Berta," Maggie gasped, reaching through the air for something to hold. Berta was at her side in a heartbeat. Jed's brain spun out of control remembering the things Lucy had said to him. She'd told him her life had been hell, but he never thought she'd meant it literally. Everyone's life was hell once in a while.

The rest of his thoughts were drowned out by the sound of pounding hooves. What now?

Reverend Conroy, clinging desperately to the horse's mane, raced toward them, his white collar standing out in stark contrast to his black suit.

And sitting behind him, with her arms wrapped around his waist, was Lucy. Her long black hair blew behind her, and her eyes—those deep emerald pools Jed had loved so much—focused on two things: Maggie and Deacon.

Deacon sucked in a sharp breath, stopped moving, and seemed struck dumb, but not for long. "What have you done, Lucille?" he bellowed, his voice hard and brittle.

Reverend Conroy jerked the animal to a stop, jumped off, and quickly helped Lucy down. He cast a quick, terrified glance in Deacon's direction, then skirted around him to where Maggie lay in the hay. The horse reared and shot off back down the road.

Reverend Conroy knelt beside Maggie, clutched his Bible to his chest and began to make the sign of the cross. "In the name o-of the Father . . ." His voice shook slightly, but he kept on, "and the Son—"

"And the Holy Spirit," Berta's voice, strong and steady, joined his.

"Jed." Lucy hurried toward him, but he backed away. How could he have been so stupid?

"Do you know what you've done?" Deacon cried, his hands flailing. "Do you have any idea what *he*'s going to do to you?"

The emphasis on the word *he* made it perfectly clear to Jed who Deacon meant, but Lucy didn't so much as spare her brother a glance.

"You have to listen to me," she pleaded, her eyes already full of unshed tears. "Please!"

Jed shook his head and tried to back away more, but she continued to match him step for step.

"I'm sure Deacon has told you everything." Her voice shook with each word. "I know it's horrible, and I know you probably hate me, but Deacon doesn't know what really happened."

Jed swallowed as hard as she did.

"Jed." She reached for his arm, but he jerked out of the way. "I love you."

Deacon stepped right up close to her, until his face was mere inches away. "You brought a preacher!" he yelled. "A preacher!"

Lucy turned on her brother with such ferocity, it sent a rip of fear through Jed's veins.

"Yes!" she yelled back. "I brought a preacher."

"But the child . . ."

An evil little smile tugged at Lucy's lips. "You lose."

"But—"

Lucy didn't wait for him to finish. She turned back to Jed, her expression softer, her eyes pleading. "I did it," she said. "I'm so sorry, but I did. I came here . . . to you . . . to make you love me and then take your soul. And the baby's. And yes, I tried my hardest to seduce you. But you—" She hiccupped on a sob, then dashed away more tears. "You were so damned stubborn. You insisted we had to respect each other, to build trust between us before we could . . ."

Her voice tripped, but she stopped only long enough to catch her breath.

"And somehow, Jed, you did it. You made me respect you. You made *me* love *you*."

Jed couldn't think clearly. He pressed his back against the tree, then slid to a crouch. In the back of his mind, the preacher's voice droned on, first through the Lord's Prayer, then on through the Psalms. And Berta's voice matched his word for word.

"I didn't make you do anything." The throbbing pain in his chest reflected back in her eyes.

"Yes, you did." She fell to the ground beside him, and gripped his hands in hers. "You made me work, and I don't just mean around the house. You made me work for your love, for your respect. And somehow, it turned around on me."

He stared at their hands, twined around each other. God, what he wouldn't give to go back a couple hours. Back to before he waved Berta and Dwight on their way, and his whole world caved in on him. Back to before his wife said she loved him, and then in the next breath told him she was the devil's daughter.

He pulled his hands away.

"Don't." How could he have been so stupid? He knew from the first second he'd seen Lucy at the damned auction that she was nothing but trouble.

Eyes that had once snapped with green flames now pleaded with him in desperation. Gone was the distrust he'd seen those first days. All that remained was raw emotion, begging him to love her. To forget who she was and that she'd done nothing but lie to him from the start.

He should have run from that auction and never looked back. He never should have let himself be swayed into taking her for his wife.

Jed dropped his chin to his chest and ground the heels of his hands against his eyes. Who was he trying to fool? No one had swayed him into marrying Lucy. He'd done it himself. He had taken her as his wife and then fallen head-over-heels-stupid in love with her.

CHAPTER
TWENTY-TWO

Deacon paced like a madman, making quick turns, chewing his thumbnail and muttering to himself. Lucy ignored him and focused completely on Jed. She took his hands back in hers, willing him to feel her love. If she could do that, maybe he wouldn't hate her quite so much. It would make the eternity she faced in Hell slightly more bearable.

"I had no idea that what I felt for you—what was scaring me so badly—was love." She squeezed his hands, milking them for the warmth only he could give her. "It was Berta who made me see it.

"If it hadn't been for Berta . . ." Lucy's voice hitched in her throat. "I might never have known that I could love."

If only Jed would look at her.

"I might never have known that what I felt for you, what filled me with so much light, was love."

Deacon stopped his pacing and snorted loudly behind her. "Yes," he said, his voice dripping with sarcasm. "She loved you so much, she was willing to condemn you and the rest of your family to an eternity in Hell."

Lucy lifted her chin and forced her voice to stop

trembling. "Not anymore. I won't do this, Deacon, and I won't let you do it either."

His laughter was anything but joyful. Instead, it was the same condescending sound it always was when he spoke to Lucy. "Have you forgotten—again—who we're dealing with? Our father will not be left empty-handed."

"He won't be." She squared her shoulders. "He sent you to make sure I failed, and I did." She swallowed a stomach full of bile and forced the quiver out of her voice. "So do it. Take me back."

Jed was on his feet, realization flooding his face. He grabbed Lucy by the shoulders and held on. "No."

"Yes." She couldn't swallow fast enough to stop the tears. "We have no other choice. Reverend Conroy is here, so the baby is protected. Deacon can't touch it."

They both looked down at Maggie, her face red, her muscles straining; and Berta who knelt beside her, praying as hard and as fast as Reverend Conroy.

Fury raged in Deacon's eyes, but before he could move, Lucy caught him in an invisible grip, freezing him.

There was no telling how long her hold on Deacon would last. He'd always been much stronger than she was.

"Jed, listen to me."

She stepped closer, hating the fear she saw in his eyes; fear of her and what she was, and fear of what he thought she would do to him.

"We don't have much time," she said. "But you have to believe I love you, Jed. If I didn't, I would have finished you and Maggie off last night and you never would have known what happened."

The pain etched across his face ripped through her.

"I needed you to love me, and you did. The only thing missing were the words."

A stifled grunt sounded from Deacon, but his lips remained frozen.

"I tried . . ." Jed trailed off, his frown deep.

"I know." She reached for his hands, willing her love to flow through them. "But I couldn't let you. I was so confused, I didn't know what I was feeling or what I would do if you said it."

She dared a glance back at her brother. His face had turned a fiery red. He'd soon be free. "I was stupid enough to believe my father when he said I could be free. But he was never going to let me go, even if I did take the child."

"You knew about Sam." Torment twisted Jed's features. "And you didn't say anything."

"It happened before I came here, and there was nothing I could do about it."

"But you knew." He spun away, raked his hands through his hair, and muttered more curses than Lucy had ever heard—even in Hell. After a long moment, he turned back to her. "Are Maggie and the baby really safe?" he asked warily.

She pressed her palms flat against his chest. "Yes." She choked on a sob. "But you're not."

His head hung low, his shoulders slumped. "Maggie knew. She *knew* and I didn't believe her." Jed shook his head slowly; every ounce of his pain seeped into Lucy, searing her from the inside out.

"I'm sorry," she whispered. "I wanted to be free of it all, and I didn't care who got hurt."

Very slowly, Jed lifted his face to hers.

"And now?" He seized her wrists and narrowed his eyes at her. "What about now?"

Her wrists pinched in his grasp, but she didn't try to escape.

"Now I know Deacon was right. I was stupid."

"To Hell with Deacon," he growled. "I'm talking about us. What happens to us?"

A blast of warmth shot through her heart, followed immediately by a rip so painful it made her gasp. "If you trust me and believe me when I say I love you more than anything else, then you can save yourself."

Darkness clouded Jed's face. "What do you mean? What about you?"

She tried to free herself from the heat of his touch, but he refused to release her. "Deacon will never let me go. His power—his hatred—is too strong."

"Deacon has nothing to do with you two." Berta's voice made them both jump. Her face was flushed and sweat trickled down her cheeks. "You can win this—you just have to trust in what you know."

Deacon burst out of his freeze and stumbled face-first to the ground. Horrified, he pushed to his feet and stared at the toe of his boot and his once-white ferret, both now covered in a thin layer of brown dust.

"Ugh," he grunted as he pulled a handkerchief from his pocket and began wiping the dust from his pet.

"Sonuvabitch." Jed whirled, swinging his fist toward Deacon, but he'd already moved.

A smug little smile lifted Deacon's mouth. "Temper temper, human."

Before Jed could swing again, Lucy moved herself between him and Deacon. "Don't." She wrapped her hand around his fist and eased it back to his side. "If you can believe that I love you, if you can hold that in your heart, Deacon can never take you."

Deacon settled his ferret back inside his coat pocket and stood with his arms crossed over his chest, his bowler hat sitting slightly off-center and his fancy black suit looking like he'd just had it cleaned and pressed.

"Lovely words coming from you," Deacon scoffed. "Considering you're the one who put the human in this situation to start with. If that's what you call love—"

Jed lunged for him again, but Lucy pulled him back.

"Look at me," she repeated.

He resisted. His hatred for Deacon poured out of him as fast as Lucy's tears fell. She could feel darkness falling over him, but she had to stop it. She couldn't let his light be snuffed out as hers was about to be.

She took his hand and pressed it flat against her left breast. Jed stared at it for a minute, then locked gazes with her. Those deep, dark eyes that had warmed her through so many times were now flooded with confusion and doubt.

"You gave it light," she murmured. "And you made it grow. There's nothing Deacon can say to make that any different."

Jed swallowed. His gaze flickered to their hands, his brow furrowed. Maybe, just maybe he was beginning to believe her.

"How touching." Deacon rolled his eyes. "Jedidiah, perhaps it's time for you to come clean with Lucille, too."

"What is he talking about?" Lucy asked haltingly. Jed would never lie to her. Would he? If only he'd look at her, she'd feel a lot better.

"Tell her," Deacon said. "Tell her about your relationship with your sister-in-law. Or I will."

Reverend Conroy continued to read from the Bible, his left hand clutching its binding, while his right hand lifted in prayer over Maggie's head.

Lucy frowned. Why did Jed seem so unnerved?

"There's nothing to tell," he said, his voice flat. "She married my brother."

"You were not the first woman your beloved human

proposed to," Deacon began. "Unless I'm mistaken, his dear sister-in-law is his first love."

Jed's eyes squeezed shut for a moment, before he blinked down at her.

"Jed?" Lucy stepped back a bit.

"That's not all, is it, Jedidiah?" Deacon's taunting voice echoed through Lucy's heart. "His brother hadn't been gone but a few days before he proposed a second time."

"You sonuvabitch," Jed ground out. "That's not how it was."

Deacon snorted. "No? Are you saying you didn't propose to her? And not just once, but twice?"

Jed's dark eyes gazed desperately at Lucy. His only answer was a brief nod.

A sharp sob ripped out of Lucy's throat.

"It was before I knew you," he said, reaching for her hands. "I never loved her."

"But—"

"No." He shook his head and sighed heavily. "I thought she would make a good wife, a sensible one who'd work hard and not question me at every turn. And even though she refused to believe Sam was gone, I knew it. I could feel it in my gut, and I knew Sam would want his wife and child taken care of."

Lucy's heart began to soften again. The Jed Caine she'd first met, the one at the auction, had been looking for the same thing in a wife.

"I never loved her," he repeated quietly, then choked on his next breath. "I've only ever loved you."

A low growl started in Deacon's throat. His anger was a double-edged sword. Good, because it meant Jed wasn't going along with what Deacon wanted; bad because his anger made him stronger, which would make it more difficult for Jed to defend himself.

Lucy dashed her arm across her eyes.

"And I've only ever loved you," she said, pouring everything she had into the touch of their hands. "Hold on to that."

She leaned up and kissed his mouth, soft and slow. Tears ran over her lips and when she looked up, it nearly killed her to see wet streaks down Jed's cheeks. "I'm so sorry," she whispered. "I hope someday you can forgive me."

She stepped back from him and started toward Deacon.

✽　✽　✽

"No!" Jed's voice thundered across the yard. "Lucy stays with me."

Lucy took a long time to face him. "I can't."

The pain in her eyes matched that in his heart. She was scared, too. Terrified.

But Jed wasn't. Not anymore. He'd gone way beyond scared and moved right on to burning anger.

Fury.

"Yes, you can." He stood straight, kept his voice calm and held out his hand for her to take.

"Humans." Deacon's laughter chilled the air. "You have no idea what you're up against."

Jed snorted. "You think I'm scared of you—a cowardly little rat who hides behind his fear?"

"Jed." Lucy gasped his name.

"Careful, human," Deacon said, his voice rising. "Lucille warned you about my powers. I can just as easily take you, too."

"So do it."

Lucy gasped again.

"He won't." Jed kept his eyes focused on Deacon. "He can't."

"Jed, please."

"Best listen to your wife, human," Deacon warned. "I can hurt you in ways you can't even imagine."

"Go ahead." He stepped closer to Deacon, daring him with each breath. "I'll still love Lucy. And she'll still love me."

Deacon's features darkened, his eyes bulged, and for a second, Jed wondered if he'd sprout horns. "She was willing to whore herself to get your soul."

Though Lucy remained upright, Jed felt a tiny part of her slip away.

"That's right," Deacon went on, curling his lips into an evil smile at Lucy. "A lying whore. That's all she was. That's all she'll ever be."

She slipped again. Deacon's smile widened. What the hell was going on?

"You're wrong." Jed fought to remain strong. He couldn't let Deacon's words hurt him or Lucy. He had to hold on. But to what?

"The baby's coming!" Berta's cry froze everyone where they stood.

Reverend Conroy's voice grew louder, stronger. "Then your light will break forth like the dawn, and your healing will quickly appear; then your righteousness will go before you and the glory of the Lord will be your rear guard."

Every muscle in Maggie's body contracted at the same time. Jed and Lucy stepped closer, but Deacon remained back, his growing fury almost palpable.

"Bear down, Maggie." Berta's soft, calm voice spoke over the reverend's. Kneeling between Maggie's legs, Berta kept one hand on her contracting belly and the other on the baby's crowning head. "Good. Do it again."

Jed stared in awe at everything going on around him. If

Lucy was lying to him still, this baby would soon be ripped from its family. And that would no doubt be Maggie's undoing.

Lucy was struggling to unbutton her dress. *What the hell . . . ?*

"Help me." She backed toward Jed, who took over undoing the buttons, but why he had no idea. When he was done, she pulled her arms out of the dress and struggled to keep it up. She turned to Jed. "Hold this."

He did as instructed, and while he held her dress up, she managed to somehow wiggle out of her chemise, slip her arms back in the sleeves, and jerked her thumb at the buttons. As if in a trance, his fingers skittered over each button, fumbling to find its matching hole.

Deacon's fuming grew louder, and though Jed didn't look at him, he wouldn't have been surprised to see flames coming out Deacon's ears. If the baby was safe, as Lucy said, why was Deacon still there? He could have taken Lucy and Jed at any time, so what was he waiting for?

Lucy knelt next to Berta, her chemise draped over her arms, waiting for the child.

There was a collective gasp as Maggie pushed the wailing baby out and into Lucy's waiting hands.

"No," Maggie sobbed. "Give me my baby!"

Reverend Conroy fumbled beneath his trouser leg and pulled a small knife from inside his sock. With a guilty shrug, he handed it to Berta.

"No!" Maggie continued to wail. "Don't hurt my baby!"

Jed held his breath. This was Lucy's chance to save herself. This was what she'd come for, and everyone's lives rested in what she did next. And now it made sense; this is what Deacon was waiting for.

Would Lucy give him the child?

With deft hands, Berta knotted the umbilical cord and

used the preacher's knife to cut it. Lucy snuggled the wriggling infant deeper into her embrace and gently tucked the edges of her chemise over its head and around its tiny body.

"Lucille." Deacon's voice wavered slightly. "Give it to me."

Tears coursed down her cheeks as she leaned closer and pressed a soft kiss to the baby's forehead. Then, smiling brilliantly, she shuffled forward and leaned down to Maggie. "You have a beautiful baby girl."

Maggie struggled to sit up while reaching for her child at the same time. Lucy waited until the baby was secure in Maggie's arms before completely releasing her, and stepping away.

"No!" Deacon's fury bounced off the tree and echoed off into the distance. "Lucille!"

CHAPTER
TWENTY-THREE

*L*ucy. Jed watched in horror as she began to back away from Maggie, past where Jed stood, and closer to Deacon. It was as though everything was happening in slow motion. He reached toward her, but missed; she slipped past, shaking her head and smiling back at him through her tears.

"Jed." Berta's one word, like a distant echo in his mind, shocked him back to his senses.

Lucy was going to leave him. Worse than that, Deacon was going to take her back to . . .

The hell with that.

"Lucy." He grasped her by the shoulders, glanced behind him at Maggie's baby, then focused everything he had on Lucy. His wife. "Why did you do that?"

Lucy dashed away her tears and gazed lovingly at the baby now curled up to its mother's breast.

"Look at that, Jed," she murmured. "It's a miracle."

He didn't need to follow her gaze to understand. "Yes," he nodded. "It is."

After a long moment, she sighed and turned back to him. The ache he saw in her eyes ripped a hole a mile wide across his heart.

"You're my miracle," she said quietly, her hands pressed flat against his chest. "Because of you I know what love is. And I'll carry that with me for the rest of my life."

She made to pull out of Jed's hold, but he tightened his grip. "Lucy."

"I love you," she sniffed. "I'm so sorry."

Berta's voice beckoned. "Jed, we need to get Maggie some proper care. We can't leave her out here like this."

"Go to Maggie," Lucy whispered. "She needs you."

"Perhaps one of us should walk back to town," Reverend Conroy suggested hesitantly.

"You're not going anywhere, Reverend," Berta snapped. "I'll go."

But nobody moved. Not a footstep sounded behind Jed. He hadn't taken his eyes off Lucy through any of it. Even through her ocean of tears, he felt her strength, felt the love she had for not only him, but his family. Her family.

"Go," she whispered again. "It's the right thing."

Deacon moved forward to take her by the arm, but Jed was quicker. "She stays."

"Lucille." Deacon's voice grew tighter, lower.

Jed's heart swelled. Deacon couldn't hurt them. They loved each other, and that was the one thing the devil couldn't win against.

Just as a smile began to work its way across his mouth, Lucy moved. Jed's smile faded as one began to spread across Deacon's face.

"Lucy?"

"I'm sorry," she said. "I can't let him hurt you, Jed."

"He can't!"

"You don't understand—"

"I understand he's a spineless coward."

Lucy sucked in a breath.

"Careful, human," Deacon growled.

"You can't do anything to us," Jed said, surprised at the strength in his own voice. "You can't make me love her any less."

"She came to take your soul."

"And she did," Jed replied. "Whether she's here with me or not, my heart and soul belong to her."

Deacon's lips squeezed white against the burning red fury of his face.

"I won't let you take her," Jed said calmly.

Deacon laughed without humor. "You won't *let* me? Try to stop me, human."

Jed ignored him, speaking directly to Lucy. "You saved the baby, Lucy. Let me save you."

She kept her eyes cast down as she shook her head.

"Then take me with you."

"No!" Her head whipped up, her eyes huge, and she lunged toward Jed. "No."

Berta and Maggie cried out behind him, but Deacon's smile widened. "Yes." He tightened his grip on Lucy's arm, while he focused all his energy on Jed.

Jed would not live here without Lucy, and if it meant giving up everything to be with her, then so be it. Deacon coiled again, his face contorted with an angry sneer. A deafening rumble crashed through the air, shaking the ground beneath them and sending branches flying from the tree.

Maggie and Berta screamed above Reverend Conroy's booming prayers, but the rumble continued, growing in strength and intensity.

With his left hand wrapped around Lucy's arm, Deacon raised his right hand above his head and swung it down again, pointing his fingers directly at Jed's heart.

"No!" Lucy ripped free of Deacon's grip and threw herself at Jed, her body the only thing standing between the two men. Jed's arms folded around her just as Deacon's strike hit, slamming her in the back, and sending both her and Jed tumbling to the ground.

She gasped hard, a sound echoed by Deacon, and then silence.

"Lucy." Jed pushed her off, staring down at her tear-stained face, searching for . . . what? Whatever pain Deacon had meant for Jed, it had hit Lucy square in the back. He moved his hands over every inch of her arms, neck, head and back, but could find nothing.

Nothing. She was alive, she was breathing, and she was . . . smiling.

Her green eyes sparkled behind her dark lashes.

"Are you . . . ?"

"I'm fine," she smiled back at him. "I'm—Deacon!"

They spun around to see Deacon collapse to the ground in a grunting heap.

"L-Lucille," he sputtered. "How . . . ?"

"What happened?" She scrambled over to him, followed closely by Jed. There wasn't a hope in Hell of him letting her go anywhere near Deacon by herself. Not after that—whatever *that* was.

"I think . . ." Deacon said, his voice shallow and pained. "Why did you . . . ? You blocked it."

"I couldn't let you hurt him," Lucy choked on a sob. "I love him."

Deacon tried to sit up, but the effort was too much. All he could manage was to roll onto his back, pulling his hat toward him.

"But l-love makes you weak."

"No," Lucy snuffled. "It makes you strong."

The weasly little ferret poked its head out of Deacon's pocket, sniffed the air, then darted out across the dirt and disappeared in a gopher hole.

Deacon grimaced. "But no one's ever . . . It c-can't be possible. I—" With a sharp intake of breath, he gave up and fell silent. The anger, the hatred and the fear disappeared from his face, replaced with a look of disbelief, confusion and intense pain. "But he said . . . I never thought . . ."

Lucy stood and took Jed's hand. "He lied."

Jed couldn't stop staring at her; that long black glossy hair, those brilliant green eyes and those lips. God, but he loved the taste of those lips.

"I'm sorry." Lucy cupped his face in her hands and looked deep into his eyes. "I'm so very sorry."

He hesitated a second, then dipped his head closer to hers. She might be sorry, but he wasn't. His mouth hovered a breath above hers, his fingers wound their way through her hair, and she leaned into him, ready for his kiss.

Berta's sharp gasp stopped them cold.

"What?"

They all looked to where she was pointing. Deacon was gone. The impression of where he'd fallen remained in the dirt, but there was no sign of him.

"He just . . . disappeared," Berta gasped. "Just like that."

Jed watched a cloud float across Lucy's face, wishing he could ease the frown from her brow. Deacon had gone back empty-handed, and there was no telling what would happen to him.

"He doesn't deserve your love, Lucy." Jed wrapped his arms around her and breathed through her hair.

She shrugged. "He's family."

A chuckle rumbled up through Jed's chest. "God help us."

"J-Jedidiah?" Maggie watched him with wide, questioning eyes. But for the first time in weeks, those eyes were also clear and sane.

"Maggie." Jed and Lucy spoke her name at the same time, then hurried to her side.

"We need to get you to the doctor," Jed said. He squatted down beside her and brushed the hair back from her face. "I'm sorry, Maggie."

She shrugged slowly. "You couldn't have known."

He pulled the edge of the cloth back and peered down at his niece. "She's beautiful," he grinned. "Just like her mama."

Maggie started to smile, but then her lip trembled, and her whole body was wracked with sobs.

"Shh," he murmured, wrapping his arms around her. "It'll be okay."

"S-Sam . . ."

"I know." He eased the baby into his own arms, then passed her carefully to Berta. "Come on."

With steady movements, he lifted Maggie into his arms. She wrapped her arms around his neck and continued to sob against his shirt.

Moving as one, the entire group turned and began the walk into town. Reverend Conroy led the way, his Bible clutched against his chest. Berta walked next, the baby snuggled tight in her arms, and Lucy walked beside Jed.

And that was just where he wanted her.

* * *

Doc Billings set Maggie up in one of his exam rooms, where he planned to keep her for a few days. No one dared tell him what had gone on that afternoon, not even Reverend Conroy. He'd simply blessed them all, laid his hand on Lucy's head, and left.

Staring down at the soft downy head of his perfect niece and the calm hands of her mother, it hit Jed all at once: they were safe, the baby was beautiful and healthy, and Sam could finally be laid to rest.

He'd never felt such intense joy and sorrow at the same time. All he could do was stare at the baby in absolute wonder.

Who'd have thought they would ever see this day?

Lucy moved beside him, offered a sad smile, and rubbed her thumbs under his eyes to dry the sudden moistness that appeared. He sandwiched her hands between his and tucked them against his chest.

He just wanted to take his wife home and try to forget everything that had happened. But when the baby cried out, Jed knew they'd never forget. She was the miracle that would remind them every day. Berta bustled around, tucking in Maggie's blankets and making sure the pillows were positioned properly. "There now," Berta nodded. "Let's be on our way. Mama and baby need their rest."

"She'll be fine," Doc Billings assured them as he ushered them out the door. "I'll be here all night and you're welcome to come back tomorrow."

Jed and Berta both kissed Maggie and the baby goodbye, then followed Lucy outside. They stood on the walk, staring out at the passersby, for a full five minutes. No one spoke, and no one moved. It was almost as though they were all afraid to disturb the peace they'd finally found.

"Well," Berta finally said, "I'm going to take myself home." She smiled brightly at Lucy, her tears held in check, and squeezed her hand. "I knew you could do it."

They hugged each other tight, then stepped back.

"Take her home," Berta said to Jed. "I'd wager you could both use some rest."

"We'll see you tomorrow?" Jed asked, surprised at how he suddenly wanted all of them to be together.

Berta smiled, nodded, and began to walk toward her

tiny house at the edge of town. Lucy slipped her hand into Jed's and they both headed for the livery.

It was a quiet ride home. Jed struggled to accept all they'd been through in the last few hours. How would they move on from here? But then Lucy slid along the bench seat and pressed next to him. With her hand resting on his thigh, and her head resting on his shoulder, he knew exactly how they'd move on. Side by side and day by day, they'd build a life on the love they shared. There wasn't anything they couldn't face, wasn't any fight they couldn't win.

He reined the horses to a stop near the corral and set the brake.

"Come on." He took her hand, and together they moved to the edge of the bench. Without releasing her, he hopped down, then reached for her.

They stood in the stillness of the yard for a long minute, Lucy's back pressed against his chest, his arms wrapped around her middle.

Lucy's voice, a feather-soft whisper, caught on a sob. "You love me."

"Yeah." He brushed a kiss against the top of her head and held her tighter. "I do."

"But no one's ever . . ." She stopped, then swallowed. "Do you have any idea what could have happened?"

"Yes," he choked over his forced laugh. "I could have gone the rest of my life without drinking another cup of that swill you call coffee."

Lucy didn't laugh. "Weren't you scared?"

"Of Deacon?" *Tell the truth, Caine.* "No. Of losing you?" He pressed his face against her hair and inhaled a long, slow breath. "Scared the hell out of me."

She turned in his arms, pressed her face against his chest and shuddered. "Me, too."

She snuggled closer, clinging to him as though afraid he'd let her go. That would never happen. Damn but he loved this woman. How or when that happened, he couldn't be sure, but he'd wager it started at the auction, the second her hands touched his. Those hands were the first truth he knew about Lucy. He lifted them to his lips and pressed a kiss against each callous.

Lucy watched him with her wide green eyes. "I can't believe how it's all changed."

"What's changed?" he asked between kisses.

Her smile was a mixture of shame and laughter. "It was only a few weeks ago that you didn't want to touch me, no matter no matter what I did."

"Oh no," Jed groaned through his laughter. "I wanted to. Sweet Jesus, Lucy, I wanted to."

She eased her fingers from his and set to work on the first button of his shirt. A coy smile lifted her lips. "Do you still want to?"

Hard already, Jed forced a sigh over his grin. "I'm actually a little tired."

"Okay. Maybe later." Lucy laughed wickedly, spun on her heel and made for the house. "There's plenty of work needs doing."

"The hell with that." In one fluid motion, Jed lifted her in his arms and made a direct line for the barn. She wrapped her arms around his neck and sighed against his skin.

"I do love it when you hold me like this."

"Good," he growled as he kicked open the barn door. "Because it's going to happen a lot."

Lucy giggled softly. "Does that mean we're about to get lusty and impassioned, husband?"

"I'm already there, sweetheart."

EPILOGUE

1884

I made coffee." Lucy turned from the stove as Jed strode through the kitchen door. "Hot and strong, just the way you like it."

She watched the familiar grimace flicker across his face, then disappear behind his smile. Three years and that smile still melted her heart.

First things first, Jed pulled her into his arms for a long, hungry kiss. Didn't matter what she was doing or where he'd just come from, every time he walked through that door, he kissed her.

"I missed you," he murmured against her lips.

Lucy laughed. "You've been gone an hour, Jed."

He shrugged and kissed her again. "Still missed you."

"I missed you, too," she admitted happily, "but you need to get cleaned up. Maggie's waiting."

Jed frowned.

"Supper," Lucy reminded him. "For Samantha's birthday."

In the months following Samantha's birth, Lucy had tried to avoid Maggie whenever possible. The guilt of what happened hung over her like a dead weight, despite the fact Maggie had forgiven her for everything, and welcomed her into the Caine family with the first supper in her new house. Gradually, the two had formed a deep bond, and Lucy loved Samantha with a fierceness she couldn't explain.

"Right." An odd little grin spread over Jed's face. "Supper."

"What?" Staying in his embrace, Lucy pulled back a bit to study his expression. "What's going on?"

He shrugged.

"Jed."

"It's supposed to be a surprise."

This time she did pull out of his arms. He grabbed for her, but she stepped out of his reach. "Tell me."

Excitement danced in Jed's eyes, making him look more like a child on Christmas morning than a grown man. "Well, it's about George."

Almost two years ago, George had given up his position at the bank and had come to work the ranch with Jed. He'd helped them finish Maggie's house, and then worked side by side with Jed and Lucy to build theirs, then took over the dingy little lean-to as his own. His share of the herd grazed alongside Jed's. It had shocked them all, George included, to discover he was such a natural around the animals. And with his knowledge of numbers, he'd become a necessary and welcome part of the ranch.

More than that, he had become like family.

"What's he up to?" Lucy asked.

"I can't tell you," Jed teased.

Lucy sidled up to him until they were chest to chest. With a slight nudge, she backed him up into the big oak table, just where she needed him. She traced her finger down his jaw and across his bottom lip.

"Tell me."

He leaned in for a kiss, but she was too quick. All he found was her cheek. "Lucy," he pleaded, leaning in again.

"Tell me."

She curled her hands around his neck, letting her fingers play with the hair at the nape of his neck. He moaned softly, but held his tongue.

Lucy leaned closer. She slid her hands down, over his shoulders, across his chest, and lower until they found the closure of his trousers.

"Oh Lord." The words ripped from his throat on a low growl.

"Tell me." She breathed soft kisses against his Adam's apple while her fingers undid the buttons of his waistband.

He swallowed hard against her lips, but didn't speak. Very slowly, she slipped her hand inside his waistband while she continued to feather-kiss his neck and chin. Her fingers grazed over his hip, then inched toward his abdomen, pulling a harsh gasp from Jed.

"Oh, fine—he's going to propose!" he rasped, staggered, then scooped her into his arms and strode towards the bedroom. "Are you happy now?"

"That's so romantic," Lucy sighed. "Don't you think?"

Jed set her on their big feather bed and ripped his shirt open, sending buttons flying in every direction. Over the last few years, Lucy had become quite adept at sewing them back on.

"The only thing I'm thinking about right now," he said, waggling his brow at her, "is how I can get you to stop thinking about George and start thinking about me."

"It's always about you, isn't it?" She grinned.

"It should be, yeah." He lifted her right foot, pulled off her boot, then slid his fingers up her leg to the top of her stocking. "But right now," he murmured as he pressed soft kisses to the inside of her knee, "it's all about you."

"Oooh, good," she murmured on a sigh. "I love it when it's all about me."

"So do I." Jed waggled his brow at her again, and set to work on the other stocking. "So do I."

Get a sneak peek at
Deacon's story in
**DANCING WITH THE
DEVIL.**

Coming Fall 2008

CHAPTER ONE

Penance, Texas
Spring 1884

Hell hath no fury . . ." Deacon paused at the bottom of the steps and eyed the ramshackle cabin. Two years ago, he'd all but expected it to collapse under a great sigh of aged wood and chipped paint.

He should have known better.

Much like its owner, the house remained standing, determined to survive, daring something—or someone—to try and knock it over.

Sparse patches of weeds and brilliant yellow dandelions dotted the narrow yard, all fenced in by rickety wooden rails that looked like they'd blow over with the first big gust.

Deacon had no sooner lifted his freshly polished boot to the bottom step when the front door banged open, and out *she* stepped with twenty-four inches of Winchester leveled at his forehead.

Even *she* couldn't miss at this range. He could step back and allow her the upper hand, if only briefly, but she was so much fun to antagonize.

He dared to climb the first step, gazing down the length of the sleek black barrel.

"Hello, Rhea." He moved up the next step, half expecting her trigger finger to twitch in answer.

"Go to Hell."

He stopped, and chuckled softly. "Just got back, actually."

Rhea's coffee-colored eyes narrowed; much of her wavy brown mane had fallen from its braid and now hung in chaotic strands over her shoulders and across her forehead.

She shifted the rifle a little, adjusting her grip and steadying her stance. "What d'you want?"

He tipped his face up to hers and smiled slowly. "A lot of things, but I'll start with supper."

A loud snort ripped from her delicate throat. "The only meal you're gonna get outta me is a mouthful of lead."

How could such a dirt-speckled little spit of a woman have absolutely no respect for who he was or what he could do to her? And why did he find that so captivating?

"That's not very hospitable of you."

"If it's hospitality you want," she spat, "you best go see your friend Salma."

"Salma?" He frowned slightly. *Who was* . . . "Oh, her."

"Yes, *her*."

Deacon lifted his right shoulder in the barest of shrugs. "She meant nothing to me, Rhea."

Another snort. "She meant enough that you took to her bed."

"Pfft. Nothing more than the fulfillment of a man's needs." He considered moving up a step, but the look in her eyes kept him still. "I've changed."

It was true, to a certain extent, but she'd never believe it.

"So have I. Now get out."

"Rhea—"

The sound of her cranking the lever echoed across the dry, deserted yard. Deacon moved back down the steps, his palms up.

"Does this mean you're not going to offer me supper?"

The first shot sprayed loose gravel across the toe of his shiny black boots, the boots she knew perfectly well he prided on keeping clean.

The second bullet hit the dirt between his feet. Damn, but she could crank that thing fast.

"You've been practicing."

The third shot would have hit him directly in the groin if he hadn't anticipated it and leapt out of the way.

The laughter he felt creeping up his throat died when she stopped to add more cartridges.

"Can't we talk about this?"

She lifted the rifle and set the sight directly at his chest. "I'm done talkin'."

"But I need somewhere to stay."

"Don't care."

"Rhea—"

She squeezed her left eye closed, and focused her right on the gun sight. "One . . ."

"I've missed you." It wasn't until after he'd spoken the words that he realized it wasn't a lie.

"Two . . ." Her fingers curled tighter around the barrel.

"Didn't you miss me even a little?"

"Thr—"

A hair too late, Deacon jumped. Burning pain ripped through his right shoulder, sending him staggering back toward the fence.

The echo of the last shot taunted him as it repeated across the dry land.

He frowned at his shoulder, then back at Rhea. Her eyes, wide with shock, stared back in disbelief. Her mouth opened in a small *O*, but she didn't lower the rifle.

"You shot me."

After a second, she blinked hard, and gave her head a quick shake.

"You should've moved." Another blink, this one followed by a stiff swallow.

"I tried!" He pulled the neatly folded handkerchief from his breast pocket and pressed it against the open wound, never taking his eyes off Rhea.

She shook the hair back from her face. "No you didn't. You could have just . . . you know . . . appeared . . . over there."

"In case you weren't listening," he snapped. "I've *changed*."

She didn't look convinced, but her death-grip on the gun loosened slightly. "How?"

His boots were filthy, his jacket was ruined, and *now* she wanted to talk. Women!

"He took most of my powers as punishment."

"Punishment for what?"

Deacon dared look away from her, knowing full well she could easily take him down with one more shot, and probably would. But damn, his shoulder burned.

"I was supposed to . . ." His now-scarlet handkerchief dripped blood over his hand and down the sleeve of his ruined jacket. A body only had so much blood, and there seemed to be an awful lot of it flowing down his arm in warm red rivers. That couldn't be good. "I, um, my sister . . ."

All this blood was enough to make a mortal man queasy. Good thing he wasn't—oooh, what was that? Something in his stomach dipped and shifted, causing an even odder reaction in his knees. He lifted his head to look back at Rhea, and instantly regretted it. The ground beneath him began to spin in slow, lazy circles. Daylight faded to shadows until he could see nothing except a tiny dot of light directly in front of him. And in that dot stood Rhea, the rifle still cocked and ready.

He shook his head to clear it, but that made everything worse. The ground spun faster, the shadows grew darker and tighter, and his stomach threatened to revolt any second. If he didn't find his balance soon, he'd end up on his backside in the dirt.

"Maybe you should sit down." Rhea's voice, guarded but concerned, seemed a hundred miles away. "You look like you're going to faint."

"Don't . . . be . . . ridiculous." Breathing was suddenly a massive chore. "I'm not going to f—"

◦   ◦   ◦

Rhea didn't move for a full minute. She'd shot him, she'd really shot him.

Deacon.

The son of Satan.

But how . . . and why hadn't he moved? He'd always loved to do that disappearing and reappearing thing on her, but he hadn't done it this time.

And now he lay dead-still in her yard. Was he dead? No—she couldn't kill him. He was the devil's son for the love of God.

"You okay, Rhea? Heard some shootin'." Holt Schmidt, her nearest neighbor, rode slowly by on his old nag. His wrinkled face gave away nothing, but his all-seeing eyes spared a slow glance at Deacon, then back at her. "Guessin' you're a sight better 'n him."

"I'm fine, thanks, Holt."

The old man didn't even stop his horse, but kept it plodding along as though Rhea shot people in her yard every day. But if she didn't get Deacon out of her yard right quick, she'd no doubt have plenty more visitors coming to check on her.

That was the problem with living this close to town; she couldn't burp without everyone knowing.

One step at a time, she made her way down the stairs, barely blinking, and keeping the rifle cocked and at the ready. The Deacon she knew would never lower himself to allow dirt to touch his clothes, so he must really be hurt.

But she also knew Deacon wasn't to be trusted, no matter what.

His bowler hat lay a few feet away, covered in dry Texas dust; his boots were scuffed and dirty from her bullets and from scraping against the ground. And his jacket . . .

Oh no, Deacon would never allow blood to stain anything he owned—especially his own blood. He must really have fainted.

She pushed her boot against his hip, then jumped back, braced for his attack.

Nothing.

She did it a second time, but still he didn't move. Finally, she lowered the rifle and jabbed the barrels right up against his ribs. Not so much as a flinch.

After another long moment, she crouched beside him, torn between what he deserved, and what she knew must be done. Then again, after what he'd put her through, he deserved to bleed to death, out in the dirt, like the pig he was. She sighed. Not even pigs ought to suffer.

This close to him, little things about his appearance became clearer. Some of those scratches on his precious boots were too deep and worn to have been made today, even with the bullets flying. His fancy black suit, usually crisp, clean and pressed, seemed oddly faded, just slightly mind you, but faded nonetheless. Even his shirt, always brilliantly white and starched stiff, appeared a little dull.

This wasn't the Deacon she knew. And it sure as hell wasn't the Deacon she'd spent two long years cursing.

Dammit.

With great reluctance, she set the safety on the rifle, laid it on the ground and moved around to Deacon's head. She grabbed him by the shoulders and began to pull him, slowly, toward the steps.

Good grief, he was heavy! Inch by inch, she managed to drag him up the steps and in through the front door. A thick, dark streak of blood trailed down his arm, across the porch, and over the floor behind him.

With a great deal of grunting and very little grace, she managed to hoist him, one end at a time, up onto the straw tick. When she was certain he wouldn't roll off, she darted back outside, retrieved her rifle, and set it beside the front door.

Now what? She was no doctor, and the only one she knew of had sworn he'd never set foot in Penance again.

She dug around the kitchen until she found the sharpest of all her dull knives, the pot of lukewarm water from the stove, and a clean sheet. After dumping the supplies on the small table next to the bed, she went back for one more thing—the last of her whiskey.

As she gulped a large swallow, she threw another silent curse at Deacon. Just seeing him again was enough to make her chug the rest of the bottle, but he needed it more than she did.

With the knife gripped in her right hand and his jacket sleeve in the other, she began to cut. It was slow going, given the state of her blade, but she managed to hack it away, leaving the wound uncovered.

It took a great deal of effort to push him up to see the back of his shoulder. Sure enough, the bullet had sliced right through him, leaving the ragged wound to seep blood all over her quilt.

Where was that hanky he'd used?

"Never mind," she muttered as she shoved him, none too gently, until he lay half on his side, half on his stomach.

She reached for the sheet, and as evenly as she could, cut it in long strips, then set them across his hip for easy access. She used one to tie around his shoulder above the wound, and then a few others to press against both sides of the wound.

When the bleeding slowed, she eased the pressure from the back of his shoulder and tipped the whiskey bottle over the wound.

It had to hurt like hell, but Deacon was obviously too far gone to notice.

She dipped the end of one strip in the water and did her best to clean the blood from around both sides of the wound before dousing the area with more whiskey and wrapping his shoulder with the remaining strips.

Curse her bad aim. And double-curse his poor reflexes.

When she was done, she sat back on her haunches and let out an enormous gush of air. *Now what?*

Wait for him to recover? Or die?

Knowing her luck, he'd linger for years. He'd obviously been kicked out of Hell again, and there was no way Heaven would take him, so where did that leave him?

It left him on her bed, thats where. And not just lying there, either, but *bleeding* there—leaving yet one more mess for her to clean up.

Typical Deacon.

The door burst open, making her jump and knock over the whiskey bottle. In staggered a breathless man, his hat askew, his gun drawn. Lucky for her—and her intruder—she'd capped the bottle, or there'd have been hell to pay.

"Rhea!"

Ernest Miller stumbled toward her, his gaze darting all around, until he noticed Deacon's motionless form on the tick.

"Are you okay?" he asked, inhaling deeply.

"Of course." Rhea shook her head and set about gathering up the remaining supplies. "Don't I look okay?"

"Holt said you shot someone." With shaky hands, he stuffed his gun back in its holster and gripped the back of a chair for support. "What happened?"

"What does it look like?" she snapped. "I shot him."

Ernest took a moment to catch his breath, then moved closer to Deacon. "Isn't that . . . ?"

"Yup."

"What's he doing here?"

Rhea shrugged. She hadn't actually given Deacon the chance to tell her before she started shooting.

"Good thing I'm here." Ernest slumped into a chair across from Deacon and eyed the bottle in Rhea's hand. "Can I get something to drink?"

"There's water out back."

Without a second glance, Rhea set to putting the supplies away. Ernest had no doubt run the entire three miles from his place, but she didn't *need* him there, she didn't *want* him there, and she thought she'd made that perfectly clear the last time he burst in with his gun drawn.

The last thing she needed was a man—mortal or demon—taking up space in her life. Ernest was a sweet, decent fellow, and even though he'd sworn his life-long devotion to her on several occasions, she'd never felt anything more than a distant fondness for him.

And the more distant the better.

She glanced out the window as he swallowed a huge mouthful of water. A second later, it came shooting back out his nose and mouth, toppling him to his knees in a massive choking fit.

He caught her eye through the window, and held up a hand to wave off her concern. She snorted softly. Oh, she was concerned alright; concerned he'd really hurt himself and then she'd be forced to put him up in the parlor, too.

It was going to be a helluva long day.

Bonnie Vanak

"Vanak has a gift for creating exciting stories, memorable characters, and a passion hotter than the Middle Eastern sun...."
—*Romantic Times BOOKreviews*

The Scorpion & the Seducer

Jasmine Tristan was no stranger to the upper crust of London society. And yet, she knew the cruel sting of bigotry. When she took revenge, a new fear was voiced: Was Jasmine truly bad at her core, like her sultan father from whom she and her mother had fled? How could she be, when she'd known a moment of pure beauty with Lord Thomas Claradon? Their kiss had been scorching as a desert sun. But like a sandstorm, it was misdirecting: Thomas's loyalty to his family and duty put him forever out of her reach. Only a return to her birthplace, a quest to find her roots, would bring Jasmine answers—and also prove that true love could triumph over ignorance, passion over prejudice.

ISBN 13: 978-0-8439-5975-8

ELAINE BARBIERI

JUSTINE

Hoping to develop the lovely singing voice she'd inherited from her father, Justine Fitzsimmons had signed on with a troupe of touring actors heading West. But she'd wound up stranded in a seedy Oklahoma saloon with her dreams in tatters. Still worse, there were two men on her trail: one who had orders to escort her safely back East, the other to make certain she never returned. But which was which? All Justine could be sure of was that Ryder Knowles was an arrogant, interfering know-it-all, and she felt almost as powerful an urge to slap his face as to kiss those incredibly sensual, wicked lips.

CRY OF THE WOLF

AVAILABLE JUNE 2008!

ISBN 13: 978-0-8439-6013-6

Bobbi SMITH

It hadn't been easy growing up half Comanche in the small ranching town of Two Guns, Texas. But Wind Walker had always managed to keep his self-respect…and the attention of pretty Veronica Reynolds. After being sentenced to prison for a murder he didn't commit, Walker had managed to escape, and only Roni could help him track down the real killer. He hated the idea of putting her in harm's way, but still worse was the thought of going to his grave without tasting her sweet lips one more time….

WANTED:
The Half-Breed

AVAILABLE JUNE 2008!

ISBN 13: 978-0-8439-5850-8

JANE CANDIA COLEMAN

Allie Earp always said the West was no place for sissies. And that held especially true for a woman married to one of the wild Earp brothers. She had no fear of cussing a blue streak if someone crossed her, patching up a bullet wound, or defending her home against rustlers. Every day was a new adventure—from the rough streets of Deadwood to the infamous OK Corral in Tombstone. But through it all one thing remained constant: her deep and abiding love for one of the most formidable lawmen of the West.

Tumbleweed

AVAILABLE JUNE 2008!

ISBN 13: 978-0-8439-6104-1